LAS
GOOD

C000311723

ALSO BY ARLENE HUNT

Last to Die

ARLENE HUNT

LAST GOODBYE

bookouture

Published by Bookouture in 2018

An imprint of StoryFire Ltd.

Carmelite House
50 Victoria Embankment
London EC4Y 0DZ

www.bookouture.com

ISBN: 978-1-78681-282-7
eBook ISBN: 978-1-78681-281-0

For Tim

CHAPTER ONE

December

They were easy to follow undetected through the congested streets. She was wearing a bright-red jacket and perky bobble hat; he wore a cashmere overcoat with a pale-blue scarf tossed artfully around his neck. They were a distinctive couple, happy, good-looking, the kind of pairing that turned heads.

Outside the Brown Thomas department store they stopped and stood gazing in at the festive display. That year the windows were decked in crystals and giant snow-globes, white Arctic foxes and a life-size polar bear wearing a bow tie. The snooty-looking mannequins sat in a sleigh pulled by white owls.

The woman pointed to something, and as she did so she leaned her head against the man's shoulder. In response, he wrapped his arm around her, pulling her tightly to him.

He kissed the top of her head.

It was such a simple gesture, the wolf thought, grinding his back teeth; so affectionate and loving, at least to the casual observer.

But he knew better than that, he knew what the kiss signified: it was a possessive marking of territory, a display of social dominance. She's mine, the kiss said. All mine.

The wolf would enjoy proving him wrong.

'Have you got any spare change?'

The wolf turned his head. A man with a blue sleeping bag draped over his shoulders was next to him, standing a little too close for comfort. The wolf wrinkled his nose at the smell coming from the bag; it was filthy and covered in stains.

He took a single step to his left.

'I only want a bit of change for a hostel, bud.' The man held out a paper cup and shook it forlornly. 'Ah, c'mon, it's nearly Christmas, have a heart.'

'I don't have any change,' the wolf replied.

The man considered this for a moment.

'I take notes.'

The wolf's eyes widened incredulously. Something in his expression caused the man to rethink his approach.

'All right, relax, I was only asking.'

He stepped away into the crowd and vanished.

Across the street, the couple were on the move again, strolling along hand in hand, oblivious to anyone except themselves. This time the wolf let them go, unconcerned with their destination.

He knew where they lived.

He knew where they worked.

He knew everything about them.

Their fates were already sealed.

A light drizzle began. The wolf turned his collar up, shoved his hands into his pockets and set off in the opposite direction, passing beneath the sparkling Christmas lights and on towards St Stephen's Green. No one paid any attention to him, and even if they had, no one could possibly have guessed the depths of his depravity.

But they would, he thought, increasing his pace, eager to get home and prepare. Soon his manifesto would become legend, and Dublin would quake at the mere mention of his name.

He would make sure of it.

CHAPTER TWO

From a single glimpse of the man's face, Eli Quinn knew whatever waited for him inside the double-fronted red-brick cottage was going to be bad. Nobody could fake a look of sheer uncomprehending horror like that; nobody.

'Sir, I'm Detective Inspector Eli Quinn.'

He stepped forward and offered his hand. The man didn't so much as blink. He just stood with his arms hanging by his sides, blank-faced in the flashing emergency lights, mouth agape.

'Sir?'

'I think we should have a medic take a look at him. He's in shock.' Detective Sergeant Miranda Lynn stepped past Quinn and gently caught hold of the man by his elbow.

'I'll need a statement,' Quinn reminded her as she guided the man towards one of the waiting paramedics.

Quinn continued up the path. The front door was partially open, and through it he spied Detective Inspector Adam Johnson from Forensics talking to one of his team.

Quinn raised his hand and pushed the door open a little further. There was a Christmas wreath hanging from the knocker, one of the fancier kinds, sprayed silver, lit with LED lights.

Johnson noticed he was there and came to greet him.

'Quinn.'

'In the flesh. What have we got?'

'Double homicide, male and female. If I had to guess, I'd say mid twenties on her, late twenties on him.'

'ID?'

'Not so far, but we've only been here a few minutes.'

'Dispatch said you asked for me personally?'

Johnson pushed his rimless glasses up his nose with his index finger. He was a pasty-faced man with faded blue eyes that were too close together. His brown hair was sparse, so he wore it in a side parting to cover his scalp.

'There's something odd about the scene. I thought you'd be a good fit.'

'Show me.'

'You can come in if you promise not to touch anything. The pathologist is on her way and you know what she's like.'

'Scout's honour.'

Quinn snapped on a pair of blue gloves and followed Johnson inside. Halfway down the hall, they turned right and entered a brightly lit living room.

Quinn paused at the door to look around, taking it all in. It was a nice room, robustly middle-class. There was a large Christmas tree blinking in the bay window, chic furniture, bookshelves, healthy-looking houseplants, even a kilim rug. There was nothing fancy or dramatically unusual apart from the dead man sitting on a blood-drenched sofa. He was upright, fully clothed, both hands resting neatly on his lap. Were it not for the blood and the unnatural angle of his head, he might simply have been resting.

'I think the assailant attacked him from behind,' Johnson said. 'Using some sort of large blade – a machete, or possibly a sword.'

'A sword?' Quinn raised an eyebrow in surprise. 'Where the hell would someone get their hands on a sword?'

'Specialist shop, internet, take your pick.'

Johnson moved behind the sofa and raised his hands over his head. 'Right to left at an angle of approximately one hundred and twenty degrees. Severed most of the neck before embedding into the clavicle right here.' He pointed over the victim's shoulder. 'Spinal cord is intact, though.'

'Would that have taken a lot of strength?'

'Depends on how sharp the blade was. It's a single blow, so I'm thinking it was pretty sharp.'

'No defence wounds?' Quinn peered a little closer at the corpse. 'No other wounds at all.'

'None that I can see, but the pathologist might have a different story. Judging from the positioning of the body and the pattern of the blood, he didn't struggle. My guess is he died right here.'

'Would you let someone walk behind you with a sword?'

'I would not.'

'Right, so I doubt this guy sat here like a cabbage waiting to be attacked.' Quinn frowned. 'You said there were two; where's the woman?'

'Master bedroom at the back of the house.'

They left the living room, passed two technicians dusting for prints and entered the bedroom to the rear of the cottage. Again Quinn paused at the door and looked around. Like the living room, it was tastefully appointed: good-quality furniture, shuttered windows and high ceilings, the kind of room decorators called restful.

The woman's body lay on top of the bed covers. She was dressed in an ivory-coloured baby-doll nightie pulled demurely over her thighs. Her legs and feet were bare and her hair had been neatly brushed and fanned out across the pillows in a golden halo. Her face was turned away from the door, towards the window; her hands were folded over each other on her stomach.

Quinn walked around to the other side of the bed. Unlike the body in the living room, there was no sign of injury or violence that he could see. The woman's face was fully made up: blue eyeshadow, blusher, her lips slick with pink frosted lipstick. Her eyes were open, staring past him, forever sightless. They were cornflower blue; pretty, like her.

'What happened to her?'

Johnson scratched the back of his head.

'My guess is it was an overdose. If you look closer, you can see traces of vomit on the corner of her mouth. Someone cleaned her up, but they didn't get it all.'

Quinn bent down and saw Johnson was right.

'So this lipstick was applied after she was dead?'

'That would be my guess.'

'Interesting. Have you found the lipstick?'

'We're collecting samples from her make-up.'

Quinn gave the room a cursory once-over, but nothing tickled his antennae. Back in the living room, Miranda Lynn was standing by the fireplace making notes in her electronic notebook – or EN, as everyone in the force called them. She glanced up when Quinn entered the room and gestured to the body on the couch.

'The man we met outside is the father of our victim. He's Sean Kilbride, aged twenty-seven.'

'There's a second body in the bedroom, a woman.'

'That will be Lorraine Dell, twenty-five.'

'What were they? Boyfriend and girlfriend?'

'Recently engaged.'

'How recent?'

'Less than four weeks ago.'

Quinn thought about Lorraine Dell's hands folded on her stomach; her fingers had been completely bare. 'Find out if there was an engagement ring, will you?'

'Sure thing.'

'What else did the father tell you?'

'Not much. The victims were supposed to meet up with Sean's family earlier this evening for pre-Christmas drinks. Mr Kilbride became concerned when he couldn't reach his son and called in here on his way home.'

'What time was that?'

'Eight thirty.'

'When did he last talk to his son?'

'He reckons around six or seven yesterday evening.'

'He didn't notice anything out of the ordinary?'

'Not that he can remember.'

Quinn looked at his watch. 'It's Saturday and this is a residential street, so there's bound to have been people floating around all day. I want door-to-door enquiries, talk to the neighbours, the friends. Find out if anyone saw either of the victims between yesterday and today. Find out if they had any visitors, deliveries, you know the drill.'

'Got it.'

Johnson poked his head into the room.

'Just a heads-up. Edwina's pulled up outside.'

Edwina King was the state pathologist. She had more than once made it clear that she did *not* appreciate detectives tramping about at the crime scene before her initial examination.

Quinn watched another of Johnson's technicians exit the room opposite the living room carrying a hand-held recorder at hip height.

'You done?'

'It's all yours.'

He crossed the hall and entered a modern dual-aspect kitchen. It had dove-grey walls and bespoke cabinets. There was a dining area within the confines of the bay window overlooking the street. The way it had been set caught Quinn's attention. Champagne glasses, ornate candlesticks, a bouquet of yellow roses in a green vase, and next to them, an ice bucket with an open bottle resting in it. He glanced in: the ice had melted.

'Miranda,' he called.

The DS came and stood beside him.

'Check this out.'

'A romantic dinner for two.'

'Little strange, don't you think?' Quinn said.

'Why?'

'You told me they were supposed to meet family this evening. This dinner for two suggests otherwise.'

'Maybe they changed their minds.'

'Maybe.'

Using the tip of his gloved little finger, Quinn eased the bottle upright so he could read it.

'Krug.'

'Expensive.' A lock of Miranda's hair fell over her forehead as she bent forward and stared at the tableau. Quinn watched her. She was five years his junior, sharp as a tack, a no-nonsense type. 'The candles are burned all the way down.'

'So champagne, candles, flowers … but no sign of any food.' Quinn looked behind him towards the spotless kitchen. 'And no sign of any food prep. I don't think they changed their minds.'

'You think this was staged by the killer,' Miranda said, as if she were reading his thoughts.

'Yup.'

Quinn studied the roses. They were a dazzling jazzy yellow, the petals tightly bunched together. Fresh. He rummaged through the stems and found a small white envelope buried in the centre. With extreme care he plucked it out, opened it and removed a card from within. It was good-quality paper, thick, with gilded edges. One side was blank, but when he turned it over, the other contained a glittery red heart, torn in two.

He held the card up between two fingers, letting Miranda see what was printed on it.

'A broken heart,' she said.

Quinn put the card back inside the envelope, placed the envelope on the table.

'Maybe our killer was unhappy about the recent engagement.'

'Ex-lover, maybe,' Miranda said. 'I'll get cracking on a list of ex-boyfriends and girlfriends.'

Quinn looked out of the window towards the street, watching the emergency lights of the ambulance flashing for a moment, thinking.

His head told him one thing, his heart another; but Quinn was a long time working the streets, and he listened to his gut. Right now, his gut was telling him this case was not the work of a disgruntled ex-lover. Worse than that, his gut was telling him this case was only the beginning.

CHAPTER THREE

January

Roxy Malloy woke to the sound of multiple dogs barking. She waited until she heard the main dog howl (she could tell them apart at this stage) before she leaned over and hit the off button.

When they'd lived together, her ex, David, regularly complained about her choice of alarm, declaring it 'aural violence', and for a while – and mostly to avoid argument– she had set the clock to deliver the sounds of babbling brooks and birdsong: stupid, soothing noise she regularly slept through.

When David moved out, she went straight back to the dogs and hadn't overslept since.

On that freezing January morning, Roxy was twenty-seven years old, almost twenty-eight, though she looked younger. Her hair was dark, short and, despite her best efforts, perpetually unruly. It framed a narrow face; not ugly, she knew that, but it was definitely not the kind of face men wrote songs about, not that she gave a damn about *that*. Her eyes were green, the same colour as her father's. At five foot eight, she carried enough weight to escape being described as emaciated, though it was a fine margin. Her body was lean and covered in old scars, faded by time to silver threads. Like her face, it wasn't perfect, but it knew how to tackle a fifteen-stone man and wrestle him to the floor, and she could outrun the average civilian, something most of her colleagues hadn't a hope of doing.

After a shower, she opened her wardrobe, took out her neatly pressed uniform and ran her hands over it. She was one week into a six-month probationary period as a detective sergeant, one of the youngest to ever reach that position.

When she was dressed, she used the fingerprint of her right index finger to unlock the wall safe next to her nightstand, and selected the weapons she would take with her that day. She picked a Trojan smart gun, a T-Prod Taser 900, and a lightweight baton with retractable steel shaft and rubber grip, which she'd privately christened 'Old Faithful'. To finish, she snapped a pair of electronic hand clips to her belt, tightening it an extra notch to offset the weight of her equipment.

Done.

Breakfast was a banana and a cup of black coffee, which she drank standing at the kitchen sink to save time. She rinsed the cup and reprogrammed the coffee machine to coincide with her flatmate's eventual rise. Boy worked as a barman in a nightclub called Oasis in the city centre. He kept odd hours, and as a result she rarely saw him. The arrangement suited her fine. Before Boy, she'd rented the guest room to a good-natured, chatty girl from Cork who liked romantic comedies and scented candles.

That had *not* worked out.

She collected her car from the building's underground car park. It had come with the promotion and she was still a little unused to it, though she liked how quiet and efficient the electric engine was.

She drove the six miles to South Circular Road. The station had once been home to an old cigarette factory until a compulsory land purchase ceded it to the Department of Justice. These days it was the central hub of the Garda Síochána Nua, the New Guardians of the Peace (the old Garda Síochána had been more or less disbanded before Roxy's time due to overwhelming corruption from the top down. It had taken two separate elections and some heavy-handed action from the Irish government, but eventually the GSN had emerged as a bright shining beacon of hope).

A loner by nature, Roxy preferred the capital in the pre-dawn hours. The streets were clean and there was hardly any traffic apart from a few cabs travelling in the specialised public-service lanes that spanned the city. Private cars were no longer allowed within the city limits, and most of the one million citizens travelled by the Luas light-rail system, or the newly built STT (sub-terrain transport). It was impossible to fathom how Dublin had ever functioned before the new laws were put into place. She couldn't imagine travelling on streets so congested even short journeys were next to impossible. As far as Roxy was concerned, this was further evidence, if evidence was required, that the new order was a vast improvement on the old.

She flashed her badge at the armed security detail, drove down the ramp and parked the vehicle neatly in its designated space. At the lift, she waited, tapping her foot impatiently, until her index fingerprint was scanned. When the doors opened, she got in and said, clearly and distinctly:

'L3.'

The lift rose to the third floor, Homicide Division.

Roxy exited and made her way through a sea of cubicles until she reached her own, tucked away in the corner opposite one of three emergency fire exits.

Her partner, Garda Officer Cora Simmons, was already at her desk. Over her shoulder Roxy noticed Cora was reading a gossip site on her computer and cleared her throat as warning. Cora clicked it off, spun in her chair and offered her a wonderfully innocent smile.

'Good morning, Sergeant.'

'Yes,' Roxy said, and after a moment, 'Good morning.'

With promotion, all sergeants were assigned a junior officer to partner with. Given a choice, Roxy would have preferred to work alone, but protocol didn't allow it and so here she was, saddled with a colleague. Cora was twenty-six and married to an electrician called Joe. She had no children or pets. She was five foot six and slightly plump, which was odd since she seemed to be permanently on a diet. Her hair was shoulder length and mid brown with some blonde highlights. She liked dark chocolate and always tried to see the best in people, something Roxy found perplexing given the nature of their occupation.

'Did you do anything on the weekend?' Cora cocked her head to one side.

Roxy removed her jacket and hung it on the back of her chair, taking care to avoid wrinkles. She tried not to let her irritation show. Had she done anything on the weekend? It was a loaded question. Of course she had done things and they were none of anyone's business. On the other hand, Cora could be persistent, so it was better in the long run to toss something out.

'I went to the gun range.'

'Oh … that sounds like fun.'

Roxy considered a response to that.

'I shot very well.'

'Great, great.'

Roxy adjusted her chair until it was exactly how she liked it and sat down. Reaching for her computer, she realised Cora was still looking at her expectantly.

'Er … and how about you, did you do … things?'

'Funny you should ask. I had to be a referee.'

'For a game of some kind?'

'No, not that kind.' Cora laughed. 'A family referee.'

Roxy was silent. Cora took this to mean further explanation was required.

'You know my sister Katie, yeah? Well, she told her young fella she had tickets for Funderland and she'd bring him, but then Theresa found out and she said they wanted to go as well and …'

Roxy feigned polite interest as Cora rambled on. In the few days they had been working together, she had learned that Cora came from a large, rambunctious family of seemingly countless siblings, nieces, nephews, cousins, aunts and uncles. To Roxy, who did not, it sounded positively exhausting.

When Cora's story ended, Roxy took her chance and activated her computer. She logged into the interdepartmental system, registered her ID and began to read the day's assignments. Almost immediately a small yellow hazard sign flashed in the upper corner of the screen.

She clicked on the icon: a Priority 1 link opened, revealing a message from Dispatch.

'RDS Malloy.' A computerised head spoke. 'For the attention of RDS Malloy, badge number 1887. See the Code 6 at Riverside View Apartments, Dundrum. For primary contact, see … Inspector Morrissey, badge number 550.'

It repeated the message once more and vanished off screen with a tiny but audible pop.

Cora was staring at her, brown eyes shining with excitement.

'Did that thing say what I think it said?'

'Yes,' Roxy replied, typing furiously to register their acceptance of the case.

'Which one is Morrissey again?'

Roxy hesitated.

'I don't know exactly.'

'Doesn't matter, does it? Sure, we'll meet him at the scene.' Cora whipped out her personal mobile phone and held it aloft. 'Code 6! Our very first homicide. This is so exciting.'

'What are you doing?'

'Taking a picture, of course. This is for posterity, so *smile*!'

Roxy scowled; Cora rolled her eyes and took the photo anyway.

'Do not put that on social media.'

'Hashtag homicide!' Cora said, ignoring her.

Roxy put her jacket on and wondered again how she was going to get through the next six months without strangling Cora.

CHAPTER FOUR

By the time Roxy and Cora reached Riverside View, a group of gawkers had already gathered and were swarming around the main entrance of the apartment building, clogging up the footpath, phones at the ready.

'Ah here, will you look at that pack of vultures,' Cora said, wrinkling her nose in disgust. 'It's eight o'clock on a Monday morning; haven't they got anything better to be doing?'

'I don't see any sign of Inspector Morrissey,' Roxy said. She'd asked Cora to bring his service record up while they were en route. He was a big man with a ruddy face and had twenty years' service already under his belt, eight of them in Homicide.

'He's probably inside already,' Cora said. 'Come on, let's go. I don't want to miss anything.'

Roxy parked behind an ambulance and switched the engine off. She was relieved to see that someone with a lick of sense had put a Garda officer on the building door itself so no busybody was going to cha-cha their way inside undetected. The recent craze of online news sites offering ridiculous sums of money to the public for 'real-life crime' shots was causing countless problems for the GSN. Despite their best efforts, it was getting harder and harder to keep the public from sticking their unwanted oars into police business.

They got out and crossed the street. Roxy shivered and wished she had worn a heavier coat: the air was frigid and there was snow atop the nearby mountains.

'Watch your feet,' she said.

'Huh?'

'Vomit.'

Cora looked down and pulled a face.

'Ew, carrots!' She stepped over the mess. 'Why are there always carrots in sick?'

They flashed their IDs at the uniform and entered the building. The foyer was bright, clean and surprisingly large, obviously built during a time when space was not at the premium it was now. Roxy glanced at the mailboxes, counting ten in total, and shook her head, bemused. In her purpose-built apartment building there were 120 units, and you could barely swing a cat in any of them.

They exited the lift on the fifth floor and followed a curving glass brick wall, their shoes clicking on the floor tiles. A second officer stood leaning his bum against the wall outside 10A, holding an EN in his hands. He snapped to attention when he saw them approach.

Roxy identified herself and then Cora. Up close, she could see the officer was thin and jug-eared, with a vicious case of shaving rash on his neck. He didn't look old enough to be out of the Garda training college down in Templemore, let alone working on the job.

'What's your name?'

'Officer Foyle, Sergeant.'

Sergeant. She blinked. The title was going to take some getting used to.

'Dispatch reported a Code 6 at this address.'

'Yes, Sergeant, the deceased is still inside. Female.'

'Is Inspector Morrissey here?'

Foyle shook his head. 'No, ma'am.'

'Oh, who is on site?'

He told them, listing off Inspector Adam Johnson from Forensics, his tech team, an ambulance crew and Edwina King, the state pathologist. Cora's shoulders stiffened at the mention of Edwina's name and Roxy remembered a rumour she'd heard. Something about how the last time the two women had been in proximity to one another it had ended with Cora sprawled flat on her back in a dead faint.

Cora, apparently, was not good with bodies.

Roxy checked her watch. Inspectors did not have to attend the crime scene, but Morrissey had to know this was her … *their* first homicide. The bloody man might have at least given them a gentle push instead of flinging them in the deep end.

'Do we know who's registered to live here?' she asked, jerking her thumb towards the door.

Foyle glanced at the EN and tapped the screen. 'The owner is listed as Andrea Colgan.'

'Who's the landlord?'

'According to the registry, she's an owner-occupier.'

Roxy raised an eyebrow. That was unusual. Very few people these days could afford an apartment in a well-to-do leafy Southside suburb like Dundrum. Hell, very few people could afford property in the city at *all*.

'Who was the first responder?'

'Technically that would be me and Sergeant Cosgrove. We took the call.'

'Where's Cosgrove now?'

'Downstairs with a witness.'

'There's a witness?'

Foyle nodded.

'Good,' Roxy said. 'What time did you get here?'

'At approximately six ten.' He swallowed. Roxy heard how dry his mouth was. 'Sergeant Cosgrove and I entered the apartment and found the … uh …'

Cora rested a sympathetic hand on the young man's shoulder.

'Breathe, Foyle, okay?'

He nodded gratefully, took a breath.

'We found the body of the deceased and then Sergeant Cosgrove called it in and told me to stay here and make sure I recorded everyone coming in and out of the apartment.'

'You say you entered the apartment.' Roxy glanced at the door; there was a smear of blood on the frame about chest height. 'How did you gain entry?'

'The door wasn't locked. Sergeant Cosgrove just pushed it and it opened.'

The same door now opened inwards and Edwina King stepped into the hall, looking surprisingly elegant for someone wearing white overalls, a bright-blue plastic cap and matching blue booties.

'Hello, Roxanne.' The pathologist's voice was deep and melodious.

'Hello, Dr King.'

'I believe congratulations are in order. Promotion to sergeant, that's very impressive. Well done.'

'Probationary,' Roxy automatically replied, uncomfortable with the attention though vaguely flattered that the pathologist even cared. 'I won't make full sergeant for another six months.'

'Nevertheless, congratulations.'

'Thanks.' She motioned to Cora. 'Have you met Officer Simmons?'

'We've met.' Edwina nodded curtly to Cora, who managed to stammer a hello.

'So,' Roxy said. 'What have we got?'

'A nasty one, I'm afraid.' Edwina removed her cap and shook her head. Every strand of her hair fell precisely into a sleek bob, as if by magic. 'One body, female, found unresponsive in a bedroom shortly after six this morning.'

'Cause of death?'

'Yet to be determined.'

'Time of death?'

'In my opinion, she's been dead a number of hours, possibly since before midnight; I'll try to narrow the window at the lab.'

'Was it suicide?' Cora wondered aloud.

Roxy tried not to wince. Her new partner, she had discovered, had a terrible habit of blurting out whatever she was thinking without giving it some weight first. Edwina had already told them she had no information as to the cause of death, and if memory served her, the pathologist did not like to repeat herself.

Proving the point, Edwina said, 'Suicides don't generally beat themselves to death, Simmons. There are easier methods by which to leave this mortal coil.'

Two men in white overalls exited the apartment carrying a stretcher containing a shape encased in black plastic, followed immediately by the ambulance crew. Edwina and the detectives stepped aside to allow them room to pass.

'I will tell you this, Sergeant,' Edwina said. 'The victim suffered a brutal assault.'

'Do we have any identification?'

'I imagine Inspector Johnson has taken her fingerprints by now; he'll be sure to have an identity.'

At that exact moment, Johnson stuck his head around the door. He looked disappointed to find Roxy and Cora standing there.

'Just you two, is it?'

'How many detectives do you need?' Edwina asked, raising a perfectly groomed eyebrow.

'Detective Morrissey is on his way,' Roxy said, hoping it was true. Johnson was a right pain in the rear; it would be easier to work the case with a senior buffer.

'Morrissey, eh? Well if you want my advice, you'd be better served to call Inspector Eli Quinn.'

'Quinn?' Roxy looked at him. 'Why would we want to do that?'

'Trust me, he's going to want this case. Do yourself a favour and get on the blower.'

'But we—'

He ducked back inside. Roxy and Edwina exchanged a glance and a number of unspoken thoughts.

'Detectives,' Edwina said. 'I expect I'll speak with you later. I will begin the autopsy after lunch, say around two?'

Roxy watched her go, fuming. How dare Johnson talk to her that way? His arrogance was outrageous and it made her mind up. He could go to hell and take Eli Quinn with him. She was a sergeant now; she was entitled to make the call.

Cora was watching at her, little lines of worry around her eyes.

'What do you want to do, Sergeant? Do we wait for Morrissey or—'

'We do our job, Simmons,' Roxy said firmly. 'Inspector Johnson,' she called. 'We'd like to access the crime scene when you're ready.'

Cora and Roxy covered their shoes in plastic, snapped on gloves and waited. From their vantage point they watched Johnson move about the apartment, ordering his team this way and that. After twenty minutes he glanced towards the door and raised a hand to waggle an admonitory finger: he wasn't ready for them yet. Stay put.

'That man is a right bell-end,' Cora muttered. 'It's almost like he's doing this on purpose.'

'Don't give him the satisfaction of seeing you get annoyed,' Roxy said.

They waited, growing twitchy and bored. Eventually Johnson returned, wearing a self-satisfied smirk. Roxy tried to take heed of her own advice and not let his attitude rankle, but it was hard not to feel affronted, especially when she knew damn well the source of his behaviour. A few months back, Johnson had made a drunken move on her at a colleague's birthday party, embarrassing her to the point where she felt she'd no choice but to leave and go home early. He'd followed her out into the car park, pawing at her aggressively, pleading his case. Roxy had been polite right up until the moment he pushed her against the wall and tried to force his tongue into her mouth.

The resulting 'skirmish' saw Johnson spend the remainder of the night in A&E. The next day he went around telling anyone who'd listen that he'd fallen in the car park and hit his head. He made such a big deal about it that, naturally, no one believed a word he was saying, adding fuel to the smouldering gossip.

'So, Malloy.' He leaned against the doorframe and folded his arms across his pigeon chest. 'You've moved up in the world.'

'That's right.'

'Good, always nice to see the department's gender quota in full effect.'

Cora squared her shoulders, but Roxy cut across her before she could get fully fired up.

'Do we have an ID on the victim?'

'We ran her prints against her ID card. Her name is Andrea Colgan, twenty-six.'

'Can we access the scene now, Inspector?'

Johnson straightened up. She could tell he was annoyed that she hadn't taken his bait. 'We've been over the living room and the kitchen, so you can start there. You know the drill, right? Keep your hands to yourselves and don't touch anything.'

'Is there anything you can tell us?'

'I've already given you some advice: call Detective Quinn.'

She gave him a look that would sour milk.

'Anything *relevant*.'

'You've been a sergeant now, what, a week?'

'That's right.' Roxy took note of the fact that he'd been keeping track.

'Is this your first homicide?'

'Yes.'

'That's what I thought. You want some friendly advice, Malloy?'

'Not really,' Roxy replied icily.

'Suit yourself.' Johnson threw his hands up and stepped aside to let them in. 'Don't say I didn't warn you.'

'Oh, don't worry.' Roxy stepped past and shot him a dark look. 'I won't say anything about you at all. I never do.'

Johnson's cheeks went red and his eyes grew mean, but he wisely kept his mouth shut, and that suited Roxy perfectly.

CHAPTER FIVE

Andrea Colgan's apartment was huge. It was also nicer – *much* nicer, Roxy thought looking around – than anything she herself could ever hope to afford. She wondered how the hell a girl in her mid twenties had been able to pay for a place like this.

She followed Cora down the hall and stepped into a split-level living room. Polished wooden floors gleamed honey gold in the morning light; French doors led to a balcony overlooking the river and the carefully maintained parkland below. The walls were painted chalky white and covered in the type of artwork Roxy could never make head or tails of, splodges of colour and indistinct shapes that could be anything if you squinted hard enough.

'Nice digs,' Cora said, pausing to admire a vintage rosewood credenza. 'I'd love to know how people keep walls white like this. My Joe would have them destroyed with scuffmarks in less than an hour. No matter how many times I tell him, he throws his dirty work bag up against them …'

Roxy squatted on her haunches and studied the evidence tags on the floor, each one placed next to a droplet of blood. She counted twelve in all, leading back towards the hall. Violence had occurred here, but there was no sign of any other disturbance that she could see, nothing broken, nothing overthrown.

She got to her feet and skirted the rest of the room, trying to picture the type of person who lived in a home like this; she imagined them as professional, effortlessly chic, the kind of person who could walk in high heels without looking awkward. There were lots of personal touches: framed photos, books, throws and cushions. The furniture was eclectic – some vintage pieces with a smattering of modernity throughout. On the lower level two rose-coloured sofas faced each other over a good-quality rug, a glass-topped coffee table between them. A vase of incredibly bright yellow roses sat on a side table next to the sofa closest to the window. The wall-mounted curved-screen television probably cost more than Roxy's monthly take-home wages, ditto the integrated sound system. She spied a phone dock on the breakfast bar, but it was empty. No computer or laptop that she could see either.

She went through to the kitchen. It was modern, high tech, but disappointingly bland after the living room: glossy white cupboards, lots of stainless steel. Integrated shelves on either side of the oven were stuffed with cookbooks. In an ornamental wine rack next to the fridge she found some decent bottles as well as the usual supermarket plonk.

A block of Parmesan cheese and a half-sliced artisan loaf lay on a chopping board next to a bread knife. Roxy touched her fingers to the bread: it was as hard as rock. An ice bucket containing a bottle of champagne sat next to the chopping board. The label read Bollinger. She made a note of it in her EN, looked around for any sign of champagne glasses and didn't find any.

She opened doors and drawers full of cooking utensils, some she recognised and others she had no idea what they could possibly be used for. The cupboards were well stocked, the fridge too. Photos on the fridge door captured scenes from a happy, privileged life: summer holidays, winter trips, dinners, a cute picture of – she assumed – Andrea Colgan standing in this very kitchen wearing a white chef's hat and a floral apron. She was smiling, beaming actually. There was a lot of love in that smile, Roxy thought. She peered at another photo: same girl, tanned and smiling, leaning back against a bearded man. He was not conventionally handsome, but his face had a certain roguish charm. His arms were wrapped tightly around Andrea's waist, fingers interlocked. There were boats behind them, a pier somewhere, or a harbour.

She took the photo of the couple with her and went back to the living room. Cora was squatting by the corner of the coffee table, holding her gloved fingers close to her face.

'What?'

'I thought I caught a whiff of something when I came in, then I noticed this rug was wet.' She straightened back up, wrinkling her nose. 'It's pee.'

'Pee?'

'Urine, then.' She held out her fingers. Roxy declined the offer of a closer inspection with a brisk shake of her head.

'I believe you. Is there a cat or something?'

'Don't see any sign of one.'

'Weird. I'll tell Johnson.'

'Piss?' Johnson said when she told him. He turned his head a fraction and bellowed, 'Jimmy!'

A bespectacled head appeared from a closet further down the hall. 'What?'

'Did you find the piss in the living room?'

'What piss?'

'That's what I was afraid you'd say. Get back up there and collect a sample, and buck bloody up. How did you miss a puddle of piss?'

'To be fair, it was on a rug,' Roxy said.

'Doesn't matter.'

Looking suitably chastised, Jimmy lumbered past. Roxy showed Johnson the photograph she had taken from the fridge.

'Is this her, is this Andrea Colgan?'

Johnson glared. 'I thought I told you not to touch anything.'

'Is it her or not?'

'Hair's right.' Johnson lowered his glasses and squinted. 'Can't really comment on the face.'

Roxy returned the photo to her inside pocket.

'I'd like to see the bedroom next.'

'Door on the right.'

Before she went in, Roxy paused and took a deep breath to steady her nerves. All death carried with it a certain smell, a lingering trace on the air. She didn't want to think about the life that had been taken; she wanted to concentrate on what had been left behind.

She wished Johnson would stop staring at her.

It was a double bedroom, decorated in shades of grey and taupe, feminine but not overpoweringly so, luxurious without being ostentatious. High ceilings, built-in wardrobes on either side of a king-sized bed, a funky-looking dresser with brass handles against the opposite wall and a red velvet love seat wedged into the space under the window. There were several pairs of high-heeled shoes lined up against the skirting board: pretty things, and, to Roxy's mind, completely impractical.

A bedside locker contained a box of tissues, hand lotion, half a packet of tablets for a sore throat, a bronze lamp and next to that a framed photo. Roxy bent down to study it.

It was the same blonde woman from the photo in the kitchen, though several years younger. She was wearing a graduation cap and cape, beaming, clearly proud as Punch. A man and woman stood to either side of her. The man was tall, with pale eyes and thick dark brows. His hand rested on the girl's shoulder in what appeared to Roxy a strangely proprietorial gesture. There was something about him that seemed familiar but she couldn't work out what it was, so she turned her attention to the woman. There was a clear resemblance between her and Andrea, especially around the mouth, but there was distance here too. The woman stood a little apart, holding a handbag in front of her waist like a shield. She too was smiling, but only with her mouth.

Roxy opened the wardrobe and flipped through the hangers. Andrea's clothes were smart, bought from high-end stores. She favoured jewel tones and Roxy imagined she looked good in them with her colouring. Near the back she found a vintage wedding dress, carefully wrapped in tissue paper. It looked beautiful and impossibly fragile. Andrea had probably been saving this, she thought, saving it for her big day.

A day that would never come.

With a pang of sadness, she put the dress back and turned her attention at last to the bed.

The covers were stained with blood, tangled, pulled free from all four corners. A bloodstained pillow lay on the floor between the bed and the window. There were traces of blood splatter on the wall and the headboard, and a pool of blood had seeped through into the mattress, on the side closest to the locker.

'She fought him.'

'Looks that way,' Johnson said from the doorway, where he was monitoring her movements closely.

'No blood anywhere else apart from those drops in the living room?'

'No.'

She stared at the bed again.

'What was she wearing when she was found?'

'Satin gown, bra and knickers,' Johnson said. 'Lacy, pink. She had one of those frilly things around her leg.' He indicated midway up his own thigh.

'A garter?'

'Yeah.'

Roxy frowned.

'Her underwear was intact?'

'That's what I said, Malloy.'

'Was there evidence of a sexual nature?'

'We've taken swabs, we'll know soon enough.' He glanced over his shoulder when someone called his name. 'I'll be back. Don't bloody touch anything else.'

Roxy pushed the bathroom door open with her elbow. An automatic sensor triggered the lights to reveal a free-standing bath almost full to the brim with water. She tested it. Cold. Candles lined the tub; all but one had burnt down to nothing. Andrea Colgan had been expecting a romantic encounter, but something had gone wrong; something had gone terribly wrong.

Using the edge of her gloved finger, Roxy opened the mirrored cabinet over the sink and found the usual bathroom stuff: earbuds, toothpaste, moisturiser, generic painkillers, mouthwash, a box of tampons, unopened; and nearer the back, a small brown bottle of tablets.

She moved the bottle around to read the label, Citalopram, an antidepressant.

'You done?' Johnson was back. He stood in the doorway, hemming her in. In the confined space his aftershave was overpowering, something musky with an underlying note she found rather unpleasant. It reminded her a little of blue cheese.

'Yes.' She squeezed past him. 'No. I want a sample taken of the vomit on the path outside the building.'

'Outside? Why?'

She forced herself to make direct eye contact with him.

'Because it's fresh, Inspector Johnson.'

'It's probably some drunk or something.'

'And if it isn't?'

He stared at her, defiant. She stared back, equally so.

'Fine,' he said. 'Jimmy!'

It was a small victory, Roxy thought, watching him storm out of the room, but it *was* a victory.

CHAPTER SIX

The lone wolf does not operate within a pack. They have rejected him, chased him away, therefore he must look for – and exploit – weakness if he wishes to succeed.

And the wolf was determined to succeed.

That morning, with the wind chill on his face, he looked down into the empty communal seating area between the buildings and thought: Estelle Roberts is weak, Estelle Roberts is vulnerable.

Estelle Roberts is prey.

She had been married once. He remembered there had been a husband, a brutish-looking beast who scowled and glowered through the windscreen whenever he came to pick her up from work in his boring sedan. Back then Estelle had seldom smiled; she'd dressed in grey and black, worn her blonde hair scraped back from her face in a variety of uninspiring styles.

But now the brute was gone and Estelle, newly free, had blossomed from a dowdy weed into a beautiful rose.

For a long time the wolf wasn't entirely sure what to do about her. Yes, she was blonde and petite, pretty when she smiled, the kind of woman who normally caught his attention.

He liked the way she played with her hair when she laughed, her eyes darting this way and that, as though afraid to be caught enjoying a joke. Unlike the other women in the office, she was shy, timid, always careful with her manners. She said please and thank you; she didn't engage in small talk of any kind, and once, when she'd caught him staring at her, she had blushed and looked away.

He'd considered her right up until the day Lorraine Dell had put her hand on his arm, asked him to do her a favour and called him 'love'; after that he forgot about Estelle Roberts, for a little while at least.

Until he saw her with a man he later identified as Hugh Bannon.

For days he watched Estelle and Hugh walk around the sculpted green next to the main office, moving in step with each other, their bodies barely inches apart. When they touched, he felt a dull ache behind his eyes.

At night he dreamed of her; he dreamed it was he who walked beside her, he who touched her, he who made her play with her hair when she smiled.

He considered his options.

His hatred for Hugh Bannon grew.

Feeling slightly frantic, he made it his business to cross Estelle's path, to bump into her at random moments throughout the day. Sometimes he called her phone at the office, just to hear her speak.

Then it happened.

Disaster.

He overheard one of the other women make a crude joke about Estelle's burgeoning romance. He listened, invisible to them as he always was, choking down his emotions as they discussed Hugh Bannon's prowess between the sheets.

It was so disgusting he'd wanted to scream at them.

After that, the wolf knew it was pointless to even try. Estelle wasn't interested in him, not in *that* way.

At first he had been upset, depressed, down in the dumps. He'd cried twice, once in public, which mortified him, and once at home, which did not. He spent hours online, trying to fill the emptiness, but nothing worked.

She belonged to another man: she had chosen him.

After a while, he stopped feeling sad. After a while, a new emotion rose within him.

Anger.

The anger felt good, clean.

Just.

He studied Hugh too, taking careful note of his mannerisms, the way he walked, and the way he spoke to others. Within days he concluded that Hugh was a loser without ambition. Worse than that, he wasn't really *that* good-looking. As soon as his hair fell out and he put on weight, he'd be perfectly ordinary. This knowledge infuriated him. God, why were women so blind? What made them pick losers when there were so many other options in the world?

Options like him.

He had wanted Estelle to be different, but she was just like all the rest.

Weak.

That cold morning the wolf watched Estelle Roberts smile at Hugh Bannon and felt his guts twist. Hugh was standing with his broad back to him, one hand in his pocket, the other on the wall behind Estelle's head. The wolf could not see his face, but he knew the exact expression that would be on it.

Watching them filled the wolf with rage, but it was important that he wear his other face here. There were too many others who might have noticed his interest in Estelle, too many prying eyes and curious minds. He had learned long ago never to drop his guard around his co-workers. They were nothing but cattle to him, but even cattle could be dangerous when threatened.

He leaned forward, pressing his stomach against the railing, feeling it give softly under his weight. From this vantage point he fancied he could almost smell Estelle's perfume. Her hair was down, and under the heavy coat he knew she was wearing a navy dress with polka dots on it. He liked it when she wore dresses; women were supposed to look feminine. It never ceased to disgust him how many women dressed like men and thought they were attractive.

The fire-escape door clanked open behind him and the platform creaked as someone stepped out.

'Jaysus, it's Baltic out here.'

George. The wolf hated George too; the man was loud and obnoxious. He told crude jokes and laughed at them even if nobody else did. He slapped backs, stood too close and belched loudly, roaring, 'Better out than in!'

The wolf lifted the cigarette to his lips and forced himself to suck down some of the disgusting smoke. He almost gagged, but managed to keep his reflexes under control. He hated taking part in this charade. He didn't smoke, and loathed the smell of cigarettes, almost as much as he despised the fake camaraderie between smokers. Us against the nanny state, one of the tobacco-stained freaks had told him recently. He'd wanted to laugh in the man's face, ram the burning cigarette up his nostril and shove him over the railing. But as always, he'd said nothing. Besides, smoking allowed him cover to observe, to eavesdrop, and to keep a close eye on his enemies and his other interests.

He glanced over his shoulder.

'All right, big man,' George said, tipping him a wink. 'Fuck me, cold, isn't it?'

I heard you the first time, the wolf thought. He dropped the cigarette onto the platform and ground it out.

'Yes,' he said, because that was what people did. They exchanged tedious 'pleasantries' countless times a day. They 'got on'. 'Very cold.'

'Forecast reckoned it might snow.' George lit his own cigarette and inhaled with a look of deep satisfaction. He glanced at the wolf and then at the clouds. The wolf followed his gaze. The clouds were pewter grey, low, heavy. Yes, it was possible that it might snow. How profound of you, George. I'd like very much to push you over this railing and watch your back snap.

George turned, leaned his forearms on the railing and looked down. He watched Estelle and the man for a few minutes; smoke curled up along his arms.

'Bet she's a real little goer in the sack, that one,' he said. 'Them quiet ones are fucking wild when you get them revved up.'

The wolf felt heat rise to his cheeks.

So here it was. Everyone could see it. Estelle Roberts would give her body to Hugh Bannon. She would offer her sex willingly. The wolf imagined her astride him, naked, panting, her pale skin flushed, her soft breasts cupped in Hugh's hands. He imagined standing over them, watching, hearing the grunts, the moans, the slap of flesh against flesh.

He began to tremble.

Time to go.

'Right,' he said, because that was how men spoke. 'I'd better get back to it.'

'No rest for the wicked, eh?' George said, still watching Estelle.

'No,' the wolf agreed. 'None at all.'

That night he added Estelle Roberts' name to his manifesto. He wrote until his eyes burned and his fingers ached. He laid out in clear and certain terms what had led him to this decision.

Estelle Roberts, he decided, had it coming.

CHAPTER SEVEN

Roxy left Cora working the crime scene and went down a flight of stairs to the next floor to speak to the witness.

Sergeant Cosgrove was standing outside the door of 8A with one hand in his pocket, one foot on the wall behind him, reading something on his phone. When he heard her approach, he turned a square, humourless face in her direction, wearing an expression that managed to be both indolent and obnoxious in equal measure.

''Bout bloody time,' he muttered before Roxy had a chance to open her mouth. He slipped the phone into the pocket of his trousers and pushed off the wall.

'Officer Foyle said there was a witness.'

He jerked his head towards the apartment. 'In there, but word to the wise, I don't think this guy is playing with a full deck.'

Roxy heard locks rattle. The door swung wide open and a wild-eyed man clutching a small, scruffy-looking white dog to his chest peered out. He wore a yellow shirt patterned with red lobsters, red gym shorts, and a pair of tattered moccasins. The shirt was open to his navel.

'There you are! We thought you were coming back.'

'Sorry, sir,' Cosgrove said. 'I was waiting for—'

'Sergeant Malloy,' Roxy said.

'This,' Cosgrove said, managing to sound like he was smirking, even though he was not, 'is Mr Jerome Falstaff.'

Straight away Roxy could see what Cosgrove meant. There was definitely something off about Falstaff. Despite the chill in the hallway he was sweating heavily. Both his pupils were fully dilated, and he was practically fizzing with energy. She guessed him to be somewhere in his mid to late fifties. He was short and wiry, with a goatee that looked like he'd drawn it on for the occasion, and his skull was oddly shaped: narrow at the bottom and large and round at the top, a bit like an old-fashioned light bulb. What little hair he had was dyed russet orange and jutted from his head in every direction. His lips were shiny and almost indecently plump.

Reluctantly she offered her hand and tensed when he took it in his and pumped it up and down with frenetic movements. When she got it back, it felt sticky, and it took considerable effort not to wipe it against the leg of her trousers.

'Mr Falstaff, I believe you are a witness to what happened this morning,' she said, showing him her identification even though he hadn't asked to see it.

'Oh I am, I most certainly am.'

Without warning, he snatched her forearm and yanked her closer.

'I knew it would come to this, you know. I tried to warn Andrea about him.'

'About who?' Roxy carefully extracted her arm.

'Who do you think? That bloody boyfriend of hers. Oh, he had a dark aura, let me tell you. I could always sense it.'

'That's very interesting,' Roxy said. 'Could we step inside your apartment and talk?'

'I'll go and—' Cosgrove began.

'No. You won't,' Roxy said firmly, unwilling to be alone with Falstaff. 'Come with me, please.'

Though the floor plan was identical to the apartment upstairs, the two could not have been more different. Where Andrea's home was bright, chic and comfortable, the kind of apartment a person would happily kick back and unwind in, Falstaff's was dingy, old-fashioned and cluttered with boxes and stacks of … stuff. The air reeked of dog, stale cigarette smoke and something else, something like … ammonia maybe. Standing in the middle of the living room, looking around at the mess, Roxy managed not to make her distaste obvious until she saw a huge, furry orange-eyed cat sitting on a countertop next to an open pizza box. It growled at her and swished its tail threateningly.

'Er, is that cat … is it okay?'

'Hah! As long as you don't make any sudden moves she is.' Falstaff waved a hand towards the outraged animal. 'That's Cucumber. Now, Cucumber, be nice.'

'Cucumber?'

'She's a bit of an acquired taste, see.'

He tittered at his own joke and dropped the dog onto the floor. Immediately it circled around behind Roxy, sniffed at her ankles a few times and began to bark. Cosgrove took refuge on a spindly-legged stool near the cat and folded his arms, wearing a really annoying 'I told you so' smirk she didn't appreciate.

'Sir, before we begin, would you mind …?' She gestured to the dog.

Falstaff grabbed for it, but it skittered out of range and the barking increased in volume.

'Perhaps you could put it in another room.'

'Oh I really couldn't. He has terrible separation anxiety. I couldn't do that to him.'

Falstaff plopped down onto an ancient velvet sofa leaking stuffing and clucked his tongue. To Roxy's relief, the dog scrambled up into his lap, and though it continued to regard her with canine mistrust, at least it was quiet.

She looked about for somewhere to sit, decided it was safer to stand and opened her EN.

'Is it true then, about Andrea? Such a travesty,' Falstaff said. 'I'm devastated.'

Roxy glanced at him; he didn't sound remotely upset, let alone devastated, but then, she reminded herself, people grieved in different ways.

'How long have you lived here, Mr Falstaff?'

'Oh now, a long time, fifteen years at least. This place used to belong to Mother, but she's passed now, God rest her eternal soul.'

'My condolences,' Roxy said. 'Did you know Andrea well?'

'Well enough. She was polite, you know. Not stuck-up like some of them around here.'

'What can you tell me about her?'

'Well, let's see. She was young, beautiful, always well turned out. Great dresser, not like the young ones you see hanging around these days. I'll say this for the girl, she knew what worked for her.'

'I don't suppose you happen to know where she worked, do you?'

'Albas Entertainment,' he said instantly. Roxy typed that in, a little surprised at how much information he had on the tip of his tongue. She herself didn't know the first thing about any of her neighbours, not even their names.

'Sir, can you tell me exactly what happened this morning?'

'Well now.' Falstaff leaned back and swung one bony leg over the other. 'Let me think. I was working, see—'

'Sorry, what is it that you do?'

He gave her a petulant look, almost as though she had disappointed him.

'Mr Falstaff is an *actor*,' Cosgrove said.

'Oh, I see.' Roxy typed that in. 'Apologies, Mr Falstaff. I don't watch a lot of television … or films.'

'That's quite all right. To tell the truth, I don't do as much screen work these days as I used to.' He clutched the dog a little tighter. 'Times have changed, Sergeant. People don't respect the craft any more. Real acting is *dying*. Nobody has any attention span, see? So you have complete nobodies with millions of followers hanging on their …' He stopped talking suddenly and licked his lips. 'What was the question again?'

'You said you were working this morning.'

'That's right, I was working. I was reading a script for a voice-over.'

'Do you normally start work so early?'

'Oh no, dear.' He shook his head. 'I'm more owl than lark.'

'So why were you up today?'

'It was all Edgar's fault really.'

'Edgar?'

Falstaff lifted one of the dog's front paws and waggled it.

'Ah. Right.' She motioned to him to go on.

'He kept on at me to get up; right little fusspot he can be.' He kissed the dog on the back of the head. 'I thought he needed to do a widdle, see, so I threw on a shirt and took him downstairs. Next thing you know, I'm stood by the patch of grass outside and Edgar's sniffing around, taking his time, when Noel comes bursting through the front door, makes this awful sound and pukes—'

'Noel?'

'Noel Furlong.' He rolled his eyes dramatically. 'That *creature* Andrea was seeing: the boyfriend, or rather the ex-boyfriend.'

'Is this the man you're referring to?' Roxy showed him the photo she had taken from the fridge. Falstaff peered at it for a moment, wrinkling his nose.

'Oh that's him all right.'

'You say ex-boyfriend …'

'Right, they were broken up.'

'Do you know *when* they broke up exactly?'

'About six weeks ago, I'd say. Andrea finally saw the light. Don't know what she ever saw in him in the first place; he was a dreadful person. Edgar never liked him, and he's a very good judge of character.' He looked at her knowingly.

'Why didn't *you* like him, Mr Falstaff?'

'I know a fraud when I see one, Sergeant, believe me.'

'What makes you think he's a fraud?'

'You know the type: gets a dribble of fame, next thing he thinks he's bleeding Michelangelo.'

Roxy was horribly confused.

'Is Noel Furlong famous?'

'Hah, he wishes,' Falstaff sniffed. 'Noel Furlong thinks he's some kind of *enfant terrible*, see, but if you ask me, Edgar could paint better than he does.'

'Oh, he's an artist,' Roxy said.

'Huh, I'd hardly call those great ugly splattered things art.' Falstaff pulled a sour face. 'He calls them "abstract angst". You were upstairs; that's his crap on the walls.'

'I see.' Roxy typed furiously. 'You've been inside Andrea's apartment, then?'

'In the past, yes.' He looked suddenly a little wary. 'But not today.'

Roxy thought she detected the tiniest whiff of a lie, but she let it go, for now.

'When you saw Noel Furlong, did you talk to him, did he talk to you?'

'No, he was sick, then he ran across the street and jumped into a van, so I grabbed Edgar and went back inside.'

'A van.' Roxy typed that in. 'Can you tell me anything about it, the make, or the model?'

'No idea. I don't drive, see, never have.'

'Did you notice the registration number?'

Falstaff shook his head.

'Colour?'

'Dark blue.' He pursed his lips, thinking. 'I don't think it had any side windows.'

'Great.' Roxy sent the description directly to traffic control, along with a request for localised CCTV footage. 'Please go on.'

'Well, I was on my way back up in the lift when I got a premoni-tion.' He pointed to Cosgrove using the dog. 'I mentioned that to you, didn't I, Paul?'

Roxy glanced at Cosgrove, who nodded, then back to Falstaff.

'My grandmother was psychic, see.' Falstaff tugged at his ear lobe. 'She could always sense when someone passed over to the other side.'

'I see.'

'Now I'm not as powerful as she was, bless her, but there I was in the lift and suddenly all the hairs on my arms and my neck stood straight up.' His eyes widened. 'Jerome, I said, something wicked has occurred.'

'So did you act on your ... premonition?'

He nodded gravely.

'You went upstairs to Andrea's apartment?'

'Of course.'

'Did you enter the apartment?'

He was shaking his head before she had finished the sentence. 'No no no no, the door was closed. I knocked and called but there was no answer. That's when I noticed the blood on the frame and I knew sweet Andrea was now one of the angels.'

'What did you do then?'

'Well, I was in such a tizzy I could hardly think straight, and my sixth sense was *screaming*.'

Behind her, Cosgrove gave a little cough. Roxy ignored him.

'You came back downstairs?'

'I must have done, yes.'

'Is that when you called the Guards?'

'That's right.'

Roxy looked down for a moment, thinking.

'You didn't hear anything, notice any sign of a disturbance?'

'No.'

'Had you ever known Noel Furlong to be violent before?'

He shrugged, stretched his mouth into a huge arc of displeasure. 'Not as such.'

Roxy raised an inquisitive eyebrow.

'I mean, he was a shouter; I'd hear him shouting from time to time.'

'Even from down here?'

He shrugged. Roxy had a mental image of him lurking about the stairwell, ears cocked.

'But Andrea never mentioned anything to you about being afraid of him?'

'No, but then women don't, do they?'

It was a fair point, Roxy thought. She'd worked on plenty of cases were a woman would swear blind everything was perfect between her and her partner while the bruises were still fresh on her body.

She thought of the outfit Andrea had been wearing, the bath and the candles. Could it have been a reconciliation gone awry? Jealousy? New lover?

'Was Andrea seeing anyone else, do you know?'

'She had … gentlemen callers.'

Roxy looked at him.

'Gentle*men* callers?'

Falstaff reached for his cigarettes, lit one and blew a stream of smoke towards the ceiling.

'She was a young, attractive woman, Sergeant. I'm not judging her.'

Yeah, right, Roxy thought. The creep was painting a picture using broad strokes, waiting for her to join the dots.

'Can you describe any of these callers?'

He picked a piece of tobacco from his lower lip. 'Older … richer, I'd say.'

'Mr Falstaff,' she said. 'Are you trying to suggest Andrea Colgan was some kind of prostitute?'

If there had been an award for best overacting, Falstaff would surely have been the front-runner. He practically squeaked with indignation.

'Oh Sergeant, please don't misunderstand me, I'm not accusing Andrea of anything other than being beautiful.' He waved a hand, spilling ash on the sofa. 'Youth is currency, it's … power.'

'Power?'

'Oh yes,' Falstaff said, nodding. 'Believe me, whoever or whatever Andrea Colgan was involved in, I'll bet she held all the cards.'

Roxy thought of the bloodstained sheets, the droplets of blood on the honey-coloured wooden floor.

'I don't believe she did, Mr Falstaff,' she said quietly. 'I really don't believe she did.'

CHAPTER EIGHT

Inspector Morrissey arrived as Cora and Roxy were leaving. He climbed out of his car and stood squinting into the sunlight, unshaved and crumpled. His clothes looked like he'd slept in them.

He eyeballed Roxy with little by way of friendliness.

'You Sergeant Malloy?'

'Yes, sir.' Roxy drew herself up to her full height. 'This is Officer Simmons.'

Up close she noticed there were traces of dried egg on his tie.

'Forensics still here?'

'Yes, sir,' Roxy said. 'We were about to start canvassing the neighbourhood to see if anyone saw or—'

'She can do that.' He nodded to Cora, who looked slightly taken aback at his tone.

'And what will I do?' Roxy wanted to know.

'You go see her mother; name's Lillian Colgan.' He handed Roxy a slip of paper with a name and address on it. 'Talk to her, bring her to the morgue and get a formal ID on the body.'

'Sir, if I may, where did you get this information?'

'Johnson sent me the victim ID. I ran her birth cert, something you might have done.'

'I would have done it back at the station, sir.'

Morrissey's blocky head moved a fraction of an inch.

'This is homicide, Sergeant; time is of the essence.'

Roxy flushed. Morrissey ambled past them into the building.

'Hashtag fucker,' Roxy muttered under her breath, and glanced at Cora to see if she had overheard.

'He's a bit … old-school, isn't he?' Cora said, with far more kindness than Roxy could ever have mustered. 'Bit of a cheek lecturing you on time when he's turned up so late.'

Roxy set her jaw, folded the paper and tucked it into the pocket of her jacket.

'I'll see you back at the station, Officer Simmons.'

'Will you be okay?'

'Of course, why wouldn't I be?'

'Oh, it can be … Breaking that kind of news is …'

Cora took another look at Roxy's face and let the matter drop. 'The station, yes, Sergeant.'

Lillian Colgan lived in an ex-council house in Ballyfermot, a deeply close-knit community that had so far managed to avoid being fully gentrified. Roxy parked the car on the footpath and checked the address again. Yep, this was definitely it.

The front gate creaked alarmingly when she opened it. She walked up a concrete path flanked by snowdrops and rang the doorbell. While she waited, she worked on her delivery. Cora was right, breaking bad news was never easy, and she had never been one for emotional scenes. Her ex-boyfriend had once told her she had all the empathy of a brick.

A middle-aged woman opened the door, smoking a cigarette. Roxy barely recognised Lillian Colgan from Andrea's graduation photo. Her hair was dyed a harsh, unforgiving red. She wore skin-tight jeans and an off-the-shoulder pink jumper. Her feet were bare, her toenails painted red to match her hair.

Roxy removed her hat, tucked it under her arm and cleared her throat.

'Lillian Colgan?'

Lillian looked past Roxy to the street, then back to her.

'What is it?'

'Mrs Colgan, my name is Sergeant Malloy. May I come in?'

'Why? What do you want?'

'I think it would be better if we spoke inside.'

Lillian jerked her head. Roxy followed her up a narrow hall and into a kitchen at the rear of the house. It was small and sunny, but the linoleum on the floor was cracked in places and some of the cupboard doors were askew. A well-stocked aquarium took pride of place between the kitchen and a breakfast nook.

Lillian offered Roxy one of the only two kitchen chairs, pressed against the wall nearest the back door. Roxy sat, put her hat down on her knees and watched as Lillian ground out her cigarette, leaned back against the worktop and crossed her arms. She looked like a woman who could feel Damocles' sword hovering above her neck.

'I doubt you're here for anything good, so out with it.'

'I'm sorry, Mrs Colgan—'

'I'm not married, you can call me Lillian.'

'Lillian, I'm … I regret to inform you that …' Roxy swallowed, feeling her heart hammering in her chest. 'I regret to inform you that your daughter Andrea has—'

Lillian's legs folded under her. She slid down the cupboard to the floor, opened her mouth and screamed. The sound was so loud and so sudden, Roxy flinched and leaped to her feet.

She heard footsteps overhead, and moments later an older woman wearing a black kimono burst into the kitchen.

'What the hell!'

She rushed to Lillian, dropped to the floor and put her arms around her.

'Lillian, my God, what is it?'

'Oh God, Justine, Justine …'

The older woman looked up at Roxy, aghast.

'What is it, what did you say to her?'

'I … I was about to tell her that Andrea is—'

'Shut up, you shut your mouth!' Lillian cried. 'Don't say it, don't you dare say that in my house.'

Roxy picked up her hat. Oh God, this was worse than she could ever have imagined it would be. She tried to think: what would Cora do in this situation?

'Lillian.' The word came out wrong. She cleared her throat and started again. 'Lillian, listen to me. I'm so sorry, I'm so very sorry, but your daughter Andrea is dead.'

Lillian threw back her head and wailed.

'Where is she?' Justine wanted to know.

'The city morgue.'

'What happened? Did she have an accident?'

Roxy dug her fingers into the fabric of her hat.

'We believe it was an unlawful killing.'

The colour drained from the older woman's face.

'My God, are you sure?'

'Yes, but I need someone, next of kin, to make a formal identification.'

'Can I do it?'

'Are you family?'

'No, but I know—'

Lillian pushed the woman away.

'No, no! Andrea is my daughter, she's my child, I will do it.'

'Sweetheart, I don't think—'

'*Justine!*'

The older woman fell silent. Using the cupboard behind her as leverage, Lillian got unsteadily to her feet. She was no longer crying, and when she spoke, her voice was flat and drained.

'Will you take me to her?'

'Yes,' Roxy said.

'Give me a minute to get ready.'

'Of course.'

Lillian left the room. Roxy wanted to go outside, breathe some cold air, but Justine was trying to get to her feet too and needed a hand up.

'Thank you,' she said, pushing her hair back from her face. 'My God, this is so awful.'

'Yes, it's … a tragedy.'

'She's just a kid.'

Roxy thought of the photo back in the bedroom.

'Is Andrea's father still in the picture?'

It was as if she had slapped Justine across the face.

'You mean Dominic doesn't know yet?'

'If you give me his number, I will be sure to contact him.'

Justine left the room and returned moments later with her phone in her hand, wearing a pair of reading glasses. She thrust the phone at Roxy.

'Here.'

Roxy typed the number into her EN.

'You need to call him right away,' Justine said.

'Would it not be best if he heard the news from family?'

'Family?' Justine looked as if she was torn between laughing and crying. 'You don't know, do you?'

'Know what?'

'Who Andrea's father is.'

Roxy shook her head, puzzled.

'You're lucky,' Justine said bitterly. 'How I wish I had the luxury.' She shook her head and pointed at the number. 'Call him. His name is Dominic Travers.'

'You say that as though I should know him.'

'Run his name,' Justine said. 'It won't take you long to see the kind of man he is. Excuse me, I need to help Lillian.'

While she waited, Roxy ran Dominic Travers' name through the GSN database and was rewarded with an immediate hit.

Andrea Colgan's father was a career criminal – or rather he had been. His last case was fifteen years before. When Roxy tried to access it, she found the file heavily redacted; moments later an official warning report appeared saying the material she wished to retrieve was not available and that she should direct all further enquiry to the office of Superintendent Augustus O'Connor.

Weird, Roxy thought, closing her EN.

CHAPTER NINE

Terry Peel's legs were heavy as he climbed the metal steps to the cabin door. He'd rehearsed his lines on the drive over, but now that he was here he was filled with the overwhelming desire to turn round, get back into his car and drive, preferably somewhere far away, a remote island perhaps, another planet. In the yard below, men in hard hats scurried to and fro, oblivious to his pain.

He envied their ignorance. He wondered how they would feel if they knew the news he carried that morning: would they feel sorry for him, resent him?

Blame him?

The rain had plastered what little hair he had to his head, but he let it be. Somehow he doubted his appearance mattered much in the grand scheme of things. With a last miserable sigh, he knocked on the door and heard a man's voice bellow, 'Come.'

At least the cabin was warm, thanks to the small space heater in the corner pumping out hot air. His boss, Dominic Travers, sat behind a paper-strewn desk, working, always working. He had his jacket off and his sleeves rolled up to his elbows. Both arms were heavily tattooed, and the backs of his hands were cross-hatched with scars. When he looked up, his pale-grey eyes seemed to glitter in the harsh overhead light. Predator's eyes, Terry thought, merciless.

'Well?'

Terry put his briefcase on the floor, removed a handkerchief from his inside pocket and dabbed at his forehead with it. When he was done, he put it back in his pocket.

'It's not good news, I'm afraid.'

It was true, he *was* afraid. He'd spent much of that morning traipsing around a muddy field trying to talk sense into a man who for the most part responded with grunts and then total silence. For Terry, a smooth talker and used to getting his own way, it had been a demoralising experience and a complete waste of time.

Dominic Travers looked at him expectantly.

'Don't stand there like a tree; what did he say?'

'He won't sell the land. I did as you said and offered him twenty-five thousand over the previous offer, and he didn't even bat an eyelid.'

'So offer him another twenty.'

'It won't matter what I offer him. He's dug in, Dominic.'

'Then dig him out.'

Terry spread his hands and tried to adopt what he hoped was a knowing yet exasperated expression. Dominic Travers didn't understand the concept of 'no'; for him, an obstacle was a minor hindrance and nothing more, something to be tackled and shunted aside. The notion that there were people out there who were equally stubborn never seemed to occur to him. Unfortunately, John Brown was one of those people.

'He's resolute.'

'Bollocks. The old fuck is nearly seventy years old, Terry, eking out a living on scrubland; you're really going to stand there and tell me you couldn't convince him to sell?'

'He said he was born on the land, he'll die on the land.'

Dominic snorted. 'That can be fucking arranged.'

Terry blinked. It was always difficult to tell with Dominic if he was being serious or not. These days his boss was to all intents and purposes a legitimate businessman, with considerable holdings and assets. But he had never fully shed his other skin, the skin of a man who it was rumoured had so many skeletons in his closet, literally as well as figuratively, he could raise an army of bone if he felt like it.

Dominic pushed his chair back and walked to the window of the office, where he stood with his hands behind his back, looking down. Terry tracked his movement without turning his head. His boss was a big man, a shade under six feet five, broad-shouldered and powerfully built, yet he was as light on his feet as a dancer.

'I tried to reason with him, Dominic.'

'You tried,' Dominic said softly, which for some reason was more terrifying than if he had yelled. 'I have an entire crew ready to break ground, Terry, machinery, cranes, the works. You assured me you had this in hand.'

'I did, I did have it in hand,' Terry said, hating how squeaky his voice sounded.

'My land is next to worthless without the acquisition. Brown's shit-heap of a farm is slap bang in the middle of the development zone.'

'It's remarkable, really,' Terry prattled on, his nerves getting the better of him. 'I mean, like you say, he's practically living in squalor. You'd think he'd jump at the chance to move.'

'You know, for a smart man, sometimes you're as dumb as a box of rocks.'

Dumb or not, Terry had enough sense to stop talking. He was relieved when Dominic's phone chirruped. He took it out from his pocket, checked the number and cut the call.

'What he's got there, livestock and the like? Sheep? Cattle? Pigs?'

'Sheep, as far as I can tell; the land wouldn't be great for grazing.'

'Mm,' Dominic mused. 'It's January, so likely those sheep will be full of lambs.'

'Um, I imagine so.'

'Who do we know has dogs?'

'Dogs?'

'Are you deaf, man? Dogs.'

'I … What kind of dogs?'

Dominic's phone rang again. He swore, but this time he answered.

'Whatever it is, I'm not—' He stopped talking. Terry glanced his way, and wished he hadn't. 'Say that again.'

He listened in silence. When the caller was finished talking, he hung up, grabbed his coat and left the office. Terry walked to the window. He saw Dominic get into his car, gun the engine and tear out of the yard, tyres spinning, spraying wet gravel behind them.

Terry let out a long breath and leaned his forehead against the glass. He would rather fight a bear with his bare hands than be wherever the hell it was Dominic Travers was heading.

CHAPTER TEN

Eli Quinn and Miranda Lynn were standing in the street. There was a no-smoking policy operational in the station, and since brass frowned on officers hanging around outside like errant hoodlums, everyone who smoked did so across the street.

Quinn offered a cigarette to Miranda, who shook her head. She was trying to quit and had managed to ration herself down to four a day. He lit his and blew a stream of smoke into the freezing air.

'I suppose you saw the story in the paper this morning,' he said after a moment.

Miranda leaned back against the wall and crossed her legs at the ankles.

'I read it, it's trash.'

'Trash or not, it's going to put added pressure on us.' He gave a bitter laugh. 'Did you see what they're calling the killer?'

'The Sweetheart Killer, I saw it. Tabloids love a good nickname.'

'Catchy. I've already had Gussy chewing my ear about it.' Superintendent Augustus O'Connor was the station boss.

'What did he say?'

'He wants to know why after a month we're still no closer to discovering the killer or killers of Lorraine Dell and Sean Kilbride. He wants to know what we've been doing with our time.'

'Are you serious?' Miranda was angry on his behalf, and on behalf of the squad. They'd been working day and night on the double homicide; they'd spoken to neighbours, friends, colleagues, ex-lovers, ex-friends, casual friends, everyone and anyone who'd had a passing chat with the victims – and nothing. But it wasn't from a lack of effort at their end.

'Gussy should know better than to let the press push his buttons,' she said.

'I don't think it's the press. I get the feeling he's getting it in the neck from higher up the food chain, trickle-down whip-cracking.'

Miranda glanced at him. He looked tired and a little worn around the edges, his face full of new lines she hadn't noticed before. People made assumptions about Quinn, based on little more than conjecture: they thought he was aloof, arrogant, a man who needed taking down a peg. Maybe there was a grain of truth to that, maybe. But she'd worked with him on and off for almost four years, and by now she knew how he ticked. She knew that failure cost him a great deal. He took it personally; he always did.

'We're going to have to go back to the start, Sergeant, go over the evidence with a fine-tooth comb: we've missed something and we need to bloody find it.'

'You done, Inspector? It's freezing out here.'

'Yeah.' Quinn pitched what remained of his cigarette into the street and they began to walk back across the road. As they reached the footpath, his phone bleeped in his pocket. He glanced at the screen.

'That was Johnson. He wants to see us in the lab.' He gave her a weak smile. 'Who knows, maybe he has some good news for a change.'

The forensics department was housed in a square single-storey building directly behind the station house, accessed from the central courtyard. Johnson came bounding out to admin as soon as he heard Quinn and Miranda had arrived.

He looked very excited, Miranda thought, like a skinny leopard seal wearing glasses.

'What have you got?' Quinn asked.

'Follow me, my good man,' Johnson said, pushing his glasses back up his nose. 'Let me show you my goodies.'

'I hate it when he pulls this cryptic shit,' Miranda muttered as they followed him deep into the bowels of the unit. 'Why can't he answer a straight question like a normal person? Why all the hoopla?'

Quinn flapped a hand at her to be quiet before Johnson heard her. The forensic scientist was a little odd at times, but he was useful. Insulting him was foolish and no use to anyone.

'Now,' Johnson said, as he entered his office, 'wait until you see what turned up this morning.'

He unlocked the top drawer of his desk and handed a brown evidence envelope to Quinn. 'They're still detailing the video, but I thought you'd like to see a few stills I've pulled.'

Quinn undid the flap and removed a number of photos, spreading them out on Johnson's desk. Miranda leaned in, her shoulder slightly pressed against his.

'Yellow roses,' Quinn said.

'That's right,' Johnson said. 'Keep looking.'

Quinn looked at another picture.

'Champagne.'

'Champagne and roses: where have we seen this before?'

Quinn lowered the photo and looked directly at Johnson, who was grinning like the Cheshire cat. 'Where did you get these?'

'From a homicide in Dundrum.'

'Tell me about the victim.'

'She was young, pretty, blonde, in her twenties, not unlike Lorraine Dell.'

'Do we have an ID on her?'

'Andrea Colgan.'

Miranda took the photo of the roses from Quinn, her brow furrowed as she read the date on the prints. 'Whose case is this?'

'I believe Morrissey is running lead at the moment.'

'You believe?'

'Well …'

'Does he know we're looking at these?'

Johnson's grin faded a little.

'I doubt he'd object.'

Miranda gave him a long, hard look.

'This is not how we operate, Inspector. If this is Inspector Morrissey's case, you should have run these by him first.'

'It's clearly the work of the same man you're investigating.'

But Miranda was not going to be fobbed off that easily.

'Clearly? I only see one body here.'

'Yes, but the—'

'Was there a note found with the roses?'

'We haven't located one.'

She tapped the photo of Andrea. 'This woman has been violently assaulted.'

'She's wearing fancy underwear,' Johnson said. 'Look at the bathroom, see all those candles? They're burned right down, exactly like at the Dell/Kilbride murder scene.'

'So she lit some candles to take a bath, like millions of women do.'

'Still,' Quinn said, looking thoughtful. 'The flowers, the champagne, her physical description, that's too much of a coincidence for me to overlook. What about make-up? The frosted lipstick, did you find any of that?'

Johnson shook his head. 'No, but that's … It doesn't mean it wasn't used. She … Well, her face was too badly smashed up to find traces of it.'

'Exactly,' Miranda said. 'This MO is all wrong.'

'Maybe she tried to fight him off and he had to subdue her.'

'He drugged Lorraine Dell to subdue her; there were massive amounts of ketamine in her system, remember? Is there ketamine in this woman's blood?'

'We don't have toxicology results back yet,' Johnson said petulantly. He was growing annoyed with Miranda for spoiling his moment. 'But come on, what else could this be?'

'I don't know.' Miranda shrugged one shoulder. 'A copycat maybe?'

Johnson snorted.

'We mentioned the flowers and the champagne in the papers,' Quinn reminded her. 'But we never mentioned that Lorraine Dell was found in her underwear.'

'It doesn't feel right,' Miranda said, stubbornly persistent.

'Maybe he's changing up his MO, or he was disturbed or some shit. Look, we should at least consider it, okay?'

Quinn gathered up the photos and put them back in the envelope.

'Thanks for the heads-up, Adam. I really appreciate it.'

'I'm glad somebody does.'

'You did great, and don't worry about Morrissey, I'll sort it out with him.'

Johnson nodded, somewhat mollified. 'You know I told Malloy you should have been called in from the off, but she wouldn't listen to me.'

'Malloy?'

'Oh, you haven't had the pleasure?' Johnson said archly. 'Probationary Sergeant Malloy; she was there this morning throwing her weight around. I told her to contact you, but she wouldn't take my advice.'

'Roxy Malloy?' Miranda asked.

'You know her?' Quinn asked.

'I worked with her before. She's a good officer, sharp.'

'She's a loose cannon,' Johnson said. 'You know who her father is, don't you?'

As it happened, Miranda did know who Roxy's father was; she also knew *where* he was. Frank Malloy was locked up in a maximum-security jail on Lambay Island, a couple of miles off the coast of North County Dublin.

'What has her old man got to do with any of this?'

Johnson was smug, unbearably so.

'They say the apple doesn't fall far from the tree, Sergeant, but if you ask me, Malloy is still attached to the bloody branch.'

CHAPTER ELEVEN

As buildings went, Roxy normally liked the city morgue. It was quiet and clean, and the air smelled faintly of antiseptic. The waiting room always had the best up-to-date scientific magazines, and if she didn't feel like reading, she liked to watch the assistants bustle about the place with clipboards in hand, everybody moving silently on the weird rubber-soled shoes they all seemed to wear.

Roxy approved of practical footwear.

But that day she could find no comfort in her surroundings, and the tension headache building behind her eyes was not helped by the fact that she couldn't stop thinking about Dominic Travers.

After she'd called him to break the news, she'd run his name again, trawling online newspaper articles about him. Andrea's father was a fascinating, terrible man, a criminal who was now considered a legitimate businessman, or so the story went. So why was his last file redacted. What had this man done to warrant that kind of secrecy?

She heard voices approaching and got to her feet as Lillian and Justine reached the administration desk. Lillian's face was the colour of ash, and had it not been for Justine holding her up, it looked like she might collapse at any moment.

'Is there anything I can do?'

Lillian looked at her. 'Can you raise the dead?'

Roxy shook her head.

'Then there's nothing you can do.'

*

Back at the station, there was no sign of Cora, but there was a message from Superintendent Augustus 'Gussy' O'Connor. He wanted to see her asap.

Feeling a little apprehensive, Roxy took her place on a hard plastic chair outside his office. She sat ramrod straight, legs together with her hands on her knees. Gussy's secretary, Nancy, sat behind her desk, typing and scrupulously avoiding making eye contact. Both women were acutely aware of the raised voice coming from behind Gussy's half-glass door.

As brass went, Gussy was generally liked and considered pretty fair-minded … for a boss. He was a committed Christian, the last of a dying breed; and unlike the hypocrites who proudly proclaimed their moral superiority in church, his Christianity manifested itself in a quiet, muscular kind of decency.

Roxy had always respected Gussy a great deal, and not just because he'd had a large hand to play in her promotion to Homicide. Under normal circumstances she believed he understood policing better than most, and ergo understood the pressures the Gardai faced daily.

A green light on Nancy's desk phone flashed. She cleared her throat before she picked up the receiver.

'Yes, sir, she's here … Certainly.'

She hung up and looked over at Roxy.

'You may go in now.'

Roxy got to her feet and tugged at the hem of her jacket. After a moment, she raked her fingers through her hair, trying to tidy it up a little, and tucked her hat under her elbow.

'How do I look?'

At least Nancy's smile was kind.

Roxy opened the inner door and entered.

Gussy was on the phone, listening, bristling with anger. He was a tall man, with a slight paunch and long limbs. He wore a sparse, unfashionable moustache on his upper lip, and from the eyebrows up he was bald as an egg.

'What?' he demanded. 'Irrelevant … No, absolutely not … I don't give a damn. The press office will not be bullied, Gavin. No releases until further notice.'

He slammed the phone down and rubbed his eyes with his heels of his hands. 'This place is like a bloody sieve sometimes. Sit down, Sergeant.'

Roxy sat.

He lowered his hands and looked at her. 'You accessed Dominic Travers' records.'

It was a statement, not a question. She gaped at him in mild surprise.

'I did, sir.'

'May I ask why?'

'His name came up in connection to a case I'm working on.'

'What case?'

She explained about her morning, how she and Cora had processed the crime scene in Dundrum; she told him about Lillian Colgan, she told him every detail she could think of except the part where Johnson tried to get her to call Eli Quinn.

When she was finished speaking, Gussy leaned back in his chair and pinched the bridge of his nose as though he'd been hit by a wave of sudden fatigue.

'Sir,' Roxy said after a moment of silence. 'Why are Dominic Travers' records redacted?'

Gussy ignored the question.

'Are you sure Andrea Colgan is his daughter?'

'Yes, sir. He's not on her birth certificate, but he is her father.'

He sat silent again, chewing his bottom lip.

'Right, where's Inspector Morrissey now?'

'I don't know, sir, I just got back.'

'Okay, return to your workstation, Sergeant Malloy.' Gussy reached for his phone.

'Sir, what about—'

'That will be all for now, Sergeant.'

Roxy took the not-so-subtle hint and left, baffled. What the hell was going on?

Downstairs, Cora was back at their cubicle, eating a yoghurt with little enthusiasm. She looked miserable.

'What's wrong?'

'People are what's wrong; society. A young woman is killed like that, you'd think they'd be queuing up to help.'

'Let me guess: no one saw anything, no one heard anything.'

Cora's expression told her she was bang on the money.

'It's so depressing.'

'Human nature. People don't want to get involved.'

'Well that's depressing too.'

'Edwina said she was going to start Andrea's autopsy at two, didn't she? I should probably be there for it.' Roxy gathered up her things and put her hat on. 'You can stay here if you like. I understand.'

Cora put her spoon down and looked offended.

'Why would I stay here?'

'You know.' Roxy waved a hand. 'In case you keel over or something.'

'Oh for heaven's sake, I knew that stupid rumour had gone round. I didn't keel over; I was a little light-headed, that's all.' Cora rubbed her temples. After a moment, she reached for her jacket. 'You certainly live up to your reputation, Sergeant Malloy, you really do.'

'What reputation is that?'

Cora pretended she didn't hear the question.

CHAPTER TWELVE

For the second time that day, the receptionist told Roxy to take a seat in the waiting room next to the administration office. To distract herself from Cora, who was whistling the same four bars of some unrecognisable tune over and over again through the gap in her lower teeth, Roxy opened her EN and read what she could on Dominic Travers, alternating between various news sources and court reports.

The more she read, the less she understood.

From what she could piece together, Travers had grown up in the system, the product of an alcoholic mother and a dangerous, violent father with gang connections. By age six, he was an orphan, his father murdered, his mother dead by her own hand. No one came forward to claim the little boy and so he spent the next twelve years shunted from one institute to another with time off for some fostering that never worked out. By the time he reached eighteen years of age, Dominic Travers was practically feral.

Yet something must have happened, because between the age of nineteen and twenty-six there were no further tangles with the law. For seven years, Travers managed to vanish off the map. Then he was back, and back with a bang. Over the next ten years he clocked up an impressive number of arrests and convictions: assault, robbery, affray, assault with a weapon, battery, affray, assault … Roxy shook her head.

The man was clearly a violent thug.

Yet strangely, there was nothing again until four years later, when Dominic Travers was arrested outside the salubrious Shelbourne Hotel on St Stephen's Green at three in the morning, blood on his hands, his coat, his face. Only there was no mention of him going to trial and this was the file that was redacted.

Weird.

Roxy leaned her head back against the wall and stared up at the ceiling tiles.

Why redacted?

Her own father had been covered in blood when he was arrested.

No, she told herself, not today. This has nothing to do with him.

Truthfully, it had been a long time since she'd allowed herself to think of her father. Thinking of him brought other memories to the surface, memories she would prefer to keep buried. She wondered if he knew about her promotion. She wondered if he kept abreast of such matters. She wondered if he was remotely interested in anything she did.

Cora cracked her knuckles, startling her. The noise was uncommonly loud in the silence.

'I hate waiting,' Cora said.

'I noticed.'

'I don't think she likes me.'

'Who?'

'Edwina.'

Roxy did not want to be drawn into a conversation about the pathologist, so looked down at her EN again, hoping Cora would get the message.

'She likes you, though,' Cora said after a while. 'She's not married, is she?'

'I have no idea.'

'I don't think she is. I don't think she's the type.'

'What type is that?'

'You know what I mean.'

'I don't.'

Roxy was glad when an assistant appeared and asked them to follow her. She showed them to the viewing booth, a small chamber with an internal window overlooking the autopsy theatre. The booth had a rubber floor and contained two rows of connected seats. Roxy took one in the front at the end of the row. Cora remained standing by the wall, close to the door. Her body language was telling.

'You don't have to be here, you know,' Roxy reminded her.

'I *know* that.'

Roxy turned back round, eyes forward. She was learning it was pointless trying to reason with Cora when she was doing that thing she did with her eyebrows.

In the autopsy room, the double plastic doors buckled inwards and a figure clad in white backed in through them pulling a gurney. Edwina brought up the rear, also wearing white. Without seeming to glance in their direction, she flicked a switch on the wall and a speaker over their heads crackled.

'You made it, Detectives,' she said.

'Yes,' Roxy replied.

'Officer Simmons, would you be more comfortable waiting in the staff canteen?'

Cora's cheeks flared pink with embarrassment.

'I'm fine, thank you.'

'Good, but should you feel faint, there's also a water cooler down the hall.'

'I said I'm fine,' Cora replied with a defiant edge to her voice.

'As you wish.' Edwina turned to her assistant. 'Rebecca, shall we?'

Rebecca unzipped the body bag and folded back the sides.

'Oh my God.' Cora put her hand to her mouth.

In life, Andrea Colgan had been a beautiful, vivacious young woman, with honey-blonde hair and dimples in her cheeks when she laughed. What lay exposed under the dazzling lights was as far from that as could be imagined. Bloodied, battered, bruised, disfigured, broken and torn, it did not look like Andrea Colgan; it barely looked human at all.

Edwina glanced at the clock, called out the time and reached for her camera. She took photos from every angle, reporting what she saw to Rebecca, who made notes.

Roxy watched the women work, fascinated by how they moved around one another with such practised ease and grace. When she was done taking pictures, Edwina put the camera down and began to comb through Andrea's hair. She scraped under her nails, measured wounds and grazes. With Rebecca's help, she removed the gown, the underwear and the garter, placing each item into a separate clear plastic bag.

Words like 'blunt-force trauma', 'abrasions' and 'lacerations' filtered through the speaker; polite words, accurate even, yet they bothered Roxy. Each time Edwina pointed out some bruise or wound, she thought of the young woman in the photo with the beautiful smile, her eyes filled with love. It didn't seem right, somehow, referring to her in such clinical terms.

When Edwina reached for her scalpel, Cora, who had not moved a muscle up until this point, abruptly left the room.

Edwina made a deep incision into Andrea Colgan's sternum, carving down and under her right breast, then repeated the same on the left side. She worked the scalpel down towards the groin and folded the skin back, revealing a thin layer of bright yellow fat, the colour of grass-fed butter.

The door behind Roxy opened. Thinking it was Cora coming back, she turned in her seat and found herself staring into a face she recognised from her earlier online snooping.

Dominic Travers.

She jumped up quickly to block his view.

'Sir, I don't think you should be here.'

Travers grabbed her shoulders and forcibly moved her out of his way.

'Dr King,' Roxy called.

Edwina glanced up, put down her scalpel and drew a sheet up over the body.

'This is a closed environment,' Edwina said.

Travers raised his right hand and placed it on the glass. Roxy noticed that the back of it was cross-hatched with scars.

'That's my daughter.'

Edwina glanced at Roxy, who nodded.

'Let me see her face.'

Edwina hesitated. 'Sir, your daughter has sustained a number of injuries that—'

'Let me see her, damn you.'

Edwina peeled the sheet back as far as Andrea's shoulders, above the incisions. Travers made a strange choking sound and sank down into one of the chairs as though all the strength had drained from his lower body.

'You have my condolences. I think it would be best if you let us take care of her now,' Edwina said. 'Sergeant Malloy, could you escort him outside, please?'

Roxy put her hand on his shoulder.

'Will you come with me? Please.'

Wordlessly he stood up and followed her out of the room. Out in the hall he pressed his forehead against the wall and made a low groaning sound that sent the hair on Roxy's neck straight up.

'Sir, I am sorry for your loss …'

The sound stopped. Before her eyes he seemed to gather himself. He stood straight, squared his shoulders and stared down at her.

'Where's Noel Furlong? Is he in in custody?'

She blinked, alarmed by the sudden one-eighty he'd pulled, no longer grieving, no longer vulnerable.

'I asked you a question.'

'I don't know,' she replied. 'I imagine by now there is a warrant out for his …'

Beneath his skin, muscles seemed to move independently of one another, forming, hardening. His eyes were unreadable.

'Sir, listen to me for a moment. Whatever you're thinking …'

He walked off before she could finish.

Roxy didn't like it. She hurried to find Cora and tracked her down in the canteen, sitting at the end of a long table, messaging someone on her phone.

'There you are. I think we'd better skedaddle. Dominic Travers was here and he looked like he …'

She stopped. Cora's hands were shaking.

'Are you okay, Simmons?'

'I can't look at dead bodies,' Cora said after a moment. 'I know people laugh about it and I know I'm supposed to be objective, and believe me I'm trying, but—'

'It's okay.'

'I don't know how you can sit there and watch her cut people up like that. There's something so … They're people, you know? They're still people.'

Roxy nodded. There was no shame in not wanting to watch an autopsy. There was nothing pleasant about reducing a human being to organs and cavities.

'It gets easier,' she said after a while. 'Honestly.'

'I don't want it to get easier,' Cora replied, giving her a strange look. 'I don't ever want to be okay with cutting people up.'

'Right.'

Edwina appeared at the door. Along the way she had ditched the scrubs and was now back wearing her casual clothes, though

Edwina's version of casual was Roxy's version of dolled up to the nines. Roxy hoped she didn't notice how upset Cora looked, and was surprised to find she cared.

'Come with me.'

They followed the pathologist to her office on the next floor. It was a square room, neat and tidy, devoid of anything that might be remotely personal: no photos, no plants, no quirky mugs saying *You don't have to be mad to work here but it helps.*

'Take a seat,' Edwina said, taking her own chair behind her desk. She put her glasses on.

They sat.

'We have a little dilemma,' Edwina said without preamble.

'What kind of dilemma?' Roxy asked.

'Andrea Colgan was pregnant.'

Cora gasped. 'Oh my God, that's terrible.'

'How long?' Roxy wanted to know.

'By my estimate, the gestational age of the foetus is roughly eleven weeks.' Edwina linked her fingers together and tilted her head back slightly. 'As I said, a dilemma.'

'Ah,' Roxy said.

Cora looked confused. Edwina noticed.

'Officer Simmons, I suspect you have a question.'

'I don't understand, what's the problem?'

'The problem is the foetus: do we take DNA from it or not?'

'What? That's ridiculous. Why wouldn't you take DNA?'

'During the first trimester, a foetus is considered the biological property of the mother; only after twelve weeks can it be considered an individual, legally speaking. There was a referendum held about it a number of years ago.'

'Hold on a second,' Cora said. 'Andrea Colgan was beaten to death and her baby died as a direct result of that. There are two victims here, so this is a double homicide.'

'Foetus,' Edwina corrected. 'And technically it isn't. The law is quite clear on the subject. Before twelve weeks, legal precedent holds that the contents of Andrea Colgan's uterus belong to her and her alone. There is no other victim.'

'So you're telling me we can't charge this fucker with killing a baby because we're out by a few days? We can't tell her family she was pregnant because of a *week*?' Cora's voice rose alarmingly. 'What if you're wrong, what if the baby – oh, sorry – what if the *foetus* is actually twelve weeks, does that magically make it human?'

'Legally it changes things,' Edwina said with a shrug. 'It would have personhood from that point. We wouldn't need a court order to extract DNA, for a start.'

'This is ridiculous,' Cora snapped. 'She was alive until her mother was killed. Her death deserves to be investigated.'

Roxy was astounded to see there were tears in her colleague's eyes. What on earth was going on? And why was Cora using the pronouns 'she' and 'her'?

'You're taking this personally, Officer Simmons, when you need to be objective.' Edwina sighed. 'Look, I am not an ob-gyn. My estimate is eleven weeks based on foetal development. If it makes you more comfortable, I will allow another opinion.'

'There's that word again. God forbid we consider a little baby to be a human.'

'Officer Simmons,' Roxy said, 'I think you should go outside and get some air.'

Cora practically ran out of the office.

When she was gone, Roxy glanced at Edwina, embarrassed and confused by the display.

'I'm sorry about that. I don't know what has got into her today.'

'Never apologise for the behaviour of a colleague,' Edwina said, switching on her computer. 'Now, since you left before the autopsy was complete, perhaps you'd like to hear the rest of my findings.'

'Yes, I'd also like a copy of your report.'

'Of course.' Edwina began to type. 'Tell me, how are you enjoy-ing your new position?'

'Oh.' Roxy leaned back in her chair and gave a mirthless chuckle. 'It's been a laugh a minute so far.'

CHAPTER THIRTEEN

The wolf returned to his lair before dark. He was so excited by his plan he almost forget to check his various security systems, and was halfway to his bedroom on the second floor when he remembered.

He left his bag on the stairs and went back down. He checked the basement first, testing the tension of the thin wires he had stretched along the tiny hall leading to the garden door. Next he went to the wrought-iron conservatory off the kitchen, taking care not to step into the path of the shotgun aimed squarely at the conservatory door. The door opened outwards, should anyone wish to try it. And should they try, little would remain of their head.

Satisfied the boundaries were in order, he returned to the main hall and double-checked the bolts on the front door. The house was large, uncommonly so, a classical detached two-storey-with-basement Victorian. It had belonged to his parents, both deceased.

It had never been a happy home; certainly the wolf had little memory of joyous occasions. His parents were dour people, snarled up in a bitter, loveless marriage; a life spent sniping at each other when they weren't avoiding each other like the plague. Despite this, the wolf did not feel hard done by. Their benign neglect of him, their lack of interest in their only child, had been freeing in many way, a gift of sorts. There was nobody to watch over him, no one to demand he go to school, eat at regular hours. A smattering of guilt on his mother's side meant he had a healthy weekly allowance, and he used it to buy junk food, video games and electronic equipment. With no one to force him into hateful activities, the wolf spent hours alone in his room, surfing the Web, playing games with like-minded souls across the globe. He was not lonely.

He was never lonely. His bedroom was his fiefdom, and he was king.

Then he hit puberty.

Suddenly everything changed.

Almost overnight he became dissatisfied. His games seemed childish; his room felt claustrophobic. Hormones, exacerbated by a diet of junk and pop, ran wild through his body. Daily he seemed to widen. His skin developed acne and hair began to sprout where there had been no hair before. His voice was untrustworthy, low one minute, cracking into a semi-shriek the next. His clothes became too tight, too short, and he was too embarrassed to ask his mother to take him shopping for more. Conscious of how he looked, he stopped going out during daylight hours, suddenly aware that people noticed him now, and not just people, other kids.

Boys were cruel. They called him names like Fatso and Fuckface; sometimes they held their noses as he walked by, pretending they were gagging, making grunting noises like he was a pig. He would ignore them and speed up, but he hated the way his thighs rubbed together and was in constant fear that he might trip and fall in front of them.

But as much as he hated and feared the boys, it was the girls who struck dumb terror into his heart.

There was something other-worldly about girls; they were a mystery to him, with their perfumed heat and sly glances. He had never noticed them much before, never had any need of them, but now, all of sudden, they infiltrated his nights and his waking hours. He saw them everywhere and found himself transfixed by their glossy hair, bright shiny lips and coltish legs. He hated them, yet he yearned for them. He wanted them to notice him, to speak to him, but even the idea of making a connection terrified him.

Most of all, he wanted to touch them.

Alone in his room he became obsessed with porn, favouring hentai, a strange brand of Japanese cartoon porn, where young women were raped by tentacled monsters and strange alien beings. The women were frequently bound, often gagged. Their pathetic struggles against the monsters exited him, thrilled him.

Gave him ideas.

Yet his inner world might never have broken through into reality had it not been for the 'the incident'.

Afterwards he would tell himself that none of it was his fault; his mission was preordained, it had to be.

The incident happened late summer, early autumn; that much he was sure of.

His father, a penny-pincher if ever there was one, saw that the gutters were clogged from falling leaves and decided they needed cleaning before winter set in. Instead of calling in a professional, Richard Williams took a notion that he would do the job himself, and fetched the extra-length ladder from the basement.

The fall did not kill him. The dry fountain had broken his trajectory. But he was in a coma for weeks, and then rehab. When he came home, he was unable to walk without assistance and spent his days forgetful and weepy, sometimes angry.

By the second month, the wolf's mother had had enough. She claimed mental exhaustion and left, packing more bags than she might need for two weeks. She kissed the wolf goodbye and told him to be good.

Good?

Three days later, Celine arrived.

The wolf had not known she was coming until he heard the rusty rasp of the doorbell and wandered down to answer it.

'Hello,' she said, smiling, her pink frosted lipstick glistening in the morning light. 'I'm Celine. Aren't you going to ask me in?'

In that single moment, the wolf fell hopelessly in love.

CHAPTER FOURTEEN

Dominic Travers was numb with grief.

He pushed open the glass doors of the morgue and walked around the corner to where the taxi he had overpaid still waited, the driver reading his phone with one hand, vaping with the other.

He thought about calling Lillian, and rejected the idea instantly. There would be time for that; there would be time to deal with her. Right now he had information and he needed to act on it.

Noel Furlong was at large.

Unbeknownst to Andrea, Dominic had had Furlong vetted thoroughly when he started seeing her first, so now he knew his friends, his place of work, and his family, even the name of his coke dealer. The prick would not be able to stay hidden for long. Still, it wouldn't hurt to start applying pressure where it counted.

He yanked open the door of the taxi, startling the driver.

'Rathmines,' he said.

'You got it.'

Travers made a number of calls as they drove, talking in a low voice to people who listened and said little. When he was finished, he hung up and stared through the tinted windows, unseeing. He had no interest in his surroundings; he wasn't capable of interest. All he could think about was the last time he'd seen Andrea alive.

They'd met for lunch at White's, a high-end restaurant near Andrea's work. Andrea had arrived late and didn't apologise. This surprised him, because it was rude, and his daughter was not a rude person. Throughout the meal she hardly spoke and seemed distracted, checking her phone with increasing regularity; she refused a glass of wine, which was unusual for her, and barely touched her food, which was not. When he asked about Noel, she waved the question away and told him it was over between them.

Privately he was delighted to hear it, although he *said* he was sorry.

When he asked for the bill, she reached across the table and took his left hand in hers.

'Do you remember when I came to live with you?'

'Sure,' he said. He'd collected her from a sobbing Justine and loaded her into the back of his car, his face grim, oblivious to Justine's pleas. Andrea had a version of the truth, of course: her mother was sick and needed time to get well.

Afterwards, when Lillian was clean again, it was too late to change things back. That was how he saw it.

That was how he *chose* to see it.

'I was terrified of you for the longest time.' She traced her thumb over the scars on the back of his hand.

'Why?'

She smiled, more to herself than to him.

'I don't know. I was little and you were ...'

'Big.'

'And hairy, like a monster.' When she lifted her face and smiled at him, he thought it was the saddest smile he had ever seen.

'Kiddo, is everything all right? Is this guy Furlong bothering you? If that little shit has done anything, you tell me and I'll—'

She withdrew her hand.

'Forget about Noel, please, Dad. I have.'

'You can talk to me, you know, about anything.'

'I know.' She looked away. 'Isn't it funny how easy it is to mistake a book by its cover?'

Later, outside the restaurant, he'd offered to share a taxi with her and she had refused, telling him she'd rather walk and get some air.

He remembered now how he'd kissed the top of her head and said goodbye. It was the last time he would ever see her alive, standing by the side of a busy street, staring at her phone.

If he'd known that, he would never have left her.

'Buddy?'

The driver was watching him in the rear-view mirror.

'What?'

'I said we're here. Would you like me to park in—'

'Pull over on the left.'

He was out of the taxi before it came to a stop. With his coat flapping behind him, he ran across the road, trotted through the arched doors of the red-brick corner building and up the stone steps.

There was something church-like about libraries, he thought, passing through the next set of doors; something about the manu-factured silence, the smell of bodies and aged paper.

He went straight to the central desk, where a dainty woman in a colourful dress was scanning barcodes with a hand-held machine.

'I'm looking for Caroline Furlong.'

'Oh, she's not back from lunch yet.'

'Where did she go?'

Her smile faltered a little.

'She won't be long if you'd like to …'

He turned on his heel and walked away.

He checked the nearby cafés, entering the Swan shopping centre last. It was surprisingly busy. Pockets of teenagers stood about talking, shouting and throwing McDonald's fries at each other's heads. A boy of about fifteen bumped into him as he swept past, turned to say something and swallowed his words whole when their eyes met.

He spotted Caroline Furlong, Noel's older sister, in the café two doors down from a discount bookshop and checked her photo from the one he had on file on his phone. She was older and plainer in person, flicking through a gossip magazine, eating some kind of sticky-looking cake with her fingers. She wore glasses. Her phone lay on the table beside her coffee cup. It had a snazzy orange cover.

He entered the café, walked to her table and stood over her. After a moment she glanced up, puzzled.

'Can I help you?'

'Where's Noel?'

'Who?'

His hand twitched at the stupidity of her reply. He wanted to slap her as hard as he could. He wanted to knock the glasses right off her face and grind them to paste under his heel.

'Where is he?'

'How should I know? He's probably at work.'

'He's not.'

Behind the thick lenses, her eyes grew wary.

'How do you know that?'

'Because if he was, I wouldn't be here.'

'What's happened?'

'Andrea is dead.'

There wasn't a single flicker of emotion on her face, good or bad. That angered him.

'Do you know who I'm talking about?'

'His girlfriend – his *ex*-girlfriend.'

Pointed, like she had thoughts about that. He picked her phone up and shoved it under her chin.

'Call him.'

'No, I don't think I will.'

With his other hand he grabbed her upper arm, squeezing it so hard she yelped in pain.

'Call him.'

'You're hurting me.'

'Make the fucking call.'

Two women at the next table abruptly got up and moved away, but an old man sitting on the other side was watching the exchange. He got unsteadily to his feet and waved his walking stick threateningly.

'You leave that lady alone.'

'Stay out of it.'

'I'm going to call the police.' He patted his pockets, searching for his phone. 'I'm going to call them right now.'

Travers tightened his grip. Caroline gasped, her pupils blooming with pain.

'Call him or I'll snap your arm like a twig.'

His fingers kneaded the limb, angling expertly between muscle and tendon. She was thin, not fleshy; he knew what he was doing. She'd be black and blue the next day. He knew she was terrified; he could practically smell the fear pumping from her pores.

But she still shook her head.

Disgusted, he let go. She fell back, clutching her arm. Beads of sweat stood out on her face.

'I'll find him.' He leaned down, pushed his face close to hers. 'And I'll remember your lack of cooperation when I do, you can trust me on that.'

He turned and began to leave.

'You stay away from him,' she screamed after him. 'Do you hear me: don't you touch him.'

Outside the shopping centre, Travers waved for the car, got in and made another call.

'Your offer still stands?' he asked. 'All resources, yes, thank you.' He hung up.

How easy it is to mistake a book by its cover.

Curious. *Mistake*, not judge.

He mulled the line over and over again.

Mistake.

Andrea had made a mistake.

Someone had broken her trust, someone close to her.

If it was the last thing he ever did, he would find that person. They would get what was coming to them, he would see to it personally.

CHAPTER FIFTEEN

Conversation on the drive back from the morgue was pretty much non-existent. Cora sat slumped in the passenger seat with her arms folded and her face set towards the window.

She was upset, Roxy could see that, but she had no idea what she was so upset about or how best to address the issue, so she said nothing. Somehow this only seemed to make matters worse.

When Roxy parked in the underground car park at the station, Cora got out, slammed the door and stalked up the ramp without saying a word, leaving her to take the lift upstairs alone. She went straight to find Morrissey. He was in his cubicle, leaning back in his chair, arms folded, eyes closed and his mouth slightly open. Inspectors did not have to share with anyone, so the space was all his. She noticed he had added a number of stains to the egg from earlier.

'Sir.'

He jerked upright.

'What?'

'Sir,' she said, 'is Noel Furlong in custody yet?'

'Where the fuck were you?' Morrissey demanded, his face redder than ever. 'I was looking for you.'

She doubted that, but she went along with it.

'I was at Andrea Colgan's autopsy, sir.'

'For what?'

Roxy frowned. Was this a trick question? 'Sir?'

'Waste of time.'

'Sir, I don't believe it was, Dr King was—'

'Anyway, it's not our problem any more.' He leaned back and belched softly. Roxy smelled roast chicken on his breath and tried not to gag.

'I don't know what you mean, Inspector.'

'I mean,' he said, 'it's not our problem any more. Inspector Eli Quinn is taking over the case.'

'Quinn, sir?'

'Yeah, and by the way, I've had a complaint about you.'

'Me?' She was genuinely shocked. 'What complaint? From who?'

'You withheld information.'

Roxy was totally confused. Had Edwina called ahead already, broken the news about the pregnancy despite her view to the contrary?

'You're on probation, yeah?'

'Yes, sir.'

'Want some advice?'

It was on the tip of her tongue to say no when she remembered how much she had wanted this gig.

'Sure.'

'If a superior officer tells you he wants a particular detective on the case, don't let your ego get in the fucking way. We don't have room in Homicide for glory hounds.'

Johnson, that miserable cockroach. Roxy's expression remained stoic, but her temper was boiling. This was politics, pure and simple. She could smell the stench of it. Johnson had tagged Quinn, who had bullied Morrissey and snagged their case right out from under them.

'I'll do my best to remember that, sir.'

'See to it that you do. Now bugger off, Malloy, some of us have work to do.'

She hesitated. 'Sir, I met the victim's father at the morgue. I think Noel Furlong might be in considerable danger.'

'Who?'

Roxy tried not to scream. 'Noel Furlong, sir, he was Andrea Colgan's boyfriend.'

'Oh yeah.' Morrissey's lids were drooping with apathy. 'Don't worry about him. Quinn's crew will pick him up for questioning. Now go on, Malloy, keep your eye on Dispatch; something new is bound to come in on the wire.'

Seething, Roxy walked back to her cubicle, but she was too restless to work. She couldn't get Dominic Travers out of her mind, or the look on his face.

Fuck it.

She ran Furlong's details, went downstairs to the main floor and looked around for a patsy.

'You,' she barked, doing her best impression of Morrissey.

A young Garda struggling with a stab vest looked at her, saw her stripes and snapped to attention.

'Ma'am.'

'What's your name?'

'Gant, ma'am.'

'Are you starting or finishing your shift?'

'Starting, Sergeant.'

She thrust an address into his hand.

'I need eyes and ears on this address, Gant. If you see anything odd, you call it in, got it?'

'Now?' He looked a little scared. 'Only I'm supposed to be accompanying Officer Keegan on patrol at—'

'This takes precedence, Officer.'

'Yes, ma'am. Can I ask what it is I'm looking for?'

Roxy remembered the photo she had taken from the apartment. She took it out and showed him. 'This guy, his name is Noel Furlong. If you see him, detain him and call it in.'

'Yes, ma'am.'

'Good.' She nodded approvingly, turned and began to walk away. She was halfway to the door when she heard, 'Ma'am?'

'What?'

He looked at her, his face pink and apologetic.

'Who are you, ma'am?'

For the first time that day, Roxy Malloy laughed.

Roxy collected Edwina King's autopsy report from her cubicle and went upstairs. Nancy was nowhere to be seen, so Roxy tapped on Gussy's door. Gussy roared, 'Come in.'

He didn't look up from his paperwork, even when she stood at his desk. As the seconds ticked by, Roxy decided she was tired of his act and cleared her throat.

'Sir, I have a request.'

Gussy sighed. 'I assume by now you've spoken to Inspector Morrissey?'

'Yes, sir.'

'Sit down, Sergeant Malloy.'

She sat in the same chair she had sat in earlier that day and put Edwina's report down on his desk.

'I've just come from the morgue.'

Gussy put his pen down, leaned back in his chair and gave her a long, appraising look.

'The morgue?'

'Officer Simmons and I went to witness Andrea Colgan's autopsy. Dominic Travers, the victim's father, was there. I spoke to him briefly.'

'Why?'

'Sir?'

'Why did you speak to him?'

'Er, it seemed prudent.'

'Do you like aggravating me, Malloy?'

'Not especially, sir.'

'If you've spoken to Morrissey then you know this is no longer your case.'

'I know it's no longer *Morrissey's* case, but with your permission I would like to stay with it.'

'Oh you would, would you?'

'I assure you, sir, it is not my intention to create any difficulties.'

'You know what they say about intentions: the road to hell is paved with them.' Gussy smoothed his moustache with his thumb and forefinger. 'Quinn has a squad in place.'

'He'll take me if you tell him to.'

'Why would I do that?'

Roxy kept her gaze steady.

'Sir, with respect, I have already established a relationship with Andrea Colgan's mother, I believe I would be beneficial to the investigation.'

'You mean you want to get out from under Inspector Morrissey.'

Roxy let her gaze wander to the plaque on the wall behind Gussy's head. Say nothing, she thought, don't blow this by bitching about a senior officer.

Gussy's chin jutted towards the file.

'What's that you have there?'

'Edwina King's preliminary report on Andrea Colgan.'

'Hand it over.'

She passed it to him. Gussy opened it, sat back and read silently and with great concentration. At one point the muscles around his mouth tightened and his lips thinned to a line. When he was done, he sat for a little while digesting all that he had read.

'She was pregnant?'

'Yes, sir. Edwina estimates the foetus to be eleven weeks, but she's getting a second opinion. There will be an issue over DNA extraction.'

'Of course there will.' Gussy closed the folder and pinched the bridge of his nose. 'We live in a repugnant time, Malloy, a sinful, wicked and fallen time.'

Roxy didn't know what to say to that, so decided it was better she said nothing.

'This is a mess, an unholy mess.'

'Yes, sir, it is.'

He stared at his desk for so long, she wondered if she should remind him of her presence with another throat clearance. But then he looked up.

'All right, talk to Quinn, see if he can find a place for you on the squad.'

'Yes, sir, thank you, sir.'

Roxy got up and walked to the door. Her fingers had barely grazed the doorknob when Gussy spoke again.

'You're ambitious, Malloy, and that's a good thing.'

Roxy heard the 'but' before he said it and tensed her shoulders.

'But listen to me, Sergeant, take it from an old dog who has seen more than his fair share of ambitious officers come and go. Learn to play with others; it will benefit you in the fullness of time.'

Roxy bristled. 'Was that it, sir?'

'And remember this.' Gussy smiled so benevolently, she wanted to slap him. '"When justice is done it is a joy to the righteous but a terror to the evildoers."'

'Sir?'

'Proverbs 21:15.' Gussy picked up his pen and pretended to write something. 'Good afternoon, Sergeant, don't let me keep you.'

CHAPTER SIXTEEN

By late afternoon, dark clouds had rolled across the city, carried on a rising wind, and the rain soon followed.

Noel Furlong was soaked to the skin by the time he ducked into the side door of Grogan's pub and went straight to the men's bathroom. Luckily the single cubicle was empty. He locked the door, pulled the toilet seat down and dug his phone out of his pocket, shivering from a combination of cold and shock.

He pressed the phone to his lips. Who could he call? Who could he trust? Where could he lie low for a few days?

The Rank would be all over his sister, Caroline, he was sure of that. It was probably the first place they'd look for him.

Droplets of rain ran from his face. He ripped a few sheets of tissue from the holder and wiped his forehead, leaving little pieces stuck to his skin. When he closed his eyes, he felt sick to his stomach.

His phone rang in his hand, scaring him so badly he almost screamed. He checked caller ID and saw that it was Mags, his boss at the tattoo parlour.

He answered.

'Hey girl.'

'Don't you dare hey girl me,' she said, sounding not in the least bit friendly. 'I've had the fucking Rank in here asking me all kind of questions about you. You asshole, you told me you wanted to borrow my van for a job.'

'Look, Mags—'

'No, you look, this is serious. You're all over the news; my *shop* is all over the news.'

'Mags, listen to me, I can explain …'

'I don't know what you're up to, Noel, but you better turn yourself in. This is some serious shit. They told me you were a person of interest in a murder!'

'Mags, you have to believe me, I'm innocent.'

'Yeah, well, where there's smoke there's fire in my view. So don't come near me or the shop until this shit is sorted out. I don't need *this* kind of exposure.'

She hung up.

A person of interest?

He went on to a news site and read in mute horror.

Body found earlier in Dundrum: The female found bludgeoned to death in an apartment shortly after six a.m. this morning has been named as Andrea Colgan. Gardai are treating the death as homicide and have issued an appeal for any witnesses. A special hotline is now open.

Update: Gardai are particularly interested in speaking with a man named locally as Noel Furlong. Mr Furlong is considered a person of interest.

Homicide, shit … and his name plastered all over the place, which meant Dominic Travers was probably combing the city looking for him.

He chewed the skin of his knuckle. This changed things. Travers was a bloody madman. If he found him before the Rank, there was no telling what he would do. Noel had heard the stories, of course he had, but up until now they hadn't mattered, they were just stories.

Now, suddenly, they mattered a lot.

Someone came into the toilet and stood outside the door, breathing heavily.

Noel froze, head cocked, listening. Had someone spotted him, followed him? He looked around, but there was no window: no way out.

He was trapped.

He yelped when whoever it was pounded on the door.

'Y'right in there?'

'I'll be out in a minute.'

'Hurry up, man. I'm touching cloth here.'

'Fuck off, will you.'

He heard muttering, the sound of the door opening and closing again.

Time, he needed time, somewhere he could lie low while he figured out his next move. Somewhere close by, someone he could trust not to dob him in. Someone who didn't know Andrea, or wouldn't be interested in—

Storm.

Frantically he scrolled through his contacts, praying he still had her number, sagging with relief when he found it. He made the call but the phone rang out. Why did the silly bint never answer calls?

Swearing, he sent a message.

U home?

He waited, eyes fixed on the screen so hard they ached. Come on come on come on.

Then, finally, there was a reply, of sorts.

Dis?

He typed: *Noel. We partied at Risen.*

Sup?

Need to C U.

This time the wait was longer. He tried to remember how he'd left things with her and couldn't. The last time they'd been together he'd been so high he could barely remember his own name.

A horrifying thought occurred to him. Travers was connected to some bigwig in the Department of Justice. They probably had access to all kinds of weird spy intel or some shit. Could they trace phones? Maybe they could; maybe Travers or his goons were on their way to Grogan's right now.

Plz! he typed.

He clung to the phone, aware his heart was going way too fast for comfort. If she said no, he was totally screwed. He'd be dead before dusk, he could feel it in his bones.

U holding?

Bless you, you greedy junkie bitch, he thought as his thumbs whirled over the keys. He left the toilet, pulled up his hood and hurried towards the quays.

Fifteen minutes later, he was standing outside a security gate, bouncing up and down on his toes. He was slightly breathless, having run all the way there. Beneath his jacket, his shirt was stuck to the small of his back with sweat.

He rang the bell a second time, then a third. In frustration he kicked the gate, then stopped in case any passers-by saw him and thought he was trying to break in.

In desperation he turned his phone back on and sent another text. *At gate!*

Eventually her voice, tinny and cranky, came over the intercom. 'You there?'

He almost screamed but managed – just – to stay calm.

'I'm here, I've been ringing the buzzer for ages!'

'Oh, didn't I tell you?'

'Tell me what?'

'S'broken. I got to come get you.'

'Right, well I'm here, so let me in.'

'Well hold on, first you got to apologise. Can't come in till you apologise.'

Noel pressed his forehead against the bars; they were deliciously cool against his skin.

'What?'

'Apologise.'

'For what … No, look, never mind. I'm sorry.'

'For what?'

'Jesus, is this a multiple-choice test?'

'A wha'?'

'Never mind,' he said again. 'I'm sorry for everything, okay, for *everything*.'

'Everything?' She sounded sceptical.

'Yes, all of it, everything I've ever done, okay? Everything. Will you let me in?'

'Even for Zee's party?'

'Especially for Zee's party.'

It helped that he had no idea who Zee was or what party she was talking about. Ever since Andrea had dumped him, his life had become one long continuous party, and now he felt like dying.

''Cos that was bang out of order. Even for you.'

'I know, I'm sorry. Can you let me in, please, Storm?'

'Awright, be right down, but you better have the good stuff.'

He switched his phone off again and for a moment considered ditching it in a nearby wheelie bin, then changed his mind. He bit his lip, trying to think.

All he had to do was keep his shit together.

That was all.

The gate opened and Storm stood in the gap, peering at him. She was wearing a see-through T-shirt over yoga pants. Her multicoloured hair was tied up like a pineapple on her head.

'Blimey,' she said, looking him up and down. 'You look like a right bag of shit.'

He swooped her up, carried her inside and kicked the gate shut behind him.

CHAPTER SEVENTEEN

The wolf opened his eyes.

Night had fallen. The wolf did not mind. The night was his friend; the night had always been his friend.

He set to work. Tomorrow he would put his plan into motion, but today he would need to prepare.

The ritual was important to him; it was sacrosanct.

Wearing nothing but baggy tracksuit pants, he sat down at his computer and logged on. The boards were active, users primed and ready.

He typed and hit send.

The responses came in fast. He read each one, savouring the words of encouragement from his brethren. Where once he had been alone, now he was not; that was why the mission was so important, so vital. Men like him were suffering daily through no fault of their own. It was cruel. It was disgusting.

It would no longer be tolerated.

Celine.

It had been weeks since he'd thought of her, but now she was foremost in his mind.

He closed his eyes and let his thoughts wander. Memories, never too far from the surface, flooded in.

Celine.

He had opened the door and there she was, standing on the top step, a canvas bag by her feet.

'I'm Celine,' she said, and held out her hand.

The wolf could not believe it. He stared at her, eyes on stalks. Surely this was some kind of mistake.

'Don't leave me hanging,' she said, and he put his hand in hers, felt the strength and warmth of her fingers as they closed around his. She was the first woman, apart from his mother, to ever touch him.

It was electrifying.

'So,' she said. 'You going to ask me in?'

Dumbstruck, he stepped aside. She picked up her bag and moved past him into the hall. He caught the trace of her perfume; it reminded him of an orchard in October.

'What a beautiful house you have!' She gave a low whistle, and turned in a full circle.

Watching her, he held his breath. Any moment now, she would see that she was in the wrong place, had come to the wrong address. She would leave and never come back, this woman with her beautiful hair and warm fingers.

'Oh yeah, where are my manners?' She opened her bag and removed a purse from inside: it was blue with a gold clasp.

'Here.' She handed him a laminated card. He took it and read it.

It said her name was Celine Dwyer and she was a qualified physiotherapist. There were letters after her name, a phone number.

He handed the card back.

'So,' she said, and smiled. 'You don't talk much, do you?'

He could see his reflection in the hall mirror, hers too, at least her back. If he squinted, their bodies seemed to merge into one.

Gradually he became aware of the silence.

She was looking at him. Was it his turn to speak? What did she want to hear?

Panicked, he felt his cheeks begin to flame as they always did.

'Don't worry,' she said. She reached out and touched his arm. 'You don't have to talk if you don't want to. I'm here to see your dad. Richard, right? Had an accident?'

'My dad.'

God, he wanted to punch himself in the face. His first words to a woman and he said that?

She smiled again. He stared at her lips, mesmerised. She had small teeth, very white.

'Tell you what, you show me where he is and we'll take it from there.'

It had been that simple. He brought her upstairs and lurked about in the hall, listening to the murmurs of conversation from his father's bedroom. The scent of her apple perfume lingered on the air, vying with the dust motes.

When she left that afternoon, he felt her loss as keenly as if he had known her his entire life. That night he tried to watch his usual fare, but nothing worked. He was no longer interested in cartoon figures, or the moaning cries of smooth fake-breasted women. It wasn't real, none of it was.

Celine was real.

Celine had spoken to him.

Celine had held his hand in hers.

Celine had touched his arm.

Celine smelled of apples.

Celine.

CHAPTER EIGHTEEN

Cora was at her desk when Roxy returned to the cubicle, writing something in a blue notebook Roxy had never seen her use before. She closed it and put it away when she heard Roxy coming.

'Inspector Morrissey told me we were no longer on the case.'

'I know, he told me.' Roxy sat down. 'Look, about earlier …'

'My apologies, Sergeant.' Cora was downright icy. 'It won't happen again.'

'I get it, you have empathy for the victim. I understand that, Officer Simmons, but as hard as it can be, we must remain professional at all times. We must follow protocol.'

Cora was silent for so long, Roxy thought she was ignoring her, then she realised her shoulders were shaking.

She was crying.

'Officer Simmons … Cora, oh now, now stop that.'

'We've been trying, you know? For a baby.' Cora's voice was tight with pain. 'Twice I thought I was … then it didn't stick. They say what's for you won't pass you by, but people say really stupid things, you know? They don't realise how hard it is.'

Alarm bells rang in Roxy's head. She was on very thin ice here. One false move and she was in danger of messing this up.

'Mm,' she said. 'That must be very upsetting.'

Cora leaned her head on her arms and sobbed as though her heart would break. In blind panic, Roxy pulled open her drawer looking for tissues, paper, anything, but all she had was a packet of mints and a stapler.

Gradually, however Cora pulled herself together and produced a hanky from somewhere. She blew her nose, then turned and looked at Roxy. Her face was blotchy, her eyes red.

'Does *anything* ever get to you?'

Roxy furrowed her brow. 'Of course things get to me.'

Cora looked disbelieving. 'Really? Because you never seem upset, you never seem to get emotional at all.'

Roxy leaned forwards, resting her forearms on her knees.

'Listen to me, Officer Simmons. I know life can throw stuff at you when you least expect it. And I'm sorry you've been going through the mill with … with your …'

'Fertility.'

'Right, that.'

Without thinking she reached out and patted Cora on the thigh. It was an awkward gesture, but it was the best she had.

'Things will get better.'

'How?' Cora sniffed.

'Trust me,' Roxy said, getting to her feet. 'I'll be right back.'

Quinn's cubicle was empty when she got there, but his coat was draped across the back of his chair and there was a packet of cigarettes by the keyboard, so she figured he hadn't gone too far.

'Where is Inspector Quinn?' he asked the man in the cubicle next to his.

'How should I know? He's probably gone for a piss.'

Roxy headed straight for the locker rooms.

'Hey, you're not supposed to be in here,' cried a naked man with a towel draped over his shoulder as she skirted the aisles.

'Sorry.'

In the toilets, she checked the stall doors until she came to one that was locked. From behind the door she could hear the sound of a video game being played.

She knocked. 'Inspector Quinn?'

The music stopped abruptly.

'Who's that?'

'It's Sergeant Malloy, sir.'

'Get the hell out of here, Malloy. I'm busy.'

'I've been to see the superintendent, sir, and—'

'Not interested, Malloy. Inspector Morrissey has already signed off. I'm taking the case.'

'If you don't mind my asking, why are you interested in Andrea Colgan's murder?'

She heard him sigh.

'Look, can we talk about this later?'

Roxy put her hands on her hips and stared at a crack in the floor tiles. Quinn had an ego the size of a rhino; that had to be a way in.

'I want to work this case with you.'

'I already have a squad.'

'This was my first homicide as a sergeant, sir. I want to learn, I want to do things the right way. The super suggested I talk to you; he told me I'd learn a *lot* from you.'

'Gussy said that?'

Someone came in behind her, muttered a startled 'excuse me' and hurried out again.

'He did.'

'Fine, incident room four in twenty minutes.'

The music started up again.

'I'd like it if Officer Simmons could come too. She's keen, and she works hard.' She grimaced, hoping she hadn't pushed her luck too far. 'You'd get two birds with one stone.'

Seconds ticked by. Roxy held her breath. She heard him swear softly.

'All right, if I take the two of you, will you get the hell out of here? Please?'

She made a fist and silently punched the air.

'Thank you, sir, you won't regret it.'

'I'd better not.'

She bolted. Retreat in victory was never a bad idea.

CHAPTER NINETEEN

Roxy told a delighted Cora the news, then made her way to the incident room, hoping to be seated and as unobtrusive as possible before the others arrived. She was surprised when she opened the door to find it was already fairly packed.

All eyes turned her way.

She muttered a soft 'hi' and took a seat at the back, uncomfortably aware of the traded looks.

In truth, though she had been at the station for three years, Roxy had not bothered to befriend many of her colleagues. Maybe Gussy was right; maybe she did need to learn how to play with others. Still, she thought, looking around, at least she recognised a few faces.

Sitting beside the radiator, wearing a biker jacket, black jeans and boots, was Quinn's second in command, Sergeant Miranda Lynn. Roxy had worked with her on a case before and liked her. She was blunt and uncompromising, a straight talker.

On the opposite side of the room was Sergeant Eoin Fletcher. He was a transfer from Galway and the subject of much chatter at the station, certainly amongst the women. He was above average height, and strongly built. His hair was so blonde it was hardly a colour at all, and he wore it military style, shorn at the back and sides, a little longer on top, but not by much. His clothes were well made, and they fitted him perfectly. Roxy supposed he was handsome, in that he ticked all the right boxes, but there was a vagueness to his eyes that she found perplexing, and whenever she had occasion to speak to him, she sometimes felt the lights were on but it was hard to judge if anyone was home or not.

She looked around for Cora: where was she?

Miranda leaned her chair back on two legs to talk to her.

'You cutting in on our dance?'

'Yes, the superintendent thought it would be beneficial.'

'Oh yeah? Whose idea was that, yours or his?'

'His.'

'Then don't look so nervous. Despite what you might have heard, we don't bite.'

Roxy tried a smile. 'Thanks.'

'Want some advice?'

Roxy sighed. What was it about her face that made people so willing to offer her advice?

'Sure.'

'Don't think Quinn's like Morrissey; he's not. He's a decent man, but he's a two-striker.'

Before she could ask what *that* was supposed to mean, a door at the top of the room opened and Eli Quinn walked in; or rather, Roxy thought crankily, he waltzed in like he owned the place. He looked around, came straight to Roxy and dropped a thick file on the desk in front of her with a thump.

'You want in, you need to familiarise yourself with this. We don't have any room for hitch-hikers.'

She stared at the mound of cardboard in surprise.

'Why not send the files to my EN?'

'You'll absorb them better this way.'

He took his position behind the podium, moving like a man comfortable in his own skin. Roxy watched him. Six foot one, lean-built, with a handsome face and thick, slightly shaggy dark-blonde hair; no wonder the media couldn't get enough of him.

'*Hola, amigos,*' he said.

'*Hola, jefe!*' the squad called back. Miranda blew a pink bubble until it burst and put her phone away.

'I trust you bade welcome to our new colleague?' Quinn waved a hand towards Roxy, then looked around. 'I thought I was getting two birds for the price of one stone?'

Just as he said that, the door burst open and Cora practically spilled into the room, looking a little breathless and flustered.

'Glad you could join us,' Quinn said. 'In this squad I expect you to be punctual, and I'm not interested in excuses.'

He said this with a smile on his face, but there was no mistaking the fact that he was also deadly serious. Cora straightened up and blushed clear to the tips of her ears.

'I'm so sorry, it won't happen again.'

'Sit down.'

Mortified, she slid into the first chair she found and spent what felt to Roxy like an age fumbling with her EN.

'Right,' Quinn said. 'Fletch, hit the lights, would you?'

Fletcher got up and dimmed the overheads. Quinn opened his own EN and tapped it a number of times until a large screen hanging on the wall behind him came to life.

Miranda raised a hand.

'For the record, I want it made clear that I have some reservations.'

Roxy looked at her, surprised.

'Noted,' Quinn said curtly. 'Let's begin.'

Behind him, Andrea Colgan's official ID photo appeared on screen. Roxy stared at her face, trying not to compare it with what she had seen at the morgue.

'This is Andrea Colgan, twenty-six years old. She was found unresponsive at 6.05 this morning. Cause of death is cerebral hypoxia, which for the benefit of the less scientifically minded means a lack of oxygen to the brain.'

'So she was strangled?' Fletcher asked.

'Yes, but there are no ligature marks.' He cleared his throat and glanced around the room. 'At the time of her death, Andrea Colgan was also eleven to twelve weeks pregnant.'

That changed things. The mood, already sombre, darkened further.

'All right,' Quinn said. 'I know you're all working long hours and probably wondering why I'm breaking your backs by adding another case.' He glanced at Miranda as he spoke. 'So here's why: found at the crime scene was a large bouquet of yellow roses,' they appeared on screen behind him, 'and this.'

The screen revealed the bottle of champagne Roxy had noticed in the kitchen of Andrea's apartment.

Fletcher leaned forward and whistled between his teeth. 'Those are his calling cards all right: it's the Sweetheart Killer.'

'Fletcher, don't let me hear you use that name in my presence again,' Quinn said.

'Sorry, but that's what the papers are calling him.'

'Exactly, tabloid muck,' Quinn said. 'Leave that shit at the door.'

'Sorry, sir.'

'Sergeant Lynn has reservations, and there is merit to them. First, there was no card found at the scene; second, there is only one victim.' Quinn looked Roxy. 'You've had this longer than me; is there anything else to add?'

'Um …' Roxy consulted her EN. 'She had recently broken up with her boyfriend and a neighbour put him at the scene this morning. I can send you the witness's statement.'

'Do so. Continue.'

'Andrea worked for a company called Albas Entertainment as a PR consultant.'

'How long had she been there?' Miranda asked.

'Two years.'

Quinn typed the name into his EN; seconds later a photo of the company's logo appeared on screen.

'Is that all?'

'No. I met her parents. Her mother's name is Lillian Colgan, and her father is in the system.'

'He's got a record?'

'A pretty extensive one, actually.'

'What's his name?'

'Dominic Travers.'

Quinn's expression didn't change, but Miranda's sure did. She looked at her boss as if she expected his head to spin three hundred and sixty degrees.

'Dominic Travers?' he said eventually. 'Are you sure?'

'Yes, sir, I met him at the morgue.'

'Describe him.'

'About six foot five, big, dark hair. He had unusual eyes, very pale grey—'

'Okay, that will do.'

Quinn looked at his notes again for a few minutes. Roxy could tell he was shaken; so could everyone else.

'Okay,' he said eventually. 'Word of warning, the next set of photos is pretty graphic in nature.'

'That's all right,' someone said. 'We're all big boys here, aren't we, Miranda?'

'That's not what I've heard about you,' Miranda replied without missing a beat. And everybody laughed a little too long and a little too loud.

'All right, settle down.' Quinn brought up the photos from the crime scene and some from the autopsy. Roxy glanced at Cora and hoped she would keep it together.

'Andrea Colgan was struck hard enough to fracture the right orbital bone. It's hard to tell from the damage, but this section here,' he pointed to the right side of her jaw, 'was also broken, as were several bones in her neck.'

'Overkill,' Fletcher muttered. 'Interesting.'

'Was she raped?' Miranda wanted to know. 'Lorraine Dell was raped. We collected DNA from the scene.'

'According to Pathology, there was no sign of forced sexual activity, though obviously we're waiting on Forensics to—'

'She's wearing a garter on her leg,' someone said.

'Relevance?'

'Women don't go around wearing garters unless there's a man in the picture willing to take it off with his teeth.'

'We don't know that *she* put it on,' Quinn said. 'Remember, in our other case the victim was dressed and her body staged after death. As I said, I'm waiting on Forensics; perhaps there is evidence outside the body to indicate—'

'Maybe he tossed a load freestyle.' It was the same man again.

Roxy glanced at him, annoyed. Was he deliberately being as crass as possible? A young woman was dead; where was his respect?

Quinn carried on as if nothing had happened.

'Three of Colgan's ribs were broken on the right side of her body. If you observe closely, you can see a faint imprint on her skin.'

'What is that?' Fletcher asked, squinting. 'Looks like … looks like an E or a W, maybe?'

'I think it's a buckle mark or something similar. I think she fell when she was struck and was then kicked in the side.'

'Could have happened if she was crawling away,' Miranda said.

Roxy spoke up. 'There were blood spots on the floor leading towards the hall that support that theory.'

'Which floor? The living room?' Miranda looked over her shoulder.

'Yes.'

'So no forced entry and blood found in the living room.' Miranda turned back to Quinn. 'What's our thinking here? Are we thinking this is someone she knew, someone she invited in? What's the deal with the ex-boyfriend?'

'I put out a person-of-interest on him,' Roxy said. 'And there's an officer watching his sister's house in case he returns there. He's been living with her since the breakup.'

'Good.' Quinn clapped his hands. 'So, let's recap. Andrea Colgan was young, pretty and blonde. She was killed in her home, found atop her bed wearing lingerie. Discovered at the scene was a bottle of champagne and a bunch of yellow roses.' He looked around at his team and opened his arms. 'All right, so until we know otherwise, we're going to assume she's one of ours.' He frowned. 'It's going to be an all-out circus – the media are already breathing down our necks as it is – so bearing that in mind, if anyone feels like they might want to sit this one out, I need to know now.'

He looked around at the faces: nobody gave any indication that they were daunted by the task ahead.

'Okay, same rules apply. You will report to me or Sergeant Lynn; it doesn't matter how odd or banal the information you discover, I want to know about it. I expect discretion and commitment. I don't want to read anything, and I mean *anything*, about this case in the media, social or otherwise. If you can't agree to these terms, there's the door.'

He waited; nobody moved. Roxy felt a surge of excitement despite herself.

'We need to move fast on this. Half of you are going to go back over the Dell and Kilbride case. The rest of you, we need Colgan's communications history, her personal history, family, friends, work and clients. Fletcher, you and Malloy organise a canvass of the apartment building. It's a residential building with a number of owner-occupiers, so someone is bound to have noticed something. If there are security cameras, I want them viewed.'

Roxy furrowed her brow. 'Officer Simmons already canvassed the building.'

Quinn looked at Cora. 'Is that right? You have statements for me?'

'Not really,' Cora said meekly, looking embarrassed.

'What do you mean?'

'Well, it's … people were reluctant to talk, apart from this one lady, but she hadn't actually seen anything.' Cora looked down. 'I think she was just lonely really.'

'Not good enough,' Quinn said. 'Right. Malloy, you're with Fletcher.'

'I was hoping to speak to Dominic Travers again and see if—'

'In my squad,' Quinn snapped, 'there's a chain of command.' He tapped his chest with his thumb. 'Me chief, Malloy.'

Roxy scowled. 'It's Sergeant Malloy, Inspector.'

'Well, *Sergeant*, you wanted in, you're in. You can't abide by the rules, you know what to do.'

She stared at him, feeling the heat rise to her face. You wanted this, a tiny voice reminded her.

'All right,' she managed to grind out.

'Splendid. Officer Simmons?'

Cora jerked bolt upright. 'Sir!'

'Check out local CCTV, that sort of thing. See if there's security on the apartment building or any of the surrounding buildings.'

'Yes, sir.'

'This neighbour you spoke to – what's his name, Falstaff,' Miranda said, reading through Roxy's notes. 'You have an asterisk next to his name. What's that about?'

'I don't know, maybe nothing, but something about him rubbed me the wrong way.' Roxy unconsciously wiped the palm of her hand against the leg of her trousers. 'I mean he called it in, but…' She shrugged.

'There's nothing wrong with following your instincts. Have you run a background check on him?'

'Honestly, I haven't had time.'

'Tell you what, I'll do one while you and Fletcher canvass.'

'I would appreciate that.'

'What about Travers?' Fletcher wanted to know. 'I knew I recognised the name. That man has plenty of enemies. You know a lot of people lost their homes when the apartment complex he owned was condemned by the city council.'

'For now we consider him off limits,' Quinn replied.

'What? Why?'

'Because I say so. Now listen, the press office will release a short statement after five, and that's going to turn the heat up. This murder was different: I want to know why, I want to know what happened, I want to know what changed.'

Roxy looked around her. All eyes were on Quinn, even Miranda's. He was the general and they were his willing army.

When they filed out, Cora caught Roxy by the arm.

'Isn't this so exciting?'

'Sure.'

'I thought for sure we'd be shafted; now we're part of the A-Team.'

Roxy snorted. 'The A-Team?'

'That's what the press call them, didn't you know that?'

'No.'

'Oh come on, aren't you the least bit excited? Our first homicide, and now this.'

'Excited?' Roxy raised an eyebrow. 'Didn't you hear the chief? This is his gig. We're along for the ride.'

Cora grinned. 'Then buckle up, Sergeant, I have a feeling this will be our big break.'

CHAPTER TWENTY

Dressed head to toe in black, the wolf waited in the shadows across the street from the bar. It was cold, but that did not bother him unduly. The wolf in winter must accept the conditions of the hunt.

When Estelle and the man– he could no longer bear to use Bannon's given name – stepped out onto the street, he could see straight away that they were drunk. It was obvious from the way Estelle swayed a little, leaning into the man's body for support.

Good, he thought, it would be easier that way.

He waited for them to walk to the corner and began to follow.

It never ceased to amaze him how people took such little notice of their surroundings. Maybe it was because they'd grown up accepting they were part of the status quo. He doubted the man ever had to plan routes to avoid his so-called peers; he doubted it had ever crossed his mind that he was in danger simply by existing in a hostile world.

Sometimes he wondered what it must be like, moving through the world unencumbered by animosity and hatred. He couldn't imagine it.

They were going to the man's house. The wolf was glad about that. Estelle lived in shared accommodation with three other women. For a while he'd fantasised about breaking in, making them watch as he dispatched each of them one by one. That had sustained him for a while, but ultimately he was forced to accept that it was too dangerous. He could control two, possibly three, but more than that and the risk far outweighed the execution.

Look at them, he thought, watching them pause for a kiss. Estelle rose onto her tiptoes, tilted her head back and allowed the man to cup her face with his hands.

The wolf raised his hand and fondled his own face, he ran his tongue over his own lips, imagining the sensation, feeling a mix of desire and burning hatred.

Potent.

He felt potent.

Do not rush this, he warned himself. Let them get inside, let them shed their clothes; let them think there's nobody else in the world except them.

The wolf shivered, not from cold but from certainty.

This was going to be exquisite.

They began to walk again, and turned into the gateway of the man's house, talking softly. Without increasing his stride, the wolf strolled on past; heard her laugh, like the sound of a tinkling bell. He carried on walking, turned the corner and immediately picked up the pace.

On the next street over, he counted down until he reached the house backing directly onto the man's home. There was no dog – he had made sure of it – and no sign of the owner's car in the drive. Earlier that evening he'd taken the security light out with a well-aimed rock, and now, under cover of darkness, he entered the garden, boosted himself over the wall of the man's property and hurried up his garden to the house.

The lights were on downstairs, and if he strained his ears, he could hear the faint sound of music. It was a narrow house, single-fronted, with a flat-roofed extension on the back.

The windows of the house were good, double-glazed and solid. Fortunately, the back door was secured by a single Chubb lock: a doddle to someone like him.

He was inside in seconds, standing in the hall, next to the kitchen.

He could hear the music clearly now, a woman singing in a husky voice about ordinary love. Though he had no clue who the singer was, he thought the choice was perfectly apt.

Working quickly, he slid the gym bag from his back and removed from it the tools of his trade. Champagne, mask, flowers, syringe.

Next he opened his coat and withdrew his sword from its scabbard, feeling a ripple of something almost sexual at the sound it made.

He crept down the hall and used the tip of the sword to push open the living room door. If it creaked, so be it.

But it did not.

They were on the sofa, him on top of her. His jacket was on the floor, hers thrown over an armchair. A fake gas fire threw flickering light into the room, one lamp lit in the corner.

She saw him first. Her eyes grew huge and she made a sound, tried to move, but the stupid disgusting man clearly thought this meant something else entirely. He groaned, moved his hands to the back of her head, forcing her mouth closer to his.

The wolf waited until she broke free.

It seemed only polite.

Finally she had enough air to scream.

The man looked up, eyes glazed by beer and lust. There was a bulge in his trousers, straining to be free of the material.

'Huh?' he said.

The wolf brought the sword down in a well-practised move, right to left. Earlier that day, using the whetstone in his father's workshop, he had sharpened the blade to a scalpel's edge. But not even he could have predicted what happened next.

Estelle Roberts stared at the rolling head in stunned silence. While her brain scrambled to make sense of what her eyes were telling her, the wolf took the syringe from his coat pocket and jabbed it into the side of her neck. Then he clamped his hand over her mouth and pushed her backwards, pinning her down with his weight. The drug would need time to do its work.

'Celine,' he said, as her struggles weakened and her eyes began to roll up into her head. 'Celine, it's me. Don't be afraid, you're having a bad dream. Here, let me help, you, Celine … Listen to my voice.'

CHAPTER TWENTY-ONE

Roxy drained the last dregs of the industrial-strength coffee and rolled her neck from one side to the other, trying to ease the cramp between her shoulders. She felt someone breathing on her; when she turned round, she found Quinn leaning over her, reading her notes.

'Don't do that.'

'What?' He looked at her, surprised.

'That.'

'I didn't realise you were so jumpy.' He nodded to the screen. 'What are you looking at?'

'It's an antidepressant. I found a bottle of it in Andrea Colgan's bathroom. I was cross-referencing it to see if there was any mention of it in the Dell/Kilbride case.'

'And was there?'

'Not that I could find.'

'Andrea Colgan was depressed, was she? I wonder what about?'

'A lot of people take some kind of anti-anxiety medication; it's the world we live in.'

'Do you?'

'No.'

'Any word on Noel Furlong?'

'No, not yet, but we've got a trace on his phone. If he uses it, we've got him.'

'He'd hardly be that stupid.'

'People can surprise you.'

Quinn glanced at his watch. 'Want to go for a ride?'

She hesitated. He noticed.

'It's a ride, Sergeant Malloy. I'm not asking you to go paragliding in the nip.'

'Where?'

'I want to talk to Furlong's sister.'

She pushed her chair back and reached for her jacket.

Caroline Furlong lived in a cottage on a quiet residential street in Inchicore, less than half a mile from the bank of the Grand Canal. Roxy guessed she was in her early forties, but she looked older. It was her styling. Her clothes were old-fashioned and kind of prim: grey skirt, cream blouse, grey cardigan. She wore no make-up and her hair was short, cut in a no-nonsense style. A silver crucifix glinted on a chain around her neck; no wedding band that Roxy could see.

She looked scared when she opened the door to Quinn's knock.

'I'm going to tell you what I told Dominic Travers,' she said, physically placing her body between them and the hall as she pulled the door behind her. 'Noel is not here and I don't know where he is, so unless you have a warrant—'

'Dominic Travers came to see you?' Quinn asked.

'That's right.' Her voice thrummed with anger. 'I suppose you're going to threaten me too, is that how this works?'

'Miss Furlong, if someone has threatened you, you are within your rights to make a formal complaint.'

'What good would that do?' she fired back. 'You lot can't be here twenty-four/seven, can you?'

'Come on now,' Quinn said. 'Miss Furlong – or Caroline, can I call you Caroline?'

'If you like,' she said, though it was clear she would prefer he did not.

'Caroline, we're not here to upset you or threaten you, I promise. We understand how difficult this must be for you.'

'Noel didn't kill that girl,' she said, her voice trembling slightly. 'The daft eejit loved her, even after she threw him out.'

'Course he did. Look.' Quinn's voice was as soft as warm butter. 'Why don't we go inside and sit down. Then you can tell us what's going on. I want to hear your side of the story.'

She hesitated.

'I want to hear Noel's side of the story too.'

That was the key, and it worked her lock perfectly. Moments later, they were following her down a hallway and into a small kitchen at the back of the house. It was decked out in pine; a lot of pine. Roxy looked around: pine panelling, pine furniture, pine benches. The blinds were down and she was surprised to see they weren't pine too.

She immediately felt claustrophobic.

'Great room,' Quinn said, looking around as if he was staring up at the Sistine Chapel ceiling itself. 'You don't see craftsmanship like this any more.'

'My father built this extension himself, with his own hands.'

'Yeah?' Quinn nodded, impressed.

Caroline had been eating before they arrived: a bowl of watery-looking soup sat on the table, a single plate containing a thin slice of brown bread beside it. There was a cocker spaniel dozing in a basket by the cooker. It offered a half-hearted woof, but didn't bother getting up to investigate them any further.

'That's Teddy.' Caroline carried the remains of her meagre dinner to the sink. 'He won't bother you; he's stone deaf.' She turned around, clutching her upper arm. Roxy noticed her wince and wondered if she was in pain. 'Do you have any pets?'

Roxy shook her head.

'I have a cat,' Quinn said.

'Oh, probably more suited to your line of work. Dogs need a routine, exercise. Cats are a lot less trouble.'

'Not mine. He's a holy terror, likes to bring in all kinds of things. Woke up the other day and he'd dragged a bloody great crow in through the bathroom window. Had a hell of a job trying to catch it. Should have seen the mess it left behind too.'

'What did you do with it?'

'Threw a towel over it in the end. Brought it outside and let it go.'

'Was it hurt?'

Quinn shrugged. 'Dunno, it seemed okay to me. It flew off.'

'Cat bites can be toxic, you see.'

'Yeah? I didn't know that. I'll have to remember for the future.'

With the ice broken, Caroline remembered her manners and offered them tea. Roxy, following Quinn's example, accepted it to be polite, though she didn't really want any. Caroline made it in a teapot, using leaves, not bags, and when she was finished, she put it in the middle of the table with a cosy over it.

'It's best to give it a few minutes to draw,' she said, putting out cups and saucers. Again her arm seemed to be troubling her.

'Love a good cup of tea, me.' Quinn rubbed his hands together. 'Nothing beats it on a cold day. This is a nice house, real cosy. Great location.'

'It used to belong to my parents.'

'Oh yeah?'

'I was working in England when Mammy died. Daddy lived here by himself for a while. He was always very independent, but then he fell and broke his hip.' She shrugged. 'You know, he needed minding.'

'So you came back home to look after him.'

She nodded and began to pour the tea.

'Was Noel not around?'

'He was … living elsewhere at the time.'

So were you, Roxy thought, yet you came home.

'Noel's younger than you, is he?' Quinn asked, even though Roxy knew exactly how old he was.

'He'll be thirty in March. He was a surprise baby.' When she smiled, her features softened and the years fell from her face. 'Though not an unwelcome one, I should add. My parents adored him.'

'A late lamb.'

'What a lovely expression.'

'You must be close.'

'We were; not so much lately.'

She made a big fuss of putting milk in her tea. Then she removed a handkerchief from the sleeve of her cardigan, blew her nose and put it back.

'How long did Noel live with Andrea Colgan?' Quinn asked, taking a long slurp of his tea and sighing with satisfaction.

'A little over a year.'

'Was it a good relationship?'

'You'd have to ask Noel.' Caroline's fingernails were short and blunt, and she tapped them very gently on the rim of her saucer. 'You never met her, of course. Andrea.'

'No.'

'She was very beautiful, in a showy way. Determined, *very* ambitious.'

'You make her sound almost predatory,' Roxy said. Under the table, Quinn pressed his foot against hers until she moved it out of range.

'What does he do, your brother?'

'He's an artist; he's very talented.'

'Yeah?' Quinn grinned. 'I always wanted to draw.' He raised his hands. 'Unfortunately these are the hand version of two left feet.'

'We never knew where he got it from,' Caroline said. 'No one in the family is particularly artistic. I can barely draw a straight line.'

'Does he do shows and the like?'

She nodded. 'Small ones, but he's developing quite a following. That's how he met Andrea, you know, at an art show. She was doing the PR for Nathan Fila; do you know him?'

They both shook their heads.

'Sculptor, works with metals and precious stones.'

'Is that all Noel does? Art?' Roxy asked, getting a scowl from Quinn for her trouble.

'Well obviously he does other work as well. Art is … It takes time to develop it into a business.'

'What does he do to make ends meet?'

'He works at a tattoo parlour in the city centre.'

'Which one?'

'The Black Cat.'

'In Temple Bar?'

Caroline was growing defensive. 'Yes, he's very much in demand, actually.'

'It's another kind of art really, if you think about it,' Quinn said. 'On a different canvas.'

'That's what Noel says. And actually it *is* very creative. I was surprised when I saw some of his design work; it's very intricate.'

Roxy couldn't bear it, not another second longer.

'Was he here last night?'

'Yes.'

'All night?'

'Until I went to bed.'

'What time was that?'

'Nine, nine thirty?'

'That's pretty early. He could have gone out after that.'

'He could have, but I don't think he did.'

'Was he here when you got up?'

She hesitated before she answered. 'No.'

'So you can't really vouch for him after nine or nine thirty?'

'No, I can't.' Caroline got to her feet. 'It's been a long day, Detectives. If you don't mind, I'd like you both to leave now.'

Outside, on the way to the car, Quinn told Roxy he'd join her in a minute. He went back, knocked on the door and spoke briefly to Caroline. Roxy saw him put something in her hand and squeeze her shoulder before he walked back.

'What was that about?' she asked when he drew alongside.

'I gave her my card in case he gets in contact.'

Roxy snorted. 'Good luck with that.'

Quinn stopped short and glared at her.

'When was the last time you hugged someone, Malloy?'

'Excuse me?'

'Hug, it's a verb; it means when one human puts their arms around another human to offer comfort or solace. People do it all the time; hell, even monkeys do it.'

'Monkeys?'

'Answer the question. When was the last time you hugged someone?'

'I'm not answering it; it's irrelevant to anything.'

'That woman,' Quinn pointed in the direction of the house, 'has had her life torn asunder today. Two seconds of talking to her, you can tell she's a minder, a carer. Noel Furlong is nearly fifteen years her junior, so he's like a son to her rather than a brother.'

'So?'

'So you don't go barking questions at her like that. Look at it from her point of view. She got up this morning and went to work and it was a normal boring Monday. Since then she's been threatened, frightened and insulted. We need her to trust us, to think we're her best option if Noel Furlong contacts her. We need her cooperation.'

'We are her *only* option,' Roxy said. 'Noel Furlong has no alibi and he was seen fleeing the scene. Why does it matter if he can paint or not? Who gives a damn about that?'

Quinn stared at her, his hands on his hips.

'How the hell did you make it to sergeant with that attitude? Whose toast did you butter?'

'*Excuse* me?'

'Gussy's right, you have a *lot* to learn.'

Roxy blinked, offended.

'I am doing the best I can,' she said after a moment.

'I was afraid you were going to say that,' Quinn said, and walked away.

CHAPTER TWENTY-TWO

A different taxi brought Dominic Travers home to the grand Regency house he owned on Dalkey's exclusive Nerano Road. It was a huge double-fronted mansion, surrounded by almost half an acre of sculpted lawns, set back from the road behind electronic gates and high walls. The previous owner, a well-known musician, had been particularly proud of the Tuscan fountain installed in the front garden. Dominic, when he won the place in a high-stakes game of poker, now enjoyed it in his stead.

His earlier anger had given way to exhaustion and then to a vague sense of helplessness, an emotion he had not felt for so long he'd almost forgotten how poisonous it was.

He had spent the day calling in favours and searching the city, anything to distract himself from his pain, but still his mind had other ideas, sending memory after memory to the surface, some he hadn't even realised he'd kept. Andrea running to find him when she lost her first tooth, full of excitement, determined to stay awake and see the tooth fairy for herself. Her face when he brought home a small tabby kitten for her ninth birthday, trying not to laugh at her staggeringly solemn promises to feed it and care for it by 'my own self'. Andrea as a teen, crying because a boy she liked preferred another girl in school. As a young woman, beautiful and confident, kissing him on the cheek, going out for the night with her friends, complaining about how scratchy his beard was.

Andrea lying on the stainless-steel table in the morgue, her hair stiff with blood, her face almost unrecognisable.

The nearer he got to the house, the more he wanted to tell the taxi driver to keep going, drive forever, drive to a place where Andrea was not dead. Don't stop here, he wanted to shout, don't stop.

His housekeeper, Frederick, was waiting for him out on the front steps, his neat little face tense and fretful. His eyes were red.

'Sir,' he said, when Travers climbed out. 'My deepest and sincerest condolences.'

Travers patted him on the shoulder.

'Andrea's mother is waiting for you inside.' Frederick waited a beat. 'She is not alone. Her friend Justine is with her.'

Dominic swore under his breath. He removed his coat and handed it to Frederick, smoothed his hair down with his hands.

'How is she?'

'Upset, as you can imagine.'

Dominic grimaced.

His relationship with Lillian was complicated. It was hard to reconcile his feelings for her. He'd loved her once and cared for her deeply. In return, she had all but destroyed him.

For the longest time she had been his rock, his lighthouse in the storm. Intelligent, beautiful, she'd helped him found the empire he presided over now. There was nothing he wouldn't have done for her; he would have slain dragons to see her smile.

He was never able to pinpoint the exact moment he knew something was wrong. She was such a consummate liar, such an incredible actress that he ignored the quiet warning voice in his head.

They'd always enjoyed an active social life: money was no object; the economy was booming. Lillian liked to dress up and go out; she liked new restaurants, trendy bars, gigs, plays, anything and everything. On rare nights in she prowled the house like a cat on a hot tin roof, always carrying a glass of white wine in her hand, unable to settle down or read a book. She slept late in the day, never truly coming alive until the second cocktail of the evening.

He thought it would be different when Andrea was born, and for a while it had been, but then she began to find fault with stupid things; she was irritated and bored stuck at home with a kid while he 'gallivanted' around town. Nothing he said or did seemed to make her happy, and so the rift between them grew.

Then, disaster.

Dominic had been working in the UK when he got the call. Lillian and Andrea had been involved in a car accident; it was serious, could he come right away?

Could he come?

Sometimes even now he woke up in the middle of the night, sweat-soaked and trembling, remembering that call.

Could he come?

Seeing Andrea, tiny and frightened, hooked up to machines and wires almost broke him. Lillian out in the hall, screaming blue murder, crying, broken collar bone, yelling at the staff to get away from her: it was an accident, she cried, calling his name over and over, an accident.

Her blood alcohol reading said otherwise.

She tried to get shared custody, and cried very prettily in the family courts. But her tears were for nothing. Dominic fought her tooth and nail, using a high-priced law firm and every dirty trick in the book to win. And win he did, even if it was a bitter victory overall.

In the early days, he struggled to cope under the yoke of parenting, even after hiring Frederick to run the household. He had always been a man who had straddled two worlds, law-abiding and lawless. He spent long hours working, organising, threatening, greasing the right palms, making sure nobody from one side felt slighted by someone from the other. Now, suddenly, he was expected to come home at a reasonable hour and read stories to a sleepy child, ask about hobbies and things he had no interest in and no real desire to understand. Weekends went by in a blur of noise and shouting, of visiting local parks and feeding overweight ducks, glowering at unruly dogs and being forced to tolerate people who stopped to smile and ask after the beautiful shy child by his side.

Unthinkable.

But gradually, over time, Dominic found his footing. He would never be able to pinpoint exactly the day or the week or even the month it happened. One day he was plotting and scheming behind the scenes; the next he was anxiously awaiting news of how his girl had got on at school, enquiring after her happiness with all the eagerness of a doting granny.

If any of his associates noticed a softening to his centre, they wisely chose not to remark on it; after all, one didn't stick a fork into a socket to see if there was electricity. But privately, very privately indeed, it was agreed that the silver-edged reality of fatherhood had humanised a man long thought to be beyond reach.

And now Andrea was dead.

Dominic pushed open the door of the study.

Lillian offered no hello, of course, no greeting of any kind. Her eyes – grey like his, but darker; storm eyes, he used to call them – stared balefully from her once beautiful face. She was dressed head to toe in black. It didn't suit her; the colour washed her out.

'Did you have anything to do with what happened?'

Her eyes, he could not help notice, were bone dry, and he knew that whatever emotional snap she had suffered earlier had since evaporated. He knew that within her chest her heart was now a block of ice. He knew because she was once his soulmate; he knew because he felt the exact same way.

'Well?' She snapped the question at him.

'No.'

He made no move to go to her, knowing she would not appreciate or accept any kind of physical connection. Justine, Lillian's partner, an older woman, defiantly grey-haired and make-up-free, wearing her usual selection of cheap silver jewellery over clashing patterns, got up and tried to offer her some comfort. Lillian shoved her unceremoniously away.

'What are you going to do?' Lillian demanded.

Dominic went to the sideboard and poured a drink, noting that she had already done a number on his bourbon, his best bourbon. In all the time he'd known her, she had never picked the cheap option in anything.

He took a long swallow, went to his desk and sat down.

'You have people, you can find out who did this. You can make them pay, I know you can.'

'Oh dearest,' Justine said. 'You mustn't talk like that.'

Dearest. The word grated on his nerves. It was so fake, so affected, like Justine herself. He'd always had her pegged as a tireless champion of the underdog and a liberal twat who thought she was smarter than everyone in the room.

'Did *he* do it?' Lillian demanded.

'Who?'

'Who do you think? Noel Furlong.'

'I don't know.'

'You with all your resources and you *don't know*.' She raised her chin. 'Bullshit.'

Travers looked at her, this creature, this near stranger he'd once adored. Her anger he could take, he was used to it by now, but her sorrow he found hard to contend with.

'Andrea was seeing a shrink, did you know that?'

He looked at her coldly.

'What are you saying?'

'Simon Fitzpatrick she said his name was.'

'You lie.'

'I do *not*.' Lillian's eyes burned in her face. 'She wasn't perfect, Dominic, none of us are.'

'Why was she seeing a shrink?'

'I don't know.'

He looked sceptical.

'How do you know this?'

'I am her mother.'

He snorted. 'Only when it suited you.'

Lillian's expression changed to one of pure venom.

'All you've ever done is try to shut me out of that child's life. Maybe if you'd allowed me to have a better relationship with her she wouldn't be—'

'Don't you dare,' Dominic warned her. 'Don't you fucking dare.'

Lillian looked away, swallowed, and regained her composure. 'Something was troubling her, Dominic. Any fool could see it.'

Dominic reached for his glass, caught the side of it by accident and tipped it over.

'Bollocks.'

He took a handkerchief from his pocket and tried to blot the worst of it up.

'Look,' he said. 'I will get to the bottom of this, I promise you.'

'Promise me?' Lillian barked a high-pitched laugh. 'You *promised* me you'd look after her. I don't give a shit about your promises, Dominic.'

Justine squeezed her bicep. 'Don't, dearest, you'll upset yourself.'

'Will you stop telling me how to feel,' Lillian snapped, and yanked her arm away with such savagery the older woman recoiled. 'I *am* fucking upset. I'm entitled to be upset, Justine!'

'I'll get to the bottom of this,' Travers repeated. 'I will find who killed her and—'

'You'll what? Have them sent to a cushy prison where they can get three square meals a day and learn another language while they wait for early release for good behaviour? Isn't that what we do now in our glorious new society? Rehabilitate.' She put her empty glass down on a side table and looked at him with naked contempt. 'There's no rehabilitation that will bring our girl back.'

She got to her feet and, weaving slightly, grabbed a dark green coat, which she swung over her shoulders like a cape before storming out of the study.

Moments later he heard the front door bang.

Justine stood too.

'For what it's worth, Dominic,' she said in her weird raspy voice, 'I am very sorry for your loss. I know you loved Andrea a great deal. I hope whoever did this is brought swiftly to justice.'

'You don't need to worry about that,' Travers said.

Justine went after Lillian.

Travers nodded to Frederick, who had soundlessly appeared in the door of the study.

'You got him?'

'Line one, sir.'

He picked up the phone, cleared his throat, listened for a moment. 'Yes, thank you. Take a name down. Furlong, Noel Furlong. Hold on …' He opened his mobile and scrolled through it with his thumb. 'Yeah, sending it and his address to you. Got it? Good, off the books, Lennox, that's right. I want this man for myself.'

He hung up, reached for a photo on his desk. He had taken it when Andrea was ten, maybe eleven, leaning backwards on an old swing with her blonde hair almost hanging to the grass. If he closed his eyes and concentrated, he could still hear her laugh, still here her call, 'Higher, Daddy, higher, higher!'

CHAPTER TWENTY-THREE

By the time she got home, Roxy was almost sick with exhaustion and the knot between her shoulders felt like it had grown to the size of a baby's fist. All she wanted to do was lie face down on her bed and pass out.

It was a surprise to enter the apartment and find her flatmate Boy standing in the kitchen wearing an apron, though she wasn't sure if the surprise was a pleasant one or not. After the day she'd endured, the last thing she wanted was any kind of company.

'You're home,' she said.

Boy paused what he was doing and turned, holding a spatula mid air.

'Well it's lovely to see you too, Roxanne. Want me to go throw myself off the balcony?'

'I'm sorry, hello.'

'That's a *little* better.'

He pointed to an open bottle of red wine on the counter. 'Pour me one of those and then pour yourself a bigger one. You look like you could do with it.'

'I will in a second. I'll be right back.'

She went down the hall to her bedroom, put her weapons in the safe, stripped, hung her uniform up and changed into grey tracksuit bottoms and a white vest. By the time she got back to the kitchen, Boy was tipping the contents of the pan onto two plates.

'What is this?'

'Indian chickpeas with spicy courgette.'

'It smells incredible.'

'Grab the wine before you sit down.'

She did as she was told. Boy poured two very generous glasses, set the bottle aside and ground black pepper over both their dishes.

'Bon appétit!'

He sat down and began to eat. Roxy took a mouthful. It was delicious; she hadn't eaten since breakfast and was ravenous.

'So,' he said, after a few mouthfuls. 'Do you want to talk about it?'

'Not really.'

'That's good, 'cos I probably don't want to hear it.'

They ate for a while in companionable silence. Roxy took a sip of her wine. Like the food, it was good. She had to admit, Boy had great taste.

'I think I'm messing up my promotion.'

'How?'

Roxy felt the heat from Boy's food loosen her sinuses. Boy didn't believe in less is more when it came to spices. Everything was always subject to his personal Richter scale of heat, and this was a solid 8.

She drank some more of her wine.

'Morrissey dumped us, and now I'm working with a squad who I'm pretty sure think I'm either an idiot or a liability.'

Boy digested this for a moment.

'So prove them wrong. Show them your strengths.'

'I don't always work well with other people,' she admitted after a moment. 'I think I'm like cucumber, an acquired taste.'

Boy laughed, but not unkindly.

'Cucumber?'

'Never mind, it's your turn. What are you doing home before midnight?'

He raised his glass to his lips and waggled his eyebrows. 'I've been free since four o'clock.'

She looked at him, puzzled.

'That's when I told Annika to stuff her shitty barely-minimum-paying job where the sun will never shine.'

'You quit your job?'

'Don't look so panicky! There's plenty of jobs out there for a seasoned barman with a winning personality, believe me. I won't stiff you on rent.'

'Oh I wasn't—'

'You were, and that's okay too.' He lifted his glass. 'Let's have a toast.'

She lifted hers. 'To what?'

'To acquired tastes.'

Roxy grinned and clinked her glass against his.

'Acquired tastes.'

CHAPTER TWENTY-FOUR

Noel woke with a strangled scream and a weird stabbing pain in his calf. It felt like his entire lower leg was encased in a vice.

He straightened his leg with a kick and opened his eyes. For a single second he had no idea where he was or what was going on, then he remembered and a wave of nausea engulfed him.

Andrea was dead, and he was on the run.

Shit.

Storm lay sprawled across his chest, one arm draped on the floor. She moaned when he tried to slide out from under her but she didn't wake.

He looked around for his clothes, found his jocks on top of a plastic cactus and pulled them on. Moving made him dizzy, and he could hear his heart beating in his ears, so he sat back on the edge of the sofa and put his head in his hands to keep it from exploding.

After a while, he gingerly located his jeans and his phone. He placed the mobile on the cluttered coffee table and stared at it, chewing his thumbnail. This was the problem with technology, he thought sourly, nobody knew phone numbers by heart any more; everything was stored on this one little machine, just sitting here offering fingertip access to the world.

He tried to think, but it was hard to form thoughts when his mouth felt like asbestos and his head was pounding. Too much blow, way too much. Storm was a bloody hoover, but what could he say: he was at her mercy and the dozy cow knew it.

His sister would probably be awake now, if she'd slept at all. He thought about his room at her house, visualising it. There was a couple of hundred stashed in the mattress (she was going to do her nut over that, but it couldn't be helped now) and his passport was under his socks in the third drawer of the dresser. Clothes, other shit, none of that was important. He needed the passport and the money; that was it.

Would she bring it to him if he called her?

This was something he'd never really considered before. Caroline was his sister, she loved him, she *had* to help him; those were the blood rules.

Weren't they?

He chewed his thumbnail some more, peeling off a piece of skin in the process. On the other hand, his sister was a bit of a square, as straight as he was crooked. She might think involving her in crime was pushing his luck; she might think this was beyond her remit as family.

Behind him, Storm snorted and muttered something in her sleep. Noel ran his hands over his head. He had the strangest sensation that he was stuck in an alternate universe or a bad dream, and that he'd wake up any moment with an overwhelming sense of relief.

Andrea was the gentlest sleeper he'd ever known. She always lay on her right side, curled up like a kitten. Her breathing was soft, steady. Sometimes he'd get in late from a gig and slide in behind her, tucking his legs into the crook of hers, slipping his arms around her waist and burying his face in her hair.

Her hair always smelled like jasmine. Funny, he'd forgotten that little detail until now.

No, there was no time for that kind of thinking, not now.

Caroline would be getting ready for work soon. He needed to make a decision. Either phone her before she left the house, or risk going there after she had gone to work. What if the cops were following her? Even assuming she'd come, she might lead them right to him.

No, it would be better to leave her out of it. He'd go around the lane at the back of the cottages, skip over the wall. No one would be any the wiser.

Would they have eyes on the house? Front and back?

He hissed and slapped the side of his head in frustration. He was as paranoid as hell. It was impossible to think straight like this.

He stole another look at his phone.

How much risk could there be in a quick call?

What if Caroline said no?

What then?

He had to do something; he had to be ... what was the word? Proactive. Throw them off the scent a little.

A thought struck him. He got up, ran to the bathroom and stared at his reflection in the mirror over the sink. The beard, he thought, running his hand over it; the beard would need to go.

Using a pair of blunt toenail scissors, he cut off as much as he could, then made foam with some shower gel and hacked at his face with a disposable razor he found in the shower.

When he was done, he rinsed his face, then dried it with a pink hand towel and looked at his handiwork. His chin was covered in nick and cuts, and multiple patches of bristly hair remained.

Shit.

He looked like the world's creepiest child-molester. Had he always had that funny-looking chin?

'Babe?'

It was Storm.

'Yeah, be right out.'

'I got to pee.'

He stared at his reflection. Okay, it was bad, it was really bad, but on the other hand, it didn't look anything like him. He grabbed a hank of hair and held it aloft.

Actually, his sleep-deprived brain told him, if he shaved his head, nobody would recognise him, period.

'Storm?'

'Wha'?'

He yanked the door open. She shrieked when she saw him and leaped backwards.

'You got any more of these crappy razors?'

'What did you do?'

'I'm … improvising.'

'Yeah, whatever. Look, I'm real sorry about this and all, but you gotta go.'

'What? Why? I thought you said I could stay here for a few days.' She scratched the bird's nest she called hair.

'My boyfriend came back from Manchester early. He's gonna call over.'

'Boyfriend?' Noel stared at her, gobsmacked. 'You never mentioned anything about having a bloody boyfriend.'

'You never asked,' she said, shoving him out of the way and dropping onto the toilet with a plop.

CHAPTER TWENTY-FIVE

Dr Gregory Milton slid out from under the sun lamp and removed his protective goggles. He took a quick shower and got dressed, deliberating carefully over his choices. He was fifty-five years old and cared deeply about his appearance. A thrice-weekly game of competitive racquetball kept his belly trim and his buttocks firm. Genetics had blessed him with thick hair, and the increasing grey did not detract from his handsomeness; if anything, he felt it added a layer of distinguished charm. His clothes were subtle and expensive. He shopped exclusively at Reiss, Alias Tom and Brown Thomas. His shoes were hand-made from the best-quality leather. He would rather die than wear jeans, or trainers outside of the gym.

Downstairs in the kitchen he prepared a breakfast of organic eggs, lightly scrambled, turkey bacon and half a beef tomato, with fresh grapefruit juice and coffee, which he'd taken black ever since he was told dairy could affect his voice.

Shortly after breakfast, the studio car arrived to take him to work at the television studio. En route he read the papers on his laptop, checked his shares on the stock market and sent a message enquiring after the health of his wife, Nadine.

April, his PA, was standing waiting at the studio door with his itinerary. As always, she was decked out in the most garish of outfits; he sometimes wondered where on earth she shopped, as he had never seen anyone else wear the sort of ensemble she cobbled together. What was she wearing on her head? It looked like a crumpled paper bag.

Still, despite her dreadful clothes and her braces and her frankly hideous hairstyles, she was a superb PA. If anything, her unattractiveness made her a valuable asset; certainly nobody could ever accuse him of impropriety with *her*.

'Good morning, Greg,' she said.

'Good morning, April.' He touched his fingers to her cheek. 'How are you today?'

She giggled slightly. 'Fine.'

'Love the hat.'

'Oh, thank you, it's vintage.'

'I can tell.'

He took the itinerary, glanced along it and frowned. Walter, the station owner, had called another one of his interminable staff meetings, tedious affairs that bored him senseless. He wondered if he might be able to wriggle out of it somehow.

April leaned in close.

'Maureen was looking for you.'

The frown deepened. Maureen Kelly, the station manager, was second in command to Walter. She was a first-rate manager but a second-rate human, and for some reason she was impervious to his charm.

Over the five years he'd worked for the station he had grown to dislike Maureen enormously, and yet, he suspected, not nearly as much as she disliked him. Certainly she was always professional in her dealings with him, but she had on more than one occasion frozen him out of conversation, and she avoided him at parties. He got the distinct impression she had also been instrumental in a show he'd proposed never making it past the treatment stage.

'Did she say what for?'

'No, just that she'd like to see you in her office before this morning's meeting.' April furrowed her brow. 'Did you have an accident?'

He followed her gaze to his hands. 'Oh, this? No, nothing serious; had a little tumble playing racquetball.'

'It looks swollen; I'll send someone to you with some ice right away.'

'No need to fuss.'

'It's not a bother, honestly.'

She was gone before he could stop her. He took the lift upstairs to his office and shut the door behind him.

He liked his office. The shelves were filled with the various broadcasting awards he'd won over the years, and books he'd written and co-authored. Three framed posters depicting his image art deco style hung behind his chair; a framed photo of him and the Dali Lama took pride of place on his hand-tooled desk.

He sat down and flicked through the stack of open letters April had left for him. He read one quickly, tossed it aside and chose another. The letters mostly contained dull, pedestrian problems – low self-esteem, a cheating spouse, challenging children – but every so often a pearl appeared in the dreck and it was these he liked to incorporate into his shows.

Someone knocked on his door.

'Come in.'

A girl he'd never seen before entered carrying a bowl of ice cubes.

'Hi.' Her smile was shy, almost apologetic. 'Um … April asked me to drop this in for you.'

He put the letter to one side.

'Why, thank you, that's very kind. If you could put it on the sideboard over there, I'd be very grateful.'

He studied her closely as she did his bidding, liking very much what he saw. She had a tiny waist, larger-than-average buttocks, round breasts, tear-shaped, natural. He imagined cupping them, feeling their heft in his hands, his thumbs exploring, circling the pert nipples. She was a redhead, so her nipples would be pinkish, her skin pale …

'Do you need anything else?'

He smiled. 'Yes, there are some towels in the bottom drawer. Would you be a darling and fetch one for me?'

'Of course.'

He watched her bend over to open the drawer. He could see the outline of her underwear through her skirt; probably cotton, white no doubt.

Virginal.

'I don't remember seeing you before, and I always remember a pretty face. Are you new?'

She selected a towel and brought it over to him.

'Yes, this is my second day. I'm on work experience.'

'Really, and how are you finding it so far? Not too dull, I hope?'

'Oh no!' She shook her head vehemently. 'It's great. And can I say how much I love your work. I listen to your show all the time and I think it's amazing how you help so many people the way you do.'

'Thank you.' He gave her his most paternal kindly smile, the one he knew made the ladies tremble at the knees. 'I feel it's my privilege to help people.'

'That woman who phoned last Friday, I mean, she was such a cow, like I don't know how you kept your composure with her. I would have told her where to get off ...' She stopped and put her hand to her mouth. 'Oh my gosh, I'm so sorry, I didn't mean to sound so negative.'

'Please don't apologise for a natural and genuine reaction,' he said, laying it on thick. 'Of course, I feel it's unproductive to assign blame or shame in my clinical cases. That poor woman you refer to was hurt and angry, and anger is a naked flame. It consumes the host as readily as it consumes its surroundings. The best remedy for anger is compassion. I try to douse the flames with understanding, and most importantly, with love.'

She was staring at him, head tilted to one side, lips slightly parted, mesmerised. He wondered what she tasted like.

'That is so inspiring, Dr Milton.'

'Please, I'd like you to call me Greg; *all* my friends call me Greg.'

She blushed. 'Okay … Greg.'

'I didn't catch your name.'

'Oh, it's Olivia.'

'But of course it is, taken from the Latin *oliva*. Did you know, a branch from an olive tree has long been regarded as a sign of peace? It's no wonder you're interested in the plight of others; it shows how emotionally evolved you—'

The office door opened and the small, malignant toad that was Maureen Kelly appeared, instant disapproval and suspicion on her face.

'There you are, didn't you get my message?'

'Of course.' He smiled, but as usual it was wasted on her.

'What are you doing here?' she snapped at the girl.

'Oh, I was bringing Greg some—'

'There's a meeting in twenty minutes. Go see if the conference room is presentable. Make sure the water jugs are filled, and no lemon slices in them this time. If I see lemon, someone is going to get fired. Still water or carbonated, that's all, got it?'

'Yes.'

'What are you still doing here then?'

The girl fled.

'Goodness, Maureen.' Milton got up, walked to the sideboard and put some of the ice into the towel. 'You're testy this morning.'

'What happened to your hand?'

'Sports injury.' He went back to his chair.

She closed the door behind her and folded her arms. He dropped the smile; it was starting to make his cheeks ache.

'What do you want?'

'Does the name Andrea Colgan ring any bells with you?'

This felt like a trap. He leaned back in his chair and pursed his lips, acting nonchalant.

'I know the name … Wasn't she the woman from Albas Entertainment who handled my book tour?'

'That's right.'

So you already knew I knew her, you miserable old hag, he thought.

'What about her?'

'She's dead.'

'Oh dear, I'm sorry to hear that.' He waited a beat. 'What happened?'

'Apparently she was found murdered yesterday.'

'My God,' he said, carefully.

'How well did you know her?'

'We had a professional relationship, Maureen. I hardly think that qualifies as *knowing* her.'

'Just professional, was it?'

He didn't like the way she was looking at him; he didn't like it at all.

'That's right.'

'Well that's interesting, because as you know, I sign off on the expense accounts here, and I seem to recall shelling out a lot of Walter's money on fancy restaurants, wine bars and top-end hotels during your tour.'

'You'd rather we ate in McDonald's and drank tap water from a spigot, is that it? Slept in a camper van or pitched a tent on the side of the road?'

She smiled, showing a lot of gum. More snarl than smile really.

'You always have an answer, don't you, Milton?'

'Oh, I hadn't realised you'd asked a question.'

Maureen took a few steps closer to his desk and leaned on it with her little fists.

'I hope for your sake that the Garda don't come rat-tat-tatting on our door. I hope for your sake your relationship really was simply professional.'

'I can prepare a statement, if that's what you want.'

'I think that would be best.'

He was surprised. The bitch really did suspect him of something.

'Was that it?'

'There is one other thing.'

'Do tell.'

'That girl you were making googly eyes at …'

'What girl?'

'Shut up. Her name is Olivia and she's seventeen years old. Hear me when I tell you this: I don't want to find her behind closed doors with you again.'

He stared at her, astounded at her naked hostility.

'Who the hell do you think you are?'

'I see you,' she said, her eyes boring into him. 'I want you to know that you might have Walter and the rest of those featherheads fooled, but Nadine and I were friends, we spoke.'

'My wife was a troubled woman, you know that.'

'Was she?' Maureen's voice dripped with contempt. 'Or did she see you for what you are too?'

She left his office, deliberately leaving the door open behind her.

CHAPTER TWENTY-SIX

Roxy arrived at the station house a full hour before her shift was due to start. It was a new day and she was more determined than ever to prove to Quinn that she deserved her spot on the squad.

She opened the door to the incident room and got a surprise. Eli Quinn was sitting at a desk, hunched over his EN, pecking at it with his index finger. There were several empty coffee cups and a pile of peanut shells by his elbow. He glanced up when he heard her, and she could see from the shadows under his eyes that he hadn't slept much either. He wore a faded blue shirt open at the throat, and his chin was covered in dark stubble. Stick a cowboy hat on him and he could have stepped straight off a cattle ranch in Montana.

'What are you doing here?' he asked.

Not friendly, but not unfriendly either.

'I thought I'd get a head start on gathering intel on Andrea Colgan.' She removed her jacket and sat down.

'What we need is a new profile. Sergeant Lynn is right: there are some aspects of this latest murder that don't quite gel with what we've got so far.' He leaned back in his chair and stretched. 'Have you heard of Lizzie Brennan?'

Roxy froze. Suddenly it felt as though all the air had been sucked out of the room.

'She's a criminal profiler,' Quinn continued, seeming not to notice her shock. 'Miranda reckons she's the best.'

'Yes, I know of her.'

'Have you worked with her before?'

'No.'

'Hopefully she'll be able to give us something we've missed.'

'Missed?' Roxy said. 'We've barely had the case for twenty-four hours; we don't know what we *have*, let alone what we might have missed.'

Quinn glanced at her, frowning slightly.

'I'm not talking about just the Colgan case here ... Are you all right, Malloy? You're as white as a sheet.'

'Yes, I'm fine ... If you'll excuse me, I need to go see ...' She mumbled something inaudible and bolted from the room.

In the ladies' bathroom, she washed her face in freezing water and dried it with paper towels. Then she leaned on the sink and stared at her reflection in the mirror. This was bullshit. She was better than this, wasn't she? Why wouldn't they call her in? Lizzie Brennan was excellent at her job. Lizzie was excellent at *everything*.

Including, apparently, being the girlfriend of Roxy's ex, David.

She was completely over David, though, right? It was all water under the bridge. They were adults and they'd moved on with their lives. Stop thinking about Lizzie Brennan, she ordered her brain. It had been nearly a year since David had walked out. So why then was her heart racing in her chest? Why had she acted like a deer in the headlights in front of Quinn when he'd mentioned Lizzie's name?

She couldn't face going back to the incident room, and besides, there was something bugging her.

By the time she reached the forensics lab, she'd managed to regain a modicum of control.

'Is he here?' she asked Briana Lu, Johnson's right-hand woman in the lab. Briana didn't need to ask who 'he' was.

'Nope, can I help?'

'He was supposed to run a test on a urine sample taken from a homicide yesterday, but I didn't find it in the notes he sent over to Inspector Quinn.'

'Oh, right, that's actually done. I was going to send it over later this morning. Do you want me to go get it?'

'Please, if you wouldn't mind.'

She waited by the window looking out over the courtyard, hands behind her back, marshalling her thoughts.

'Here you go.'

Briana returned carrying a brown envelope. Roxy thanked her and left with it under her arm.

Upstairs, Quinn was nowhere to be seen, thankfully. She picked a desk, sat down and opened the envelope. She was still reading the analysis when Fletcher arrived carrying a Styrofoam cup in one hand, a leather satchel in the other.

'I thought I'd be first here.'

'You're not even second.' Roxy closed the file and tapped her index finger on the spine, thinking. She looked at Fletcher.

'We're doing the door-to-door at Andrea Colgan's apartment building, right?'

'That's right.'

'Why don't we head over there now, get ahead of the curve?'

'If you want.' He looked at his watch. 'It's a bit early, no?'

'It is, but I want to see a man about a dog.'

Fletcher wrinkled his brow.

'I'll explain on the way.' She got to her feet.

'Have you spoken to Quinn about it?'

'Yes,' Roxy said. 'He was here earlier.'

It wasn't a lie, she reasoned as they took the lift to the car park. She had spoken to Quinn that morning.

And as with everything in life, the devil was in the detail.

CHAPTER TWENTY-SEVEN

Ambrose Bailey stood at the bottom of his garden and swore under his breath. The crocuses that had been starting to push their way up through the soil were broken, the stems crushed.

Bloody kids acting the maggot, he thought, fuming. He poked at the dying flowers with the tip of his slippers. He did not like kids, not the ones that went around the place these days anyway. Didn't know they were born, half of them, rude little shits.

Muttering, he crossed the scrubby sun-starved lawn and checked the bird feeder. He was surprised to find it running low. Probably the blasted magpies; try as he might, he couldn't keep the buggers out of his garden.

Still muttering, he unlocked the shed door and fetched the little bag of birdseed he bought once a month. Mr Bailey hated almost everyone and everything, but he liked songbirds, and his garden was generally a welcome haven for them.

He was halfway through filling the feeder when the bushes beside the greenhouse began to shudder and shake. He heard a low growl, and then, cheeky as you like, a large black-and-white cat burst from the vegetation, its jaws firmly clamped around a robin.

'You bastard! You rotten bastard!' Mr Bailey screamed, and ran for the garden rake. But by the time he'd got it, the cat had hopped up on the wall and jumped down the other side.

Furious, Mr Bailey flung the rake aside and stormed back to the house to dress. This was the final straw; that wretched filthy creature of Bannon's had finally pushed him over the edge. It wasn't enough that it shat in his flower beds, it wasn't enough that it kept him up at night yowling and fighting with other cats; now it was killing his songbirds.

He would go round and have words. He wasn't a violent man, but by God, if Bannon didn't do something about that murdering creature, he'd … he'd … well, he'd think of something.

Twenty minutes later, he marched up Hugh Bannon's path and raised his fist to hammer on the door. It swung wide open at the first blow.

'Bannon?' he called. 'You in there?'

He cocked his head, listening.

'Bannon, it's Ambrose Bailey. I want to talk to you about that cat of yours.'

He waited. No one appeared. The house felt empty, yet he could hear music coming from a room to his right. Was the bugger ignoring him, hoping he'd go away?

'Bannon?'

He stepped over the threshold and walked slowly towards the door, acutely aware that he was now trespassing. Well, he thought, he had just cause, didn't he? His robin was dead.

He pushed open the living room door and stared.

It wasn't the blood that caused his heart to stutter, he would explain later to a sympathetic young nurse. It was seeing Bannon's head resting on top of some books in the middle of the coffee table that caused him to have a turn.

'He looked like he was about to ask me a favour,' he said, still horrified. 'He looked like he was going to ask me to go fetch his body.'

CHAPTER TWENTY-EIGHT

'Didn't you already interview this guy?' Fletcher wanted to know, peering at the number on Falstaff's door 'Shouldn't we start with the apartments on the ground floor and work our way up?'

'We can do that after we talk to Falstaff,' Roxy said.

She rapped on the door again, good and loud, and heard barking from somewhere inside. Eventually the door opened.

'Good morning!' She beamed the fakest smile she'd ever mustered. 'We met yesterday – Sergeant Malloy, and this is my colleague Sergeant Fletcher.'

Jerome Falstaff stood in the doorway of his apartment blinking and scratching his bare chest. He was wearing boxer shorts and nothing else. The shorts had dancing unicorns on them. His hair was wild.

'What time is it? I was sleeping.'

'Sorry about that,' Roxy replied, trying to ignore the little dog that had come out to investigate the callers and was barking up a storm. 'We didn't get a chance to finish our chat yesterday, did we, what with the kerfuffle. I thought you'd like an opportunity to revisit your statements.'

'Have you caught him then? Noel? Did he confess? I didn't hear anything about it on the news.'

'That's a nice little dog,' Fletcher said. 'What breed is it? Maltese?'

'That's right.'

'I hear they're very smart, easy to train.'

'They are!' Falstaff was no longer scowling and was in fact looking at Fletcher with something approaching civility.

'May we come in, Mr Falstaff?' Roxy asked.

They followed him up the hall to the same untidy sitting room. Falstaff plonked the dog down and swept an armload of clothes off the sofa. He looked around for somewhere else to put them, gave up and dumped them on the floor next to a stack of cardboard boxes.

'I don't think I've got any coffee, but I've got herbal tea.'

'That's okay, Mr Falstaff,' Roxy said. Fletcher got down on one knee and scratched the dog behind its ears.

'Oh, he likes you,' Falstaff said. 'You're blessed; he's a very astute judge of character, you know.'

'Dogs always like me,' Fletcher said. 'Dunno why, even as a kid.'

'Do you have one of your own?'

'No. When I retire I'm going to get two, probably Staffies, I like Staffies.'

'You live here alone, right, Mr Falstaff?' Roxy said quickly before there was any more talk of dogs. What was it with Quinn and his band of chatterboxes?

Falstaff dropped onto the sofa and crossed one pale leg over the other, exactly as he had done the day before. 'Well, apart from Edgar and my cat.'

'And this was your mother's place.'

'That's right.'

'You said yesterday that you were an actor. Are you working on something at the moment? You mentioned something about reading a script.'

'I'm between jobs at the moment.' He waved a dismissive hand. 'I mostly do voice work these days. Audio books and adverts, that sort of thing.'

'I imagine it's a difficult business.'

'It's not a business; acting is my life.' Falstaff reached for a packet of cigarettes on a side table and lit one. 'But you're right,

Sergeant, it can be difficult. Especially since every bloody halfwit with internet access thinks they're a bloody star. Amateurs: they mess it up for the rest of us, see, no understanding of the craft. Don't even get me started on them.'

'Andrea Colgan worked for Albas Entertainment. I gather a lot of actors are on their books.'

'That's right.'

'Did you and she ever work together?'

'We knew a lot of the same people.' He shrugged. 'Acting's a small world.'

'You were friends then, as well as neighbours?'

'We knew each other well enough to chat now and then. I mean, we weren't best friends or anything like that.' He took another drag on the cigarette. 'You know what they say, good fences makes good neighbours.'

'Can you remember the last time you saw Andrea?'

He looked up to the right, scratched his chest, thinking. 'Last week sometime. She'd had her hair done.'

Roxy smiled. 'You noticed?'

'She had wonderful hair, that girl. I told her she looked like a young Jeanne Moreau.' He glanced at Fletcher, who offered no comment.

'Who?' asked Roxy.

'French actress, *very* famous back in the day.'

'Oh.' She shrugged. 'Sorry, Mr Falstaff, like I said yesterday, I'm not much of a movie buff.'

'Nobody is these days,' he said sourly.

'You said that after you saw Noel Furlong downstairs, you had a premonition.'

'Did I? It was all so traumatic.' He picked a piece of tobacco off his lower lip. He had shredded the filter. 'I'm sure I told you everything yesterday.'

'I'm just making sure I have the details right. Tell me exactly what happened. You hammered on the door and …'

'I called Andrea's name, got no answer, called again, saw the blood and knew something was wrong.'

'You didn't go inside?'

'No.'

'Then you came down here and then what?'

'I made a drink…'

'You made a drink?'

'For the shock. That's not illegal, is it?' He was defensive. 'Look, I don't like these questions, Sergeant, you're making me feel like I've done something wrong.'

'Was Edgar with you when you went upstairs based on your premonition?'

'I … What do you mean?'

'Well, you'd brought him outside – for a *widdle*, I believe you said – so I'm wondering if he was with you when you went upstairs.'

'I'm sure he was.'

'Remind me again, was the door open or closed?'

Falstaff opened his mouth to speak, but before he got the chance, Roxy held her hand up.

'Mr Falstaff, before you say what I think you're going to say, let me stop you right there. Do you realise we have a forensic database?'

She was no long smiling, no longer acting chummy.

'We keep all manner of things on it, samples and the like. How long do you suppose it would take us to compare Edgar's urine sample with the urine we found on a rug upstairs?'

Falstaff blinked.

'Mr Falstaff?'

'I hope you're not suggesting—'

'I'm not suggesting a thing. But I'm curious as to what Edgar was doing inside Andrea Colgan's living room. You said you didn't enter the apartment, so why was he in there?'

'I think I've said enough.'

'Maybe you should come down to the station with us. Sergeant Fletcher, will you accompany Mr Falstaff while he gets dressed.'

'Sure.' Fletcher got to his feet. Edgar got up too and wagged his tail. 'Come on, Mr Falstaff.'

'This is outrageous, it's harassment.'

'You'll be back before you know it.'

At the station house, Roxy processed Falstaff and put him in interview room one.

'I think I'm going to have to burn these clothes,' she said to Fletcher, desperately trying to brush some of the animal hair from her uniform. Fletcher wasn't paying attention. 'What's wrong?'

'Hope little Edgar will be all right. Falstaff told me on the way here he's got separation anxiety.'

Roxy stared at him in amazement.

'Seriously?'

'Not the dog's fault, is it?' He frowned. 'Can't believe you nailed him with dog wee. Didn't know we could differentiate what breed it came from.'

'We can't.'

He looked at her.

Roxy shrugged. 'Listen, anyone stupid enough to think we keep a database of dog piss deserves whatever is coming to him.'

She left him and went upstairs to the incident room. Again there was no one there, but when she opened her EN, she discovered that Miranda had sent her a file. She opened it and read the message.

'Holy shit.'

There were fifteen pages in total.

And all of it was about Jerome Falstaff and his history of assaulting women.

CHAPTER TWENTY-NINE

Eli Quinn was sitting on a low couch in the reception of Albas Entertainment, admiring a very shapely pair of pins and wondering whether the owner of said legs had a boyfriend, and if not, whether she might be interested in taking a chance on some dinner with a slightly scruffy-looking inspector.

'Don't even waste your time trying,' Miranda said without looking up from the magazine she was flicking through. 'She is so way out of your league she might as well be in a different solar system.'

'I don't know what you're talking about.'

'Please, I can hear the little plinks of drool from here.'

To distract himself, Quinn got up and walked around, pretending to study the black-and-white headshots of the company's various clients. He thought he recognised a few faces here and there, but most were strangers to him. After a while, he got bored and sat back down.

'It's a weird job, acting.'

'Weird how?'

'Grown men and women pretending to be someone else; don't you think that's weird?'

'If you pare any job back to the basics it sounds weird.'

'Policing's not weird.'

Miranda shrugged. 'What do think undercover is if not acting?'

'That's different.'

'How?'

'It's … it's—'

'Pretending to be someone you're not.'

'It's performing a role for the greater good, Sergeant.'

He drummed his fingers on the armrest for a while.

'What do you make of our new recruits?'

'They're okay. I like Malloy.'

Quinn harrumphed.

'What?'

'Johnson says she's a loose cannon.'

'Well he would say that, wouldn't he?'

'What's that supposed to mean?'

'If you ask me, the only reason he's down on her is 'cos *she* wouldn't go down on him.'

Quinn shook his head disapprovingly. 'You do have a way with words, Sergeant.'

A few minutes later, a tall, handsome, incredibly tanned man came out to meet them. Getting to his feet, Quinn suddenly wished he'd worn a better suit, maybe shaved a little closer, grown a few extra inches overnight.

'Dy Anderson,' the man said, smiling, blinding them with a display of choppers so dazzling it was like they had harnessed the sun's energy.

'Inspector Quinn, and this is Sergeant Lynn. We're here to talk to you about Andrea Colgan.'

'Of course, I was expecting you. Please come this way.'

He led them into a conference room off the reception area and waited until they were seated around the walnut oval table before he closed the door and took a seat too.

'Can I get you anything, tea, coffee, water?'

'We're fine, thanks.'

'As you can imagine, we're all devastated, simply devastated.' He shook his magnificent head sadly. 'Andrea was a wonderful, beautiful human being. Her loss is incredibly difficult to comprehend and a real blow to all of us here at Albas.'

'How long had she worked here, Mr Anderson?' Miranda asked.

'Please, call me Dy.' He gave her the smile with extra wattage. 'She joined two years ago.'

'What did she do exactly?'

'For the most part she handled promotional work for our various clients. She was exceptionally good with the talent, great natural energy. I mean, everyone adored her.'

'Did she seem troubled by anything recently, mention any difficulties or something that might have upset her?'

'No, absolutely not. We are a growing company, but we're family, you know, and if there had been anything amiss, believe me, it would have been taken care of in house.'

'What was Andrea working on before she died?'

'She was heading up a campaign for Angel Agents. It's an American company that attends to the wishes of the dying, the terminally ill … you understand. They plan to open a branch here in Ireland.'

Miranda cocked her head to one side. 'You mean like assisted suicide, that kind of thing?'

'Yes, a little like that kind of thing.'

'Controversial,' Quinn said.

'Well, it would be the first of its kind in Ireland, and naturally there's always going to be a little push-back to what people perceive as radical change.'

'What kind of push-back?'

'You know, angry letters, protests, objections, that kind of thing.'

'Have you had any of that?'

'Not really. There again, we are in the very early stages of planning a strategic marketing campaign.' Dy leaned forward, adopting a slightly conspiratorial tone. 'Between you and me, Detectives, Andrea's *professional* life was the least of her problems.'

Quinn leaned in too. 'Do go on.'

'It's not really my place to say.'

'Andrea is dead, Mr Anderson,' Quinn said. 'If you know something, now would be the time to tell it.'

'I'm not trying to be evasive.' Dy waved his hand. Quinn noticed that his nails were pink and buffed to perfection. 'It's just … Look, PR is not a nine-to-five job. Partners don't always respect that.'

'You reckon Andrea was getting grief from her partner?'

'We were *all* getting grief from Mr Furlong,' Anderson said pointedly. 'As I said, we're expanding the business at the moment, so all of us are working long hours. Noel would regularly turn up here demanding to speak to Andrea, abusing our staff if she wasn't available. Andrea was mortified by his behaviour. He was very controlling.'

'Controlling how?'

'It seemed to me he wanted to know every detail of her working day, who she spoke to, where she dined, that sort of thing. Certainly not the behaviour of a well man.'

'She tolerated this?' Miranda asked, raising an eyebrow. The idea of any man telling her what she could and couldn't do was ridiculous to her.

'She did, but she was getting tired of having to constantly reassure him.'

'What do you mean?'

'Andrea was ambitious; she had a clear vision. I think Noel was a distraction for a while. There's no doubt that she enjoyed his company, but anyone with eyes could see they weren't suited. It was inevitable they'd split up, but I could never have believed he would do something so horrific.'

'Well, we don't know that it *was* him.'

'Oh, I thought he'd gone into hiding. The radio said—'

'We'd like a list of everyone Andrea's been working with in the last year,' Quinn said. 'Clients, other PR firms, whoever she might have had regular dealings with.'

'Is that really necessary?'

'You want us to catch her killer, don't you?'

'Oh, well you hardly think she was killed by a client, do you?'

'We don't know, that's why we're investigating. A list of her colleagues, too; was she friends with anyone in particular?'

'Not that I'm aware of, but I'd be happy to introduce you to our head of advertising, Lucy; she'd be the best person to speak with about that.' Anderson's smile was back to full wattage.

'That would be swell,' Quinn said, not quite able to keep the sarcasm from his voice. He had taken a dislike to Anderson. It happened sometimes.

Forty minutes later they left Albas Entertainment with a belly full of coffee and some of the nicest complimentary pastries they'd ever eaten, but no particularly useful information.

'Angel Agents,' Quinn said, shaking his head. 'Ghouls more like, preying on the sick. It should never have been allowed in this country. The whole system is ripe for abuse.'

'I wonder what the burn-out rate is for people working in PR,' Miranda said, accepting his offer of a cigarette. 'Can't be healthy being so upbeat all the time. Never being able to tell someone to go shove it up their arse.'

'Dunno.' Quinn lit both their cigarettes. ''Bout the same as ours?'

'Furlong is sounding more and more like a right creep, isn't he?'

'Needy for sure, but that doesn't make him a monster.'

'You don't need fangs and claws to be a monster, Quinn.'

'True.' Quinn took out his phone and looked up Angel Agents online. 'It would make our jobs a lot easier if you did, though.'

'I suppose, it would certainly cut down on the—'

Her phone and Quinn's bleeped simultaneously.

They read their messages, looked at each other and ran for the car.

CHAPTER THIRTY

Quinn stared at the woman's body and felt a strange compulsion to touch her leg to see if she was still alive. Even though he knew she was dead, it was hard to wrap his head around it.

'Jesus,' he said. 'She looks like she's sleeping.'

Johnson took another photo and handed the camera to Jimmy.

'It's the make-up. Funeral homes do it all the time; helps people appear more lifelike.'

'Macabre.'

Johnson shrugged. 'Death is never pretty.'

Quinn walked around the bed, taking in every detail. The room was functional and felt masculine. It held a large double sleigh bed, a chest of drawers and a stand-alone wardrobe. There was nothing at all to indicate a feminine touch, nothing.

'I'm guessing she didn't live here.'

'I doubt it. We found her handbag downstairs with her wallet inside. According to her identity card, her name is Estelle Roberts, with an address in Cypress Grove Road, Templeogue.'

'That's not too far from here.'

'No, she could have walked it in less than forty minutes.' Johnson pushed his glasses up his nose. 'We found a toothbrush and clean underwear in her bag too.'

'So she was planning to stay over.'

'Looks that way.'

Quinn took a number of steps backwards until his shoulder blades touched the wall.

Estelle Roberts lay in the middle of the bed with one hand over her heart, the other by her side. Like Lorraine Dell, it looked as though she'd been posed post mortem; her hair had been neatly brushed and her face was carefully painted with the same slightly garish make-up as the earlier killing.

This time the killer had decorated the scene. Hundreds of yellow rose petals surrounded the body. One of Johnson's team had already found the stems dumped in the refuse bin outside.

'Was there a card?'

'In between the ring and middle finger of her left hand,' Johnson said. 'We've bagged it already.'

Downstairs, the scene in the living was grim. The walls and soft furnishings were heavily stained with Hugh Bannon's blood, and sometime between the arrival of the ambulance and the Gardai, a large black-and-white cat had gained access to the room. There were small bloody pawprints everywhere.

'He decapitated him,' Miranda said.

Quinn squatted by the body. Bannon had been a relatively young, fit man, strong. Yet apart from the fatal blow, there was no sign of trauma. No defence wounds, nothing.

'He took them by surprise in here.'

'Yeah, the back door was jimmied. Probably he waited until they were getting busy, then he struck.'

Quinn looked around the room. 'We need to know everything about their movements last night: where they were, who they spoke to, everything.'

Miranda watched a forensics officer dust the coffee table where the head was found for prints.

'This man was able to come in, take two people out, set a stage and leave again without anyone seeing him. Why isn't he worried about being caught?'

Quinn took out his phone.

'That's it, I'm calling Lizzie Brennan in. I'm tired of chasing this guy's fucking shadow. We need a new bloody profile.'

CHAPTER THIRTY-ONE

Falstaff was sweating profusely when Roxy and Fletcher entered the interview room, despite the room not being particularly warm. Roxy wondered again if he was on some kind of drug or medication.

'Are you okay, Mr Falstaff?' she asked.

'I have agoraphobia, did you know that?'

'We can get the doctor for you if you like,' she said briskly.

Falstaff shot her a baleful look.

'Do you want anything before we start, coffee, tea, a glass of water?'

'I'm going to make an official complaint about this, and you better believe I know people. It's not right, treating a law-abiding citizen this way. I had things to do today, lots of things.'

'We won't keep you longer than necessary.'

Fletcher set up the video recorder, entered the time and date and gave all their names.

'So.' Roxy opened the folder she'd been carrying and began to read from it. 'Andrea worked for Albas Entertainment; do you know the company?'

'Yes, I know them, everybody knows them.'

'What can you tell me about them?'

'Nothing.'

'Nothing?'

'I knew the owner, back in the day.'

'That would be a man called Dy Anderson?'

'That's right.'

'What was your relationship with him?'

'Relationship?' He barked a laugh. 'We didn't *have* a relationship, Sergeant. He was an arrogant jumped-up shit who thought he was the be-all and end-all of show-business.'

'He was your agent, wasn't he, at one point?'

Falstaff narrowed his eyes. 'So?'

'What happened, why did you part ways?'

'It's common for actors to use many different agencies over the course of their careers.'

'Let's talk about your other career. You were arrested for trespass on three separate occasions.'

He threw his hands up. 'Oh my God, are you serious? I was a teenager, for Christ's sake.'

'You were nineteen.'

'Look, a little backstory might help. Alison Phillips was my girlfriend at the time, only her old man didn't like me and said he didn't want her to see me.' He glanced at Fletcher, looking for support, but Fletcher's face was impassive. 'You know how it is: she didn't want to get in trouble so she hung me out to dry and he pressed charges.'

'Did she hang you out to dry when you came to her place of work and assaulted her?'

He leaned back and crossed his arms over his chest. 'It's not … that's not how it happened, okay? We had a little argument, it was nothing really … okay, I admit voices were raised, but then next thing you know, her boss stuck his nose in and got involved, and after that everything was blown out of proportion.'

'So what happened two years later with Rita Owen? Did things get blown out of proportion then too?'

'No,' he said after a while. 'You have to understand that I was a different man back then, Sergeant. I drank, I did drugs; my life was a mess. But then I discovered acting and learned how to channel my emotions in a more healthy and productive manner.'

'You threw corrosive liquid in Miss Owen's face, Mr Falstaff; you blinded her in one eye and scarred her for life.'

He licked his lips.

'She pushed your buttons.' Fletcher spoke for the first time.

'That's right,' Falstaff said, nodding furiously. 'She did, she was a cheat. Now I'm not saying what I did was right, but yeah, she was … she … It was a long time ago.'

'You paid your dues, turned your life around.'

'That's true, I did.'

'I've had a look at your financials,' Roxy said. 'You're going through a bit of a dry spell, aren't you?'

'Sign of the times,' Falstaff said. 'What can I do?'

'Let's talk about Albas Entertainment again. They're involved with *Storycast*, an online soap series.'

'I think so.' Falstaff was very wary.

'That's your kind of thing, right? Voice work and all that jazz. Did you ever ask Andrea to put a word in, maybe get you a gig?'

'A gig?' Falstaff tried to smile, couldn't pull it off.

'That's right.'

'Well, I might have mentioned something to her in passing.' His forehead was dotted with sweat and he squirmed in the seat. 'I gave her one of my recordings.'

'You're very behind on your mortgage repayments, aren't you?'

'I see what you're trying to do.' Falstaff bunched his hands into fists. 'I do, I see it, but you're barking up the wrong tree. I didn't kill Andrea, I swear to God.'

'Then what were you doing snooping around her apartment?' Roxy asked.

Falstaff looked from one detective to the other, his mouth twisting in on itself, his expression full of hatred, self-pity and fear.

The dam broke.

'She could have fucking helped me, she had a million connections. All she needed to do was put in a word for me. There's a code, you know. We're industry, she could have helped me, but she didn't. She wouldn't even put my name forward for a single audition.'

'What were you doing in her apartment, Mr Falstaff?' Roxy repeated.

'I never said I was in there. Look, I want a solicitor. I'm not saying another word until I get one. I know my rights.'

'Okay.' Roxy sat back and regarded him coolly. 'That's absolutely your right. It's not like you did anything wrong. Well, lying to the Gardai is wrong, obstruction is wrong, interference in a criminal investigation is wrong. After we compare the urine samples, I imagine we'll get a warrant, search your place. Hope we don't find anything *wrong* there.'

Falstaff looked like he was going to be sick.

'You got to listen to me. I didn't hurt Andrea. I never … I liked her, see. She was nice to me sometimes.'

'You liked her so much you went creeping around her apartment while she lay dead in her bedroom?'

His gaze flitted between them. He reminded Roxy of a trapped wild animal, half crazed, terrified, dangerous.

'You don't understand.'

'You're right,' Fletcher said calmly. 'We don't, so explain it to us.'

'Okay, well things are really bad at the moment and I needed the money. I mean, she was already dead, you know? Cold. There wasn't anything that could be done.' His hands flapped wildly. 'But I didn't kill her, I swear. I just needed the money.'

'What money? Did you take money from the apartment? Did you take her phone and her laptop?'

'Are you crazy? I never touched her stuff. Check my apartment if you don't believe me. It's not like I could have saved her.' He was practically heaving. 'She was already dead.' His eyes darted about desperately. 'Don't look at me like that; you have no idea what it's like. The bank is threatening to take my home. I can't let them put me out on the fucking street.'

Roxy and Fletcher exchanged a look.

'What did you do, Mr Falstaff?'

'Nothing. I mean, I only took some photos. I swear, I didn't even send them!'

'You took photos of your dead neighbour?' Roxy was disgusted. 'Why would you do such a thing?'

'He was going to sell them,' Fletcher said, in a tone that made it clear he thought Falstaff was nothing short of vermin. 'There are websites that offer good money for true-crime photos, am I right, Mr Falstaff?'

'It's not like I could have done anything for her.'

'You could have afforded her some dignity,' Roxy said. 'Shown her some respect.'

'Respect?' Falstaff reared back in his chair. 'What about me, what about her respect for me? Huh? She could have helped me out. There's a code, there's supposed to be a code …'

'Where are those photographs right now?'

'At my place. I uploaded them onto my computer.'

'Do I need a warrant to retrieve them, or are you going to play ball?'

Without warning, Falstaff shot forward and grabbed Roxy's right hand.

'If I give them to you, can we keep this to ourselves?'

'What?'

'Please,' he said, pleading. There were tears in his eyes. 'Please, you don't understand. If this got out, it could ruin me. I'd never work in the industry again.'

'What a loss to society that would be,' Roxy said, extracting her hand from his and wiping it on her trouser leg under the table.

CHAPTER THIRTY-TWO

Noel Furlong lay prone on his belly, bleeding from a gash in his head that would probably need stitches. Standing beside him, bent double and breathing hard, was Officer Derek Gant.

'Ow,' Furlong said.

'Shut up.'

Officer Gant held his right hand away from his body, trying not to get blood on his uniform from a wound on his thumb. With his left, he reached for his shoulder radio and pressed the button to speak.

'Dispatch, this is Gant, badge number 3006, requesting backup. Please advise. I have a suspect, Noel Furlong, in custody; repeat, I have a suspect in custody.'

He listened to the reply, gave his location and put his radio away. More blood dribbled from the wound.

'Goddammit,' he said.

'Can I sit up?' Furlong asked. 'I swear I won't try anything.'

'No.'

'Come on, man, I'm breathing dog-shit fumes down here.'

'Good, I hope you choke on them.'

Gant searched his pockets and found a bit of scrunched-up tissue. It wasn't ideal, but it would have to do. He wrapped it about his thumb as best he could and glared at the man on the ground.

'If I let you up, you have to swear you won't try to bite me again.'

'I won't, man, I swear.'

Gant helped Furlong to his feet.

'That was completely uncalled for.' He held out his bandaged thumb. 'I'm going to have to get a tetanus jab now, and they bloody *hurt*.'

'I'm sorry. Look, man, I didn't know you were a guard. You scared the living shit out of me jumping out of nowhere like that. It was a natural reaction.'

Gant was not remotely swallowing this line of bullshit.

'I identified myself.'

'You have this all wrong anyway. I actually live in this house. I wasn't trying to break in.'

'You broke that window with that brick.' Gant pointed to the damning evidence.

'Only because I lost my keys. It's *my* window.'

'Registry says the house belongs to a Caroline Furlong; you don't look like a Caroline to me.'

'She's my sister.'

'So it's *her* house.'

Furlong sagged. He'd only known Gant ten minutes, but it was clear the man was part mule.

He leaned against the garden wall and closed his eyes. He was tired and hungry, and his feet were killing him. Storm's arsehole boyfriend had turned up at the flat while Storm was helping him shave his head; the next thing he knew, all hell had broken loose and he'd found himself tossed out onto the street with half-shaved head, no keys and no shoes.

Stupid, he had been so stupid. He'd known the Garda would have someone watching the house, but he hadn't expected them to be watching the back lane as well.

Caroline was going to be livid about the window.

'You got any cigarettes?' he asked Gant.

'I don't smoke.'

'Of course you don't.'

They heard the sound of a powerful engine, and seconds later a black BMW pulled into the lane. Furlong squinted at it. It didn't look like a Garda vehicle; come to think of it, the two behemoths that got out and began walking in their direction didn't look like Gardai either.

'You recognise them?'

'No,' Gant said.

'Shit.'

'What?'

'Listen to me, whatever you do, do not let those men take me.'

'What are you talking about?'

The behemoths stopped a few feet away. The one on the right sported a crew cut and a squashed nose; the one on the left was wall-eyed. Neither of them was ever likely to win any beauty contests.

'You got him then?' Crew Cut said. 'Nice work, Officer.'

'Thank you.'

'Quinn put you here, did he?'

'No, sir, Sergeant Malloy.'

'What a coincidence. We were talking to Sergeant Malloy a few minutes ago.' He looked at his partner. 'He said we could take it from here.'

Gant stiffened.

'That's right,' Wall Eye said. 'We'll take it from here, lad.'

Gant looked from one man to the other. Something about them made his skin crawl and his testicles want to shrivel back inside his body for safe keeping.

'That's okay,' he said. 'I've already called for backup.'

'And here we are.'

'I only sent the call a few minutes ago.'

'We were in the vicinity.' Crew Cut leaned his massive head a little closer. 'What's your name, lad?'

'Gant, sir.'

'On the job long?'

'Six months.'

'Thought so. Still wet behind the ears, no shame in that; we all started somewhere. So let me help you out, Gant. We work for your boss, which makes us teammates, if you will, and the best teams know how to play together, know when to attack and when to defend. You seem like a good lad, a good team man, so you'll understand me when I tell you it's time to pass this bleedin' ball,' he glared at Furlong, 'to a different player.'

To his eternal credit, Gant, who was less than half the size of either man, stood his ground.

'My orders are to bring Mr Furlong into the South Circular station.'

'Ask them if they have identification,' Furlong said.

'Shut up,' Gant snapped, but to the men he said, 'Let me see some identification.'

'No need for that,' Crew Cut said. 'My name is Lennox, and this is my associate, Fleming.'

'You could be making those names up. I need to see some actual ID.'

The behemoths remained unmoved by this request.

'Cut the shit,' Fleming said, looking at Gant like he'd enjoy spreading him on toast and eating him. 'We're taking him. If you're not happy about that, you can go and—'

'File an official complaint,' Lennox said.

'I made the arrest,' Gant said, standing firm even though his knees were practically knocking together. 'This man is my prisoner. I am responsible for his well-being.'

He fumbled his radio from the shoulder holder, but before he could get to use it, Fleming stepped forward and slapped it out of his hand.

'Hey!'

Furlong whimpered. It had occurred to him that these men were not the type of men who took no for an answer. Also, he didn't like the way Lennox was scanning the windows of neighbouring buildings, making sure they weren't being watched.

'Gant,' he said, feeling more than a little afraid. 'Maybe we should move towards the street.'

'It's all right, kid.' Lennox was still playing nice. He reached a huge red hand towards Furlong, who shrank back against the wall. 'We'll put in a good word for you, Gant, let our boss know you played ball.'

'If you like,' Fleming said, 'we can make it look like he got the jump on you.'

Gant licked his lips.

'Come on, son, hand him over.'

Despite the odds, Gant found himself reaching for his Taser. It was, he would later tell his friends over a number of hastily organised drinks, like he was having an out-of-body experience. He could see what he was doing, even though he had no recollection of making the decision.

'I think,' he said, pointing the Taser directly at Lennox's chest, 'you should get in your car and drive away. I'll wait here with my prisoner for the real backup to arrive.'

Furlong wanted to tell him he thought that was a splendid idea, but his mouth was too dry with terror to speak.

'You're making a big mistake here, lad,' Lennox said, sounding perfectly calm. So calm that neither Gant nor Furlong noticed how he'd shifted his weight onto his heels.

They did notice how fast he was when he snatched the Taser out of Gant's hand and clubbed him across the head with it. Almost as quickly, Fleming caught the young man as he fell and lowered him quite gently to the ground.

'Out like a light,' he said, impressed. 'You know, that's a hell of a technique you have.'

'All in the wrist,' Lennox said, returning Gant's weapon to his belt. He grabbed the officer by the back of his shirt, dragged him to the wall and leaned him against it in a relatively upright position. Fleming caught Furlong by the arm.

'Right, mate, easy way or hard way?'

'*Help*!' Furlong tried to wriggle free. 'Somebody help—'

His knees sagged and he slumped to the ground.

'All in the wrist,' Lennox repeated, waggling his sap.

'Nice.' Fleming tossed Furlong over his shoulder and carried him to the boot of the car as if he weighed nothing at all.

CHAPTER THIRTY-THREE

Quinn and Miranda called at Estelle Roberts' home, but there was no one home. A neighbour told them the house was rented to a number of 'nice' girls – nurses, he thought. One of them, Janice, worked at the Mater Hospital in Phibsboro.

'Janice, nurse, Mater Hospital,' Quinn was saying as he and Miranda entered Homicide. 'Get someone over there now. I want to know everything we can find about Estelle Roberts. When you're done, run a background check on Hugh Bannon and locate his next of kin. We need to be quick: the media already have people at the hospital trying to talk to Mr Bailey.'

'What about—'

'Sir!'

Quinn looked round. Sergeant Roxy Malloy and Sergeant Eoin Fletcher were walking towards him at speed.

'What is it?'

'We heard the news that the Sweetheart … er, the killer has struck again.'

'Looks that way.'

'Did you get my message?' Roxy asked.

'What message?'

'We arrested Jerome Falstaff and he told us he—'

'You did what?'

'We arrested Jerome Falstaff. He lied to us about yesterday. He was inside Andrea Colgan's apartment; he took photographs of her, sir.'

'What?'

'Photographs, he was planning to sell them to a media site.'

'Jesus Christ,' Miranda said.

'He's got form for battery and assault,' Fletcher offered with a shrug. 'You should see his record.'

'I don't give a shit if he's Jack the Ripper,' Quinn snapped. 'I sent you to get statements from the residents, not go off on some maverick spree. Bloody hell, Fletcher, her I understand, but I expected better from you.'

'I thought you said—'

'It's wasn't Fletcher's fault,' Roxy said, lifting her chin. 'I told him I had spoken to you.'

Quinn narrowed his eyes. 'You told him I wanted Falstaff brought in for questioning?'

'No, I told him I'd spoken to you … and I maybe gave Sergeant Fletcher the impression that that was what you wanted.'

'Lies of omission, Malloy; it didn't work for the bloody Catholic Church and it won't work for you,' Quinn said. 'Fletcher, get back to that building right now and canvass the rest of the residents.'

'Yes, sir.'

'And while you're at it, locate those damned photographs, they're evidence. After that, get your arse back here pronto; we're going to need all hands to the pump on this latest killing.'

Fletcher gave Roxy a look and left.

'What about me?' Roxy asked. 'What do you need me to do?'

'You're going to stay at a desk, Malloy, where I can keep an eye on you.'

'A desk?'

'Miranda, send her the list of Andrea Colgan's colleagues.' Quinn narrowed his eyes. 'You're going to go through every last one of those names and see if there is *any* connection, no matter how random, to *anyone* connected to the Dell/Kilbride case. I don't care if they shared a manicurist; if it's there, I want to know.'

'But that could take days.'

'Indeed it could,' he said coldly. 'So you'd better get right on it.'

Roxy slunk away and took a desk in the furthest corner of the room.

'Taking photographs of a dead woman.' Quinn looked at Miranda and shook his head. 'People never cease to disgust me. Hyenas.'

'You're leaving her on Colgan?'

Quinn sighed. 'You saw what I saw today, Miranda. There wasn't a mark on Estelle Roberts' body. It's like he wanted her to be beautiful.' He shook his head, face grim. 'You might have been right.'

'You're having doubts that it's the same killer.'

'Doubts, yes, but I'm not willing to cut Colgan loose just yet.' He glanced at Roxy. 'Besides, she wanted to work on the case so let her have it; keep her bloody busy at least and out from under my feet.'

Miranda's phone rang. She answered, listened, said, 'Thank you,' and hung up.

'We have a situation.'

Quinn groaned. 'Now what?'

'Remember yesterday Malloy said she had an officer watching Caroline Furlong's home—'

Roxy gave up all pretence of working and spun around in her chair.

'That's right, Derek Gant.'

'He went back there today, called Dispatch twenty-five minutes ago to say he'd arrested Noel Furlong attempting to break into the back of Caroline Furlong's house.'

'He has him?'

'*Had* him. When the backup unit got there for collection, they found Gant sparked out with a pretty sweet bump on his head, and Furlong gone.'

'Is he badly hurt?' Quinn asked.

'I don't know. Apparently he's downstairs. He says he wants to talk to Malloy.'

Roxy got to her feet, looked at Quinn. 'Sir …'

'Go on. Miranda, you go with her. But listen to me, Malloy, this changes nothing. I still want a comprehensive run-through of the names on the lists, you hear me?'

'Yes, sir.'

The two women hurried downstairs to the infirmary on the second floor.

Gant was sitting on an examination table wearing his uniform trousers and a T-shirt, with the rest of his uniform draped across a chair. He was holding an ice pack to the back of his head and his thumb was bleeding. Doc Keaton was in the middle of adjusting a blood pressure cuff on his left arm.

Gant tried to get off the table when he saw them, but Keaton pushed him straight back where he was.

'Sit bloody still, lad. If you won't let me X-ray that bonce of yours, the very least you can do is let me check the rest of your vitals.'

'Yes, sir.'

'I heard what happened,' Roxy said. 'Are you okay?' She looked him over, trying to see if he was injured anywhere other than his head.

He smiled sheepishly. 'I'm grand.'

Miranda introduced herself. 'Can you tell me exactly what happened, Officer Gant? Did Noel Furlong do this?'

Gant shook his head and began talking. When he was done, Roxy was seething and Miranda looked troubled.

'Was Lennox a big hulking thing with a squashed nose?'

'That's him.'

'You know him?' Roxy demanded.

'Not personally, thank God.' Miranda grimaced. 'Only by reputation. He was one of ours once.'

'He was Gardai?'

'Special Branch; part of a team that worked covert operations.'

'So what happened?'

Miranda shrugged. 'There were rumours of corruption. Next thing we knew he'd taken early retirement. He works in private security now, as far as I know.'

'He was corrupt?'

'Don't look so shocked, Malloy, there's good and bad apples in every barrel.'

'And the other guy?'

'Fleming, same deal: a brace of bastards.'

Miranda made a call. While she talked, she walked in a circle, one hand in the small of her back.

'Quinn? Yeah, he's okay, brave lad.' She winked at Gant, who blushed. 'We've got a problem, though. It was Lennox and Fleming. They've taken Furlong.' She listened for a minute. 'Copy that.'

She hung up.

'You'll be okay, Gant,' she said. 'Old Sawbones here will have you patched up and as good as new in no time, won't you, Doc?'

Keaton waved a dismissive hand and reached for his stethoscope.

Miranda patted Gant on the shoulder.

'Perhaps you'll hold off on making an official report, though.'

'Ma'am?'

Roxy could not believe what she was hearing. 'Sergeant Lynn, what the hell are you asking?'

'Officer Gant, when you're done here, nip upstairs and have a chat with Inspector Quinn, would you? He'd like to see you. Do you understand?'

'Yes, I think so.'

'Right,' Keaton said, breathing on the stethoscope to warm it. 'Now, I want you to take a deep breath when I count to three …'

Miranda jerked her head towards the door and Roxy followed her out.

'What the hell was that? We need his incident report. We have to find those men, arrest them for assault and bring Furlong in for questioning.'

Miranda shook her head. 'No we don't. Besides, we know where Furlong is.'

'I don't.'

Miranda smiled, and it was as bleak a smile as Roxy had ever seen on another living human.

'Dominic Travers has him.'

'Andrea Colgan's father?'

'Yes.'

'Then what are we waiting for? Let's go get him.'

'You need to let Quinn handle this.'

'Bullshit. Gant was my responsibility.'

Miranda grabbed Roxy by the shoulders. 'Malloy, listen to me. You're on thin ice as it is; let Quinn handle this.'

'What the hell is this about? What kind of black hold does Dominic Travers have over this department?'

'That's enough.' Miranda looked around in case anybody had overheard. 'Let it drop.'

'It's true, isn't it?' Roxy said. 'First his records are redacted, and now this? Is he … like, is he some kind of informant or something?'

'I told you to drop it.'

Roxy was so overwhelmed by anger she could barely think, let alone formulate a coherent answer.

'This is outrageous. What those men did is … it's against the law.'

'Goddammit, Malloy, don't you get it yet?' Miranda said, exasperated. 'Dominic Travers has friends in very high places, okay? He doesn't care about the law. Look, Quinn's no fool, he'll know how to handle this. If you want to stay working in this squad, learn to take advice, learn to take an order.'

'This isn't *advice*.' Roxy spat the word out as though it was poisonous. 'I'm being hamstrung.'

'You're smart, Malloy, and you have potential, but you're so bloody stupid sometimes it hurts. This is Dublin: there are layers upon layers upon layers. Dominic Travers is … let's just say he's an untouchable.'

'But why—'

Miranda shoved her back against the wall and held a threatening finger in front of her face. 'I'm telling you, but you're not listening. Travers has connections, connections that extend to people way above our station. Top brass already know this, which means top brass sanction this. Now they don't care about you; they don't care about any of us. But whether you believe me or not, Eli Quinn is a good man, and he does care, so let him handle this. Okay?'

'Is that where we stand?'

'That's where we stand.'

Roxy pushed her away. 'Then we're no better than the scum we're supposed to fight.'

'Oh dear, Malloy,' Miranda said. 'Whatever gave you the idea that we were in the first place?'

CHAPTER THIRTY-FOUR

Noel Furlong woke up and immediately felt worse.

It took him a few seconds of groaning and squinting before he worked out he was alive and being held in a garage or shed or something similar. A single light bulb hung from a beam over his head, throwing most of the room into shadow, which was terrifying, but not as terrifying as discovering he was strapped to a gurney of some kind.

He lifted his head as far as he could manage and looked down. His ankles and thighs were bound with duct tape, as were his hands, his feet and his chest; only his head was free to move.

'Hello?' he whimpered.

He heard movement from somewhere behind him and groaned as Dominic Travers emerged from the shadows.

'No no no no!'

He began to struggle, desperately trying to free himself, but he was held fast.

'Please, whatever you're thinking of doing, don't do it, man, please don't hurt me, *please*.'

He felt a small jolt and his body was tilted and began moving backwards.

Another bump and he was still. He heard Dominic clattering around behind him, and the sound of running water.

'Dom, what are you doing?'

Another jolt, then to the unmistakable hiss of hydraulics he rose slightly and stopped. The gurney tilted backwards until his head was slightly below horizontal. From this angle he could see Dominic perfectly. He was standing with a remote control in his hand.

'Please, please listen to me, I didn't do anything to your daughter, I swear.'

Dominic didn't answer. He put the remote down on a workbench, picked up a towel, shook it out, folded it twice and placed it over Furlong's face. Plunged into complete darkness, Furlong began to hyperventilate.

'If you struggle,' Dominic's voice was calm, measured, ice cold, 'you'll find it harder to breathe. My advice is not to struggle.'

The gurney began to move again. The first splash of freezing water to hit his forehead was such a shock, Furlong screamed. He continued screaming until his entire face was under the flow, then screaming became gurgling and in terror he pressed his lips tightly shut, vowing to hold his breath.

Within seconds he was gasping for air. The sodden towel was sucked into his mouth, and water ran down the back of his throat. He gagged and coughed, tried to breathe and gulped more water down. Terrified, he thrashed his head from side to side, but there was no escape, he couldn't breathe.

He was drowning.

Miraculously the water stopped and the towel was removed from his face. The relief was so intense, he burst into tears even as he retched violently.

Dominic watched him impassively.

'I'm going to ask you some questions,' he said. 'You're going to answer me.'

Furlong began babbling. Dominic slapped him across the face; not hard, but hard enough to get his attention.

'Look at me.'

Furlong stared into his silver eyes.

'I want you to listen to what I'm telling you. If you lie to me, or I think you're lying to me, I'm going to put you back under. I've seen men a lot tougher than you think they could hold out; they couldn't. I'm telling you this in case you think you're different.'

Furlong shook his head. Between sobs he tried to speak, until Dominic told him to shut his mouth and the questions began.

The interrogation took over an hour, and twice Dominic used the water to be sure what he was hearing was true. It might have gone on longer, but a light on the wall over the workbench began to blink, a signal from the house. He dried his hands and left Furlong strapped to the gurney, blubbering and exhausted.

Dominic exited the garage. The moon was high in a cloudless sky as he crossed the manicured lawn to the main house; he could see his breath with every step.

Frederick waited by the conservatory door.

'Detective Eli Quinn is here to see you. He said you'd know what it is about.'

'Where is he?'

'I put him in the front room.'

Quinn was leafing through a leather-bound encyclopaedia when Dominic opened the door.

'Nice collection you have,' he said, holding the book aloft. 'Don't see this kind of thing any more.'

Dominic grunted, looked around. The front room was cold, rather formal, and smelled of furnish polish. He rarely set foot in it. Frederick kept it spick and span regardless.

'What do you want?'

Quinn put the book back on the shelf with care and walked around the room, stopping by the ornate mantelpiece to study the various photos on it. After a while he turned.

'I'm sorry about Andrea, Dominic. I didn't realise she was your daughter.'

Dominic leaned against the wall, his face revealing nothing.

'How's Lillian doing?'

'How do you think?'

'I think she's hurting, same as you. I think she wants answers. But what you're doing won't solve anything.'

'Who says I want to solve anything?' Dominic folded his arms. 'That's your job, isn't it, Detective?'

'I can't do my job if you keep snatching witnesses out from under my nose.'

'Witnesses.' Dominic's lips twitched.

'That officer Lennox struck – his name is Gant, by the way – suffered a mild concussion.'

'So what?'

'Was that really necessary?'

'I don't know. Why don't you ask Lennox when you see him? I'm sure he'll oblige you with a run-down of his thinking.'

'Is Furlong still alive?'

Dominic wouldn't insult Quinn's intelligence by pretending he had no idea what he was talking about.

'He's alive.'

'Is he here?'

Dominic shrugged.

'Look, nobody knows you took him apart from Miranda Lynn and a new kid, Malloy. I'm trying to keep it off the books.' Quinn spread his hands. 'So unless you're starting to enjoy attention in your old age, why don't you let me handle this?'

'Are you handling Andrea's case?'

'My squad is.'

'You got any leads?'

'Not so far, but Jesus, Dominic, it's been less than twenty-four hours. I can't rule anything out, but what I can do is eliminate people from our lines of enquiry, assuming I can get to talk to them.'

'Maybe I'll get you a confession.'

Quinn looked down at the empty grate.

'Yeah, I bet you could. I bet you could get Furlong to say anything you wanted him to say.' He looked up again. 'But you and I both know I couldn't use it in court. It would kill any credibility we had.'

'You think I care about courts, about credibility?'

'I think you care about catching Andrea's killer, and so do I. I'll catch him, Dominic. You've got to let me do my job.'

'Furlong doesn't know shit.'

'That's not up to you to decide.'

Dominic thought it over for a minute.

'Get your car and meet me in the access lane out back.'

Dominic went back through the house and across the lawn. When he entered the garage, Furlong, still on the gurney, was rattling and shivering from cold and shock. Even his lips had turned blue.

Dominic walked to the rear of the garage, unlocked the door and rolled it up halfway. He waited until he heard the crunch of tyres before he went back to Furlong and cut through his ties with a knife. When he sliced the chest strap, Furlong half fell, half fainted onto the floor and lay on the concrete heaving and juddering.

'Listen to me,' Dominic said as Quinn slid under the door. 'You're going to go with …'

Furlong rolled onto his hands and knees and began to crawl away, sobbing hysterically.

'What are you doing to him?' Quinn asked.

'Nothing,' Dominic said, genuinely baffled.

Quinn hurried over and tried to grab Furlong, who pitched forward onto his side, shaking so badly Quinn could hardly hear him over the sound of his teeth rattling in his head.

'He's hypothermic; what did you do?' He looked around, saw the gurney and figured it out. 'You fucking waterboarded him?'

'I wanted answers.'

'Mr Furlong, listen to me, my name is Inspector Eli Quinn. I'm taking you into custody, you're safe, okay?' He glared over his shoulder. 'Go get a blanket out of my car, and where the hell are his shoes?'

'He didn't have any.'

'Get the blanket.'

With a sour face, Dominic fetched a blanket and flung it towards Quinn. He watched the inspector help Furlong out of the garage and load him into his car.

'This is bullshit,' Quinn said when he'd slammed the door. 'How the hell am I supposed to explain his condition?'

'Not my problem.' Dominic Travers put his hands in his pockets and tilted his head so he could see the stars and admire the constellations overhead. 'Get him out of here,' he said in a low, quiet voice. 'And if anyone asks what happened, tell them what you like.'

CHAPTER THIRTY-FIVE

Nobody dared say a word to Quinn when he entered the station house with Furlong limping and shivering by his side. Keaton was called to examine Furlong and a fresh set of dry clothing was hastily found.

The interview was bizarre and broken up by bouts of intermittent sobbing. Furlong admitted being at Andrea Colgan's apartment but said he was there to take his paintings back. He said he was broke; he admitted he had substance abuse issues and that Andrea had broken it off with him after a physical fight in which there had been blows traded, and that he was, in his own words, 'a complete fucking mess'.

'I loved her,' he told Quinn. 'I fucking loved her so much, but she didn't want me any more, you know?'

'Let me see if I have this right: you were at the apartment to steal paintings?'

'They were my paintings!'

'So why didn't you take them with you when you broke up?'

Furlong looked down at his hands.

'Well?'

'I was going to let her keep them, okay, but then … I had a buyer lined up, you know.'

'You needed the money,' Quinn said.

'But I never hurt her. I didn't even know she was there until I saw blood on the floor. I went down to our room and …' He put his hands over his eyes. 'Oh God, she was lying there with her face all smashed in.'

After the interview, Quinn took him down to be processed. While he waited, he called Adam Johnson in Forensics and asked him to take swabs and photos of Furlong's hands, looking for any sign of bruising. But as much as he disliked the young man, he sensed Furlong was telling the truth. He even waived his right to legal counsel. If anything, he seemed relieved at the idea that he would have to spend the night behind bars, safely out of harm's way.

When Quinn came back upstairs, he tossed Roxy the USB key with his recording of the interview and told her he wanted it transcribed and copied.

Roxy, still quietly steaming from earlier, took it without complaint.

'So now what?' Miranda wanted to know, walking with him to the canteen. 'Do you believe him?'

Quinn rubbed his eyes wearily. 'Yes, I believe him. I think he'd tell us everything he'd ever done in his life if it kept him out of Travers' hands.'

'He looked pretty shook up.'

'He'll live.'

'This is a really bad business, Inspector. Tampering with witnesses, assaulting an officer. Where does it end? How much more of this shit are we supposed to turn a blind eye to?'

'What would you have me do? It's fucked up, but you know the situation with Travers.' Quinn lowered his voice to a whisper. 'He turned state's evidence on the last pinch. He's got immunity; the powers-that-be want him loose.'

'If you ask me, it's like releasing a virus into the community.'

'You think I don't know that? Jesus, Patrick would turn in his grave if he knew this was how we operated.'

Something in his voice made Miranda glance at him. She was alarmed at how tired he looked, how drained. He kept walking with his head down, but she saw the muscles bunching in his jaw.

Patrick Lynch had been Quinn's boss when Quinn was starting out. Miranda had heard a lot about him. He was a big tough bastard from Cork, not much on small talk and straight as an arrow. He was a good cop too, hard but fair. Quinn had respected him a lot. Unfortunately he hadn't a lick of political sense; he was the kind of man who'd arrest a minister's son for driving under the influence as quickly as he'd arrest a cyclist for running a red light.

'The law's the law, for pauper or prince,' he'd say.

Then came what the papers nicknamed the Samsonite Case. Two little boys netting for baitfish found a battered suitcase washed up on the rocks near the harbour in the fishing village of Howth. When they dragged it onto the beach and broke open the locks, the badly decomposing parts of one Mati Prya spilled out onto the sand, sending the boys screaming down the beach in horror.

It hadn't taken long to trace Mati's place of employment. She was one of two maids working for the then Attorney General, Elliot Joyce. When interviewed, Joyce had been arrogant and dismissive. He also had multiple alibis: powerful figures who would all swear on their sainted mother's mortal soul that Joyce had nothing to do with the unfortunate woman's demise.

Patrick Lynch thought differently.

Patrick Lynch kept digging, and before long found evidence that Mati Prya had on more than one occasion complained about Joyce's intimidating sexual behaviour. Lynch also had evidence that the previous summer, a Samsonite case had been purchased by the state – no less – as part of a junket to Central Asia for Elliot Joyce. A case Joyce declared had been stolen from his home in a burglary he had curiously not reported to the Rank.

Despite repeated warnings from the Commissioner, Lynch could not be persuaded to let the matter drop. Not even when a suspect conveniently turned up dead in a shitty flat on the North Circular Road, with a suicide note in his handwriting confessing to the murder of Mati Prya left on a table. Still Lynch refused to accept

Joyce's innocence. In the end his inflexibility became a hindrance and ultimately led to his downfall.

A trumped-up charge of brutality was brought against him, witnesses were quickly found, and with very little fanfare, Lynch was found guilty, stripped of his badge and sacked from the Rank without his pension, a fine how-do-you-do for twenty-five years of service.

Within six months, he was dead; according to the coroner, the victim of a colossal heart attack. Lynch had always been a big man. Everyone knew his heart wasn't good, everyone agreed he didn't look after his health: he had high blood pressure, he ate greasy foods, drank too much.

It was sad, but unremarkable.

His demise served as a stark reminder to anyone else who might consider themselves more than mere cogs in the wheels of justice.

When you're ordered to stand down, stand down.

It was a lesson Quinn had taken to heart.

The canteen staff had long gone home. Lynn got two coffees from the machine, handed him one and sat down opposite him. She said nothing; she could see the storm brewing.

Quinn sipped the bitter brew and thought about Roxy bashing away at her keys with undisguised fury. He thought about Furlong, crying and shivering in the car all the way in, the younger man's almost hysterical relief when he saw the lights of the station. He thought about Gant's face, how stoical he had been as he listened to Quinn suggest it might be best if he let the assault go.

It sickened him.

He sickened himself.

CHAPTER THIRTY-SIX

Gregory Milton snagged a piece of sushi from the platter with his chopsticks, popped it into his mouth and closed his eyes in pleasure. God, but Cho was a marvel. Sweet and delicate, so fresh it was practically wiggling.

He opened his eyes and noticed that his dinner guest was staring into the bottom of his wine glass, deep in thought, his food untouched.

'What's the matter, don't you like it? I can have Cho bring you another plate.'

'The food is fine. It's the fucking Rank I don't like.'

'It's a formality, Dy, they have to ask their questions.'

Milton set the chopsticks aside, lifted his gin martini and took a sip. It was his fourth cocktail in less than an hour, and he was starting to feel the effects.

Dy Anderson's blue eyes flicked upwards.

'I'm worried about Delia Shawcross. She was a friend of Andrea's; what if the cops want to talk to her?'

'You told me Lucy left Delia's name off the employee list.'

'She did, but I still don't like it, I don't like any of it.'

'Why would they want to talk to her? She's been gone, what, a year?'

'They might connect her with Andrea.'

'Even if they do, so what, they worked together, that's it. Look, there's no way they'll be bothered talking to her. She's ancient history.'

'History has a way of biting people in the arse. You of all people should know that.'

Milton pulled a face and put his glass down.

'Delia's not exactly in a position to cause any trouble for us now, is she? Besides, she signed a non-disclosure when she left the firm.'

'Keep your voice down, will you?'

Milton glowered at him, but lowered his voice all the same and leaned across the table.

'Dy, listen to me. You're catastrophising – no, really, you are.'

'Don't mumbo-jumbo me, Greg. Delia Shawcross is a threat and you know it.'

Milton shook his head vehemently. 'No, she would never risk losing Charlie.'

Dy raised a perfectly sculpted eyebrow. 'How can you be so sure?'

'She's a mother bear, that one.' Milton drained his drink and waggled the empty glass at a passing waitress, who ignored him. 'Look, if you want, I can talk to her, tell her—'

'Don't even think about it,' Dy said. 'Stay away from that woman. Haven't you caused enough trouble?'

He shook his head. He wasn't angry, not really; besides, what would be the point? He had known Milton since college. He was a genius on one hand and a total and utter shit-gibbon on the other.

'Did you talk to Walter about the new show? Have we got the green light yet or what?'

'I spoke to him.' Milton waggled the glass again, scowling. 'What does a man have to do to get a drink around here?'

Anderson was not a shrink, but even he could tell when someone was being evasive.

'What?'

'It's nothing.'

'Don't give me that shit. The treatment went in weeks ago. When I pitched it to him over a round of golf at the K Club, Walter was all for it. What's changed?'

Milton gave up trying to get the waitress's attention and sighed. 'It's Maureen.'

'What about her?'

'I think she put a spoke in it.'

'You think?'

'All right, I know. I was going to tell you, but with all this other stuff about Andrea, it—'

'What? Why did she kill it?'

'Why does she do anything? She's a horrible miserable bitch, that's why. I don't know why Walter keeps her around. If it were up to me, I'd sack her. She absolutely hates me.'

Dy was furious. 'That show was gold. I had six writers work for a fucking week on the treatment. You're telling me she squashed it without even discussing it with me first?'

'Don't blame me, Dy, take it up with her.'

'I will,' Anderson said. 'I'll call Walter first thing in the morning too.'

He pushed his plate away. Milton finally caught the eye of the waitress and ordered another drink. It was definitely turning into a five-martini sort of evening.

CHAPTER THIRTY-SEVEN

'Dr Brennan, thank you so much for coming. I apologise for the short notice.' Quinn was up and moving, his right hand outstretched, a big plastic smile already in place.

'Hello, Inspector, I'm sorry I'm late.'

'Not at all, not at all, please, come in.'

Roxy kept her eyes firmly on her screen, her fingers working. She was aware of Cora's shifting attention beside her, aware of the change in her own breathing, the way the hair on her arms had lifted slightly in reaction to Lizzie's voice, a voice that startled her in its familiarity. How had she forgotten that husky rumble? It was a forty-cigarettes-a-day voice; a newsreader's voice; the kind of voice that lent itself to authority, to trust, to compliance. She wondered what kind of things that voice whispered in David's ear, and mistyped a number of words that she then had to delete.

This was stupid, she chided herself: she was a professional, and it had been over a year since … since … Dammit! She deleted another slew of incorrect words.

Quinn was making the introductions, working his way around the room.

'And these are our newest members, Officer Cora Simmons.'

Cora leaned over Roxy to shake hands.

'Hi.'

'And Sergeant Roxy Malloy.'

Roxy raised her head.

Yep, Lizzie was still beautiful, still with the same glorious wavy blonde hair, still with the perfect skin, the rosebud mouth, a Nordic queen amongst mortals. Sickening really.

You slept with my boyfriend and destroyed my life.

'We've met,' she said. She offered her hand. Lizzie took it and they shook briefly. 'Hello, Dr Brennan.'

'Hello, Roxanne. Um … congratulations on the promotion.'

'Thank you. Inspector Quinn here has been rapidly broadening my horizons.'

Quinn scowled.

'Right, well we won't keep you, Malloy, those reports won't type themselves.' He hurried Lizzie away. 'What do you need, Dr Brennan?'

'Not much. I've taken a very rudimentary look at the information you've sent me and obviously I'd need a little more time to study all the information available before I can offer any advice, but I should have something for you by tomorrow.'

'Terrific, I'll find you an office where you can work.'

'Oh, any old desk will do.'

'I think we can manage better than that. But first, Superintendent O'Connor was hoping to have a quick chat.'

They left together. When they were gone, Cora whistled under her breath.

'Wow, she's really pretty, isn't she?'

Roxy gritted her teeth. 'That's one way of putting it.'

'What's the other way?'

'Never mind.'

Cora looked sympathetic. 'He's been really rough on you lately, hasn't he?'

'Who?'

'Quinn. You know everyone thinks you did a good job nailing Falstaff the way you did.'

'For all the difference it's made.'

Cora turned back to her EN and worked for a while.

'Did you see the state of Noel Furlong, though?'

'No.'

'I wonder what happened. I wonder how Quinn knew where to find him.'

'Telepathy.'

'Huh?'

Roxy shut her mouth. Why was she being rude to Cora anyway? None of this was her fault.

'I heard Furlong's sister was downstairs earlier. Apparently she kicked up absolute blue murder after she spoke to him.

'I hope Quinn finds the time to offer her a big hug. It's what humans do; even monkeys.'

'Are you okay, Sergeant?'

'Peachy.'

'Some of the squad are saying she'll probably go to the media about her brother's treatment. Do you think she will?'

'I don't know.'

'I don't think it's him, though.'

'Who?'

'I don't think Noel Furlong is the Sweetheart Killer, do you?'

Roxy wished Cora would stop talking. She was trying very hard to concentrate on checking off the Albas employee list against that of Lorraine Dell and Estelle Roberts' places of employment. So far she'd found nothing to connect them. Roberts and Dell had both worked in Park West Business Park, but for different companies. Hugh Bannon was a freelance accountant and had worked in various places, and Sean Kilbride had been a clerk at the law library in the city centre. There were no links to Andrea Colgan as far as she could see.

The door opened and Fletcher walked in, moving at a determined clip. Out of the corner of her eye Roxy watched him march up to Miranda Lynn's desk, place a sheet of paper down in front of her and tap it. She wondered if he was still angry with her for her lie of omission.

Miranda read the page and looked up.

'That's interesting,' Roxy heard her say. 'Did they say what—'

'What's going on?' Cora asked.

'Shush.'

Miranda grabbed her jacket from the back of her chair.

'Fletch has a witness said a courier buzzed her on Friday about a flower delivery.'

'At the Dundrum apartment building?'

'Yeah, there was no one home so she held onto them for Andrea.'

'Please tell me she remembers where they came from.'

'You got it.' She strode to the door. 'Come on, Fletch.'

As Fletcher passed her desk, Roxy leaned out a little.

'Look, Fletcher, about before. I'm really sorry. I should have been clearer about wanting to bring Jerome Falstaff in from the outset.'

He kept walking as though she didn't exist.

Yep, he was still angry.

Roxy went back to her lists, feeling lower than a snake. Fletcher had found something, something they probably would have had earlier if she had done what Quinn had asked her to do in the first place.

CHAPTER THIRTY-EIGHT

The wolf phoned in sick and went back to bed. He slept until late in the afternoon, then got up, phoned for a pizza and went back to his room to eat it.

He was exhausted, but satisfied. Estelle Roberts had taken some careful coaxing, but in the end her mind had given out and they had enjoyed a wonderful experience together.

In fact it had been so wonderful it gave him an idea.

He enjoyed the hunt, obviously; he enjoyed the feeling of power it gave him, knowing his prey was oblivious to him. He enjoyed his little rituals, the sense of theatre. He enjoyed the pay-off, watching the women morph and change from the venal snakes he knew them to be to the compliant doves they became.

He enjoyed making love to them, hearing them utter his name, the feel of their bodies under his. But it was too short, the drugs wore off too soon and then it was over.

If only there was a way to extend the experience.

He lay on his back, staring at the ceiling, thinking.

Estelle had been the closest physically to Celine. She reminded him of her a lot; she even tasted like Celine. He would have liked to keep her, make her his.

Celine … he used to dream about her so often. He'd wake up and find his sheets sticky, his heart beating hard and fast in his chest.

She knew the effect she had on him, of that there was no doubt. How often had he come downstairs to find her in the kitchen in skin-tight jeans and a vest, rummaging around in the fridge?

'Your dad's thirsty,' she'd say, leaning forward, letting her breasts press against the material. 'He's getting better, you know?'

He did not know and this was hardly welcome news. If he got better, Celine would stop coming. The house would revert to how it was before, except that that was impossible.

He never remembered how he came up with the solution. It wasn't like he was involved with his father's care. The man could use a toilet by himself, and didn't have any particular needs that required his intervention. Celine made him food: soups and sandwiches. He ordered takeaway at the weekend and had her bring him a bottle of bourbon every Friday.

But suddenly his father was all he could think of; or rather, his recovery.

It had to be stopped.

The first time he drugged his father he used too much and almost killed him. He spent a miserable three hours holding ice to his father's neck and wrists, watching his chest rise and fall, waiting for him to come back to earth. After that, he was more careful. He liked to drug his father's late-night Ovaltine, knowing full well the old man had to get up several times a night to use the toilet. His father blamed his falls on the bourbon and vowed to cut back.

Still he fell.

Celine was concerned.

'I'm sure it's neurological,' she told him one day, after she found fresh bruises on the old man's legs and chest. 'He needs to go to hospital and get checked out.'

The wolf nodded, drained his can of Coke.

Hospital. Would they run tests? Discover the 'treatments' he'd been providing? Could they do that?

For a few weeks he did not drug his father.

Curiously, this made little difference. The old man had changed over the course of his illness. He talked less and stopped reading the papers. Sometimes the wolf found him out on the landing without his crutches, peering into the shadows, listening for snatches of conversation that were only available to his ears.

'He's got an infection,' Celine said. 'Probably caught it through the pressure sores. Runs through the blood and makes him seem doolally.'

A doctor came, a thin man with a pronounced lisp. He prescribed antibiotics.

'He should really be in hospital,' he told the wolf, only it came out as 'He thud really be in hothible.' The wolf showed him out.

Day after day, his father weakened. Sometimes he cried out; other times he laughed and sang songs to himself. The wolf did not know what to make of it, but he knew it was bad. Not that he cared about the old man; he could sing himself into the grave if he cared to. But Celine … Celine would no longer come if he was gone. He needed the old man alive.

He needed Celine.

CHAPTER THIRTY-NINE

Gavin, the lanky boy working in the florist, was the kind of kid that gave Miranda Lynn a pain in the rear. He had blue hair, facial piercings and an annoying snotty laugh that went with his snotty attitude.

'Last Friday, your shop delivered flowers to this address in Dundrum.' She turned her EN around so he could read the address on the screen.

'Yeah?'

'I want to know who ordered them and how they paid for them.'

'Don't you, like, need a warrant or some shit for that?'

Miranda leaned her hip against the counter and narrowed her eyes.

'This is a murder inquiry.'

He looked sceptical. 'So you're, like, investigating flower deliveries?'

'Have you ever been arrested for interfering with a Garda inquiry, Gavin?'

'No.'

'Would you like to be?'

Gavin got the picture. With an overly dramatic sigh, he turned to the shop computer and began to tap the screen. While he searched, Fletcher peered at the elaborate flower arrangement he'd been working on when they arrived.

'It's for a civil partnership,' Gavin said, noticing his interest.

'What is that?' Fletcher pointed.

'That's a king protea, *very* popular this year.'

Fletcher glanced at him to see if he was taking the proverbial, but apparently he wasn't.

'Okay, so yeah, the roses were ordered the week before, on the second of January.'

'By who?'

'It doesn't say.'

'What *does* it say?'

'It wasn't an online order or a phone order.' He shrugged. 'I guess someone came in and paid cash.'

'You don't remember?'

'I wasn't working that day, Ro was.'

'Ro?'

'Rowena Delaney, she works here too.'

'I want a number for her.' Miranda looked around. 'Do you have any security cameras in here?'

Gavin did the snotty laugh until she glared him into silence.

'Get me that number.'

'Fine, Jeez, chill.'

'Sixteen roses, long stem, that's how much?' Fletcher wanted to know.

'A hundred and forty yoyos,' Gavin replied in an instant.

'For a bunch of flowers?' Miranda was astounded. 'What are they, dipped in gold?'

'For *scented* roses,' Gavin corrected her. 'For *out-of-season* scented roses.'

He found Ro's number and read it out.

Miranda called and waited, tapping her foot impatiently. Fletcher wandered up and down the narrow aisles, peering at the shelves and pots, a little baffled at the variety. He knew next to nothing about horticulture. He'd had a plant once, a house-warming gift from his sister, but he'd over-watered it and it died.

'Rowena Delaney?' Miranda was saying. 'My name is Rank Sergeant Miranda Lynn and I wonder if I could ask you a few questions. I'm here with Gavin at the shop. He gave me your number.'

She paused, listening for what seemed like an interminably long time.

'No, you're not in any trouble.'

Gavin smirked. Miranda resisted the urge to slap him.

'I want you to think back, Ro, okay. The second of January, someone came into the shop and ordered sixteen long-stemmed yellow scented roses for delivery … That's right, the second. It's an unusual order and the customer most likely paid cash.'

She pinched the bridge of her nose.

'No, I can see how that would be difficult … Male, that's good. Try to concentrate, Rowena. Was he tall, short, fat, thin? Young or old? Did he have a beard? Did he have an accent?'

There was another long pause.

'You think he was tall, wearing a hat. That's great … No, that's okay, that's good. What about clothes … No? Okay, Rowena, could you come down to the station on South Circular Road and work with a sketch artist?'

She gave the girl her details, then hung up and looked at Gavin. 'What?'

'How often would someone order yellow roses?'

'Not often. Red are pretty popular, and white, but not yellow.'

'Once a month, once every two months, what?'

'I don't know.'

'Well can you check?'

This time he knew better than to sigh. He tapped the screen, leaned his chin on his hand and scrolled.

'Last order we got was in September of last year.'

'Cash?'

'Nah, ordered by a Mrs Margaret Pierce, note says it was for a funeral.'

'Nothing around December?' Miranda was thinking of the Dell and Kilbride murder.

'Nope.'

Fletcher reappeared, looking thoughtful. He opened his EN and went to the crime-scene photos taken at Hugh Bannon's house. He found a close-up of the rose petals, and one of the stems found in the bin.

'Can you take a look at these?'

He showed Gavin the photos. Gavin studied them, tapping his tongue piercing against his lower teeth as he did.

'Okay,' he said eventually. 'So, like, I can't help you here.'

'Why?' Miranda asked.

'Because these are, like, garden roses.'

'Aren't all roses garden roses?'

'Well yeah, I guess, but we don't order these: too thorny.'

Fletcher took the EN back and brought up the roses found at the Dell/Kilbride scene.

'What about these?'

Gavin looked.

'That's the same variety. Like I said, too thorny.'

Fletcher looked at Lynn, who grinned.

'Gavin?'

'Yeah?'

'Believe it or not, you've been very helpful.'

'Well yeah,' he said, rolling his eyes.

CHAPTER FORTY

For Falstaff, the journey home was almost as terrifying as being in custody. His usual self-medication had long worn off so by the time he got back to Dundrum, he was frightened and angry.

Very angry.

He let himself into his apartment, then slammed the door shut and leaned against it, practically hyperventilating with the stress of it all. He ran to check his computer and swore. The photos were gone, wiped. He had nothing.

Edgar danced around, going bananas with joy, but the apartment reeked of shit from his deposits all over the manky living room floor.

After opening a few windows, Falstaff grabbed some paper towels and cleaned up as best he could. When he was done, he poured a glass of gin and drank it straight down, thinking about his situation.

The nasty dark-haired sergeant had been correct. Without the photos of Andrea to sell he was in dire straits. Somewhere in the mess were letters from the bank, polite at first, increasingly threatening thereafter. The last one he'd dared open had been downright terrifying.

He had less than eight weeks to clear his arrears or they'd put him out on the street.

He drank some more gin and did some thinking.

They didn't know everything, of course; he wasn't *that* stupid.

They didn't know he had witnessed Andrea's other visitor on the day she was killed, he wasn't about to toss away that kind of ammunition. It was time to get busy. A single payment to clear his arrears was all he wanted to keep quiet, and maybe put a little spending money in his pocket.

He wasn't greedy, he explained to Edgar, who was licking his face enthusiastically. This wasn't greed; it was forward planning, yes, that's what it was.

After a third glass of gin, he set to work, scouring the newspaper for the right letters, the right words. Tongue out, he used the kitchen scissors to snip and cut, then glued the words to a sheet of blank paper. When he was finished, he stepped back to admire his handiwork.

'Look at this, Edgar,' he said, lifting the little dog up to show him. 'Isn't that glorious?'

Of course he'd have to send it, and that would necessitate another trip outdoors. But needs must.

He poured the last of the gin over a cube of ice, tossed it back and smacked his lips with satisfaction.

'Edgar, my lad,' he said squeezing the little dog. 'Everything is going to be fine.'

CHAPTER FORTY-ONE

The last patient of the day was often a difficult session. Dr Simon Fitzpatrick tried to keep an interested expression and forced his body to remain poised and attentive. His mind, however, had left the office twenty minutes before and was now in his favourite restaurant, Baroque, ordering duck rillette and a bottle of Pinot Noir.

He licked his lips and shifted his weight from one buttock to the other. His client blew her nose noisily, and glared at him as if she sensed his boredom.

'You probably think I'm exaggerating, don't you?'

'Exaggerating, no, of course not. Your emotions are yours, Emily. They are not open to denial or scrutiny. It is your responses we are here to discuss.'

'I told you,' she cried, waving her hands in the air. 'I can't help how they make me feel.'

'But you can help how you respond. Emotions, Emily, are not facts. Situational anxiety is real based on how you perceive reality, but it is not fact.'

She didn't like this; she never did.

He risked a glance at his watch and was relieved to see their time was almost up.

'Will you work on some of the exercises I gave you?'

She looked at him from under her brow, pouting, her bottom lip quivering.

'It would be easier if you just wrote me another prescription for those tablets. *They* helped.'

'Elimination therapy is merely one part of the process. We need to restructure your mind, Emily, not tamp your reactions down with beta blockers.'

'But they helped!'

'I'm sure they did and will again.' He smiled as though humouring a child. 'But this week we need to *feel* some of the stress, if only to recognise …' He waved his hand at her.

She scowled, refusing to play her part.

'… that emotions are not facts,' he finished for her. 'And on that note, let us finish.'

'Sometimes I think you enjoy knowing that I suffer,' she snapped, reaching for her handbag. She pulled out her purse, counted out his money with insulting deliberation and flung it on the low table between them. Fitzpatrick left it there, got up and went to his desk in the corner of the room. He wrote a receipt and brought it to her.

'Same time next week?'

Without replying, she snatched the receipt from his hand and stuffed it into her bag.

Proving he could be petty when he wanted to, he didn't offer to help her into her coat as he usually did, and to his internalised shame, he enjoyed watching her struggle with it.

When she was finally gone, he sighed, loosened his tie and poured himself a very large whisky over a single ice cube.

Maybe it was his age, or maybe it was this wretched society; whatever the reason, lately he had grown increasingly tired of dealing with people and their never-ending complaints. When he was a younger man – a much younger man – he'd believed in what he was doing, he'd felt his profession was an opportunity to do good in the world, make a difference, write a book that millions would clutch to their chests and feel salvation.

What a simple-minded idiot he had been back then. He should have listened to his father and learned a trade of some kind.

Actually, now that he thought about it, he rarely got carpenters, plumbers or builders as clients. Now why was that? Were they dissatisfied with their lot in life? Did they spend their evenings wondering where the hell they'd gone wrong?

Somehow he doubted it.

He tossed the last of his drink back, put his coat on and switched off the lights.

Downstairs, he put his briefcase down on the ground next to him and locked the door. The bottom lock was stiff and it took quite a bit of twisting and twiddling, but he got it at last.

When he reached for his briefcase, it was gone.

'What the …'

He turned around and found himself looking up into the unsmiling face of a large man with eyes the colour of a lake in winter.

'This must be yours,' the man said. He was holding the briefcase in a huge hand.

'Oh, I … yes, thank you.'

He reached for the case, but the man tucked it under his arm. Fitzpatrick dropped his hand to his side. He felt ridiculously stupid.

'Do you know who I am?'

Tired as he was of this life, Fitzpatrick realised his ennui was fading fast in the face of real and present danger. He looked about. But it was late and the street was empty. He could run, he supposed, but he doubted that would be very sensible.

To make matter worse, the man seemed to have the ability to read minds.

'If you shout or try to call for help, this situation will turn ugly, needlessly so. Do you understand?'

What kind of question was that? Did he say yes, or did he say no?

In the end he settled for nodding; it seemed the most prudent choice.

'Good, now do you know who I am?'

He squinted at the man's face. It *was* familiar, but he couldn't quite place him.

'*Should* I know you?' he asked.

The man smiled. It was a terrible smile and nothing in it suggested amusement or kindness or humanity.

'You should, you were treating my daughter. She was killed, murdered.'

The realisation hit Fitzpatrick like a sledgehammer. Now he recognised the face, but not from his memory; from the newspapers.

'You're Andrea's father.'

'That's right.'

Fitzpatrick grimaced. 'Look, um … Mr Travers, is it? Firstly I'd like to say how sorry I am for your loss, I was horrified to read about what happened to Andrea—'

'She was seeing you, wasn't she? I want to know why.'

'Oh, I don't think … I'm afraid I can't discuss that with you.'

'You can,' Dominic Travers said, and though his voice remained exactly the same, something shifted in his tone. 'And you will.'

A slight tremor rippled through Fitzpatrick's body. He recognised it for what it was: epinephrine and norepinephrine were being released into his bloodstream, his fight-or-flight response kicking into action. Funny, knowing the terminology and understanding the physiology didn't do a damn thing to help him.

He was still scared silly.

Oh yes, a brave man, an indignant man even, would refuse on principle, professional principle at least. But as he looked at Dominic Travers, Fitzpatrick knew he would capitulate, so why pretend? Why bother with the sham in the first place?

'Um, would you like to come upstairs?'

Dominic handed him his briefcase. Fitzpatrick took it, turned around and promptly dropped his keys. Before he could retrieve them, the big man had scooped them up.

'Which ones?'

'The long one is for the bottom, the short one for the top.'

The scarred hands did not shake and the lock did not stick. Within seconds, the door swung open.

'After you,' Dominic said.

Simon Fitzpatrick gave one last forlorn look to the empty street and went back inside, the duck and the wine completely forgotten.

CHAPTER FORTY-TWO

Lizzie Brennan worked fast, and as promised, the next day she asked to see the squad in the incident room.

When they got there, the big screen was down, displaying a photograph of a bouquet of yellow roses. Roxy thought Lizzie looked a little tired, but no less beautiful. Her hair was tied in a loose bun at the nape of her neck and her black suit was sharply tailored.

Effortless, she thought. How did people do it?

'Why did the killer choose yellow roses?' Lizzie asked, moving from one side of the podium to the other, her hands as expressive as her face.

'Because they're pretty?' Cora said, and looked embarrassed when a number of officers laughed.

'They are.' Lizzie smiled at her. 'But what do they signify?'

Nobody answered.

'We think of roses as a romantic flower, even a Valentine's gift if you will, but historically yellow roses have had a different meaning. They were often displayed by a jealous lover, or given passive-aggressively to denote a fading love; so for instance a man might give them to a woman he was about to leave for another.' She looked back at the screen. 'Our killer chose these flowers not to be romantic, but to tell us something, to warn us that romance is dead: he is literally delivering death to romance.'

She pressed the button, the screen split and a different bunch of roses appeared beside the first.

'These are the roses sent to Andrea Colgan. Notice anything unusual about them?'

Again it was Cora who spoke up.

'There are no thorns on those ones.'

'That's correct, Officer.' Lizzie turned to the screen. 'The flower on the right is a yellow banksia rose; the roses found at the first and third murder scenes are Friesia roses.'

'So he shops around for his flowers,' an officer said. 'Probably to avoid being recognised.'

'I don't think he does. I think he is very singular in his methods. Think about this: what was taken from Lorraine Dell?'

'An engagement ring.'

'What was taken from Estelle Roberts?'

Quinn spoke. 'According to her housemates, she wore a small silver necklace with an E on it, a gift from her grandmother. It was not recovered at the crime scene.'

'Right. Now think about what was taken from Andrea Colgan. A phone. A laptop. There's nothing personal in either item.'

She looked around.

'Andrea Colgan's killer left us a different message.'

'What?'

'He attacked her physically and obliterated her face. This was an extremely personal act; personal to him. She was a threat, she represented losing face, so she lost hers. Dell and Roberts were not a threat to their killer. They were prizes; in a way, he revered them.'

'Prizes?' Miranda asked.

'Look at how he treated them after he raped them. Look at how he tended to their bodies: he brushed their hair, applied make-up, made sure they were not displayed in an obscene manner when he was done with them. He scattered petals around Estelle Roberts. He wanted something from them, something tender, something he felt he deserved.'

'But he left a card with a broken heart.' Cora looked confused.

'Oh yes, there's no doubt that these women angered him in some way.'

'He's angry with them, but harbouring romantic feelings towards them too?' Roxy asked.

'This isn't romance, Sergeant, it's conquest.'

Lizzie looked around at the squad. Some of the expressions were thoughtful, some a little sceptical.

'You found ketamine in the women's bloodstreams, but the men were slaughtered. Why is that, and why does he use ketamine specifically?'

'To subdue them,' Fletcher said.

'There are many drugs you can use to knock a person out, Sergeant, but ketamine is different. It is a dissociative drug: it can alter a person's perceptions; depending on the dosage, it can even produce vivid hallucinations.'

'You think he drugged them to make them think they were in some kind of fantasy?' Miranda asked.

'Not *some* kind of fantasy, Sergeant; a very specific one, directed by him.'

'To what end?'

'I don't know.'

'Do we have anything on the make-up?'

'The make-up is interesting. Forensics has identified the lipstick as Golden Rose Frosty Baby Pink.'

'Roses again.'

'Yes, they are a huge signifier for this man.'

'So why did he change his MO with Colgan?' someone asked from the back of the room.

'I don't believe he did.'

'What do you mean?' Fletcher was frowning.

'I mean I don't believe the person who killed Andrea Colgan is responsible for the deaths of the other victims.'

There were immediate murmurs and mutterings. Miranda cast a glance at Roxy, who was sitting rigid, her heart racing.

'I believe that whoever killed Andrea wanted us to think it was the same killer.'

'So you think it could be a copycat?'

'No.' Lizzie shook her head. 'I think it's someone who saw an opportunity and went with it.'

It was Miranda who spoke next.

'So, just to be clear. We're looking for two separate killers?'

'Yes.' Lizzie leaned her hands on the podium. 'The first killer is a white male, in his twenties or very early thirties. He may have suffered a bad break-up recently, or been rejected by someone he viewed as a romantic mate. He has ready access to drugs and he works unusual hours.'

'Wait, what makes you say that?' Roxy asked.

'Apart from Andrea Colgan, the victims worked nine-to-five jobs; this man was able to study them and monitor their routines. He has time on his hands.'

'Maybe he's unemployed.'

'Maybe, but the champagne he chooses is not cheap.' She looked around. 'I don't think the suspect is on the breadline.'

'So, male, white, with disposable income.' Fletcher shook his head. 'No offence, but that hardly narrows it down.'

'I believe he studied them, the women at least. The women are his prize; the men are collateral damage.'

'And the second killer?' Quinn spoke.

'The second man is older, more calculating. If I had to make an educated guess, he's someone known to the victim. She invited him into her home, so to a degree she trusted him. This attack was violent and there were no drugs in her system, so he's pretty powerful. Andrea Colgan was not a small woman, and she was physically fit; it would have taken great strength to overpower her.'

'Or because she trusted him, he caught her completely unawares,' Miranda said.

'That is also a possibility.'

'We can't rule out the possibility that Andrea Colgan was a victim of the Sweetheart Killer,' Fletcher said, stubborn to the end.

'I told you already, Sergeant Fletcher,' Quinn snapped, 'keep that tabloid crap out of my investigation.'

'Sorry.'

Lizzie spread her hands. 'Then by all means investigate her death as such, but my feeling is you're going to get caught in another current if you concentrate on her. You asked for my opinion, Inspector. This is it.'

'All right.' Quinn got to his feet. He looked tired and despondent. 'Okay, well thank you for your time and expertise.'

The meeting was over.

As the group dispersed, Lizzie came over to where Roxy was collecting her things.

'I'm sorry if I've made a mess of your investigation.'

'Not my investigation. I knew all along she didn't fit.'

Lizzie put her hands in her pockets.

'So what do you do now?'

Roxy shrugged, put the strap of her bag over her head.

'Back to the drawing board.'

'If you need any assistance, I'm more than happy to help.'

Roxy nodded stiffly. In the background, a couple of officers were watching the exchange, both wearing the same stupid grins on their faces. Roxy scowled at them. Was nothing in this place ever private?

Oh God, why was she still standing there?

'You know,' Lizzie said, 'I've been meaning to … speak with you. It's just, with … um … everything that happened, I wasn't sure if—'

'Sergeant Malloy!' Miranda bustled up. 'Oh, sorry to interrupt, Dr Brennan. Malloy, I've asked you about interviewing Gregory Milton twice now and you still haven't got round to it. I'm sorry, but it can't wait, okay? I need you to take care of it right now.' She clapped her hands. 'Chop chop, let's go.'

Roxy nodded to Lizzie and followed Miranda out into the hall. When they were out of earshot, she glanced at her colleague.

'Who's Gregory Milton?'

'Oh, just some guy Andrea Colgan did a PR job for a few months back.'

'I'm sorry, I didn't know I was supposed to talk to him.'

Miranda grinned. 'Relax, Malloy, you weren't.'

'Then what was that about?'

'That was a rescue. You should have seen your face. You looked like you were going to be sick all over yourself.'

Roxy was genuinely touched. Before she could express her gratitude, Miranda handed her a name and address.

'Oh, you do actually want me to interview him.'

'Two birds, one stone, that's what you promised Quinn, right?' Miranda Lynn winked. 'You're my bird now, ducky. Quack quack.'

CHAPTER FORTY-THREE

Roxy stood in the shadows behind the cameras and the sound man, trying not to get in anybody's way or trip over what seemed like a million cables criss-crossing the floor.

On set a few feet away, Dr Gregory Milton was leaning back in his wing chair, his index finger pressed to his lips, one leg crossed over the other. He was wearing canary-yellow socks, Roxy noticed.

Sitting opposite him on the famous velvet sofa was a couple in their late sixties with a cold gap between them. The woman kept twisting a handkerchief between her fingers.

'It's like my needs don't matter,' she wailed, tears threatening. 'I'm tired of trying to be patient.'

'Tom.' Dr Milton gave the older man a gentle encouraging smile. 'How long have you felt this way?'

'Well,' the man said, speaking slowly and clearly. 'Ever since Bonnie died, I guess.'

'Bonnie?'

'My dog.'

'That damned dog!' the woman cried. 'I sometimes think he loved her more than me!'

Dr Milton looked at Tom, who shrugged unapologetically. 'She was a good dog,' he said. 'She certainly never belittled me every day of the week.'

Someone tapped Roxy on the shoulder. She looked around to find a smartly dressed woman standing at her shoulder. She beckoned her to follow.

Outside in the corridor, the woman introduced herself as Maureen Kelly, the station manager. Her handshake was firm, her manner efficient, even brusque. She certainly did not beat about the bush.

'You're here about Andrea.'

'That's right, but don't worry, it's a formality. We're interviewing everyone who worked with her in the last year.'

'I see, a formality.'

Something in her tone caught Roxy's interest.

'Did you know Andrea?'

'I met her a few times. Charming girl, *very* pretty.'

'Yes, I saw her photo.'

'Smart, too.'

'So I believe.'

'Of course, she wasn't the only pretty girl to work with Dr Milton. As he's fond of saying, he values beauty.'

Roxy was impressed by the injection of sheer loathing Maureen used when she mentioned his name.

'Oh?' She paused. 'He has a preference?'

'He likes them to be young, pretty. Preferably involved.'

'Is he married himself?'

'In name only.'

'I don't understand what you mean.'

'His wife, Nadine, suffered a catastrophic brain injury from an accident some years ago. She survived, but never recovered.'

'Oh, I'm sorry to hear that.' Roxy tilted her head slightly. 'Why would Dr Milton want the women who work for him to be involved?'

'Why indeed?' Maureen said. 'I've often wondered that myself.'

'I hope you don't mind my saying so, but I get the distinct impression you don't much like Dr Milton.'

'Well.' Maureen Kelly's eyes were hard and direct. 'Far be it from me to disrespect the talent – he is after all the biggest star we have currently – but let's say I find him problematic and leave it at that.'

'Albas Entertainment promoted his last book, didn't they? That's how he met Andrea Colgan.'

'That's right. Milton and Dy Anderson are very old friends. There was another pretty girl before Andrea, now that I think of it. Delia I believe her name was.'

'Delia?' Roxy said, frowning a little. She had gone through the whole list of employees Albas had given Miranda and Quinn; there had been no mention of a Delia.

'That's right. I believe she and Andrea were friends. You should talk to her.'

'I will, thank you.'

'Yes, well, best of luck with your interview, Sergeant. I hope you get to the bottom of it all. I'm not sure the world can afford to lose any more bright young things. But then I hardly need to tell you that, do I?'

And with that, Maureen left.

CHAPTER FORTY-FOUR

The idea began to take flight. Padding through the house, the wolf thought about the logistics.

The upper floors were out: too many windows, and the old fire escape was too much of a risk. But the basement could be perfectly adapted. Five rooms, two interconnected. There was even a toilet. The windows to the front were barred, and it wouldn't take much to block up the old door under the steps of the main house: some bricks, a little cement, and *voilà*.

He looked around. He could haul the mattress from his mother's room downstairs. It had some mildew, but it was serviceable.

He took the measuring tape and wrote the distances on a slip of paper. If he put a ring in the ceiling right there – he looked up and calculated – she could access the toilet, but not the door leading to the internal stairs, though it might be sensible to install a security door just in case.

All the work made him hungry. He went back upstairs and microwaved a ready meal. While he ate, he considered his evolution.

Celine had been wrong about him. He was not stupid, no indeed.

Not at all.

When he was done eating, he tossed the plastic container towards the bin and went back upstairs. He had work to do, research.

As soon as he logged on, he went to his usual online clothes store, and for the first time ever, hit women's clothes.

The array was astounding, complicated. He himself only wore black: black jeans with an elasticated panel, black T-shirts, black jumpers. But women should look bright, pretty, like tropical birds.

His woman would be feminine; she would wear dresses that showed a lot of leg, pretty blouses, white bras, white knickers. She would wear satin and lace, she would take pride in her femininity. She would wear make-up and leave her hair down. She would please him, and in return he would take care of her, feed her, love her.

It was the natural order of things.

It was, he smiled, perfect.

CHAPTER FORTY-FIVE

Gregory Milton was a real piece of work, Roxy decided, watching him accept his hot lemon from his assistant, who shot Roxy a vaguely dirty look as though she disapproved of her sharing the same oxygen as her boss.

'Ah, this is wonderful, April.' He touched his knuckles to her cheek and the girl positively glowed with delight.

'Sergeant, are you sure there's nothing we can offer you?'

'I'm fine, thank you.'

April left. Milton settled back in his swanky chair and blew on the cup.

'Lemon and honey, nature's finest balm, don't you think?'

'Sure.'

Roxy opened her EN and waited for him to stop faffing about.

'Andrea Colgan—' she began.

'You have wonderful bone structure, Sergeant. I detect some Slavic influences, perhaps?'

'Not that I'm aware of.'

'No, your colouring is too dark. Any Romanian heritage?'

'No.'

'Fascinating.'

'So, Doctor, Andrea Colgan—'

'Ah.' Milton cut her off. 'Andrea, such a beauty, a gorgeous, vital, intelligent young woman on the cusp of her life.' He sighed theatrically. 'I was devastated to learn of her passing.'

'Devastated? Did you know her well?'

'No.' He smiled. 'We worked together very briefly.'

'But you were devastated.'

He spread his hands wide. 'I am an empath by nature, Sergeant, and as much as I try to control my emotions, the death of a young woman like Andrea is a heavy burden on my soul.'

'She handled your last book tour, didn't she?'

He sprang up out of the chair so fast he scared the wits out of her. Within seconds he had plucked a book from the shelves and thrust it into her hand. She looked at it.

Rewiring the Heart by Dr Gregory Milton, 'renowned psychologist and therapist'.

She flipped it over. The back was taken up by a black-and-white photo of Milton standing at a huge window with one finger pressed to his lips. It was the exact same pose she had watched him perform on set not an hour before.

'You'll be putting the cardiologists out of business, Doctor.'

Milton threw back his head and laughed as if this was the funniest thing he'd ever heard.

'Very droll, Sergeant, I like that.'

She tried to hand the book back, but he waved it away.

'No, please, keep it. A gift.'

Roxy put it on her lap; it made balancing the EN easier.

'So before this book tour, had you ever met Andrea?'

He retook his seat.

'No, I don't believe so.'

'When exactly did you meet her?'

'About a week before the tour started. October, I think. I can get April to check the precise date.'

'How was the tour?'

'Demanding. I did various talks, shows, signings all over Ireland and the UK. It's the nature of the beast, of course: you strike while the iron is hot.'

'Andrea travelled with you?'

'Yes.'

'Did she ever talk to you about her boyfriend?'

Milton's expression went from polite to scornful in the twitch of a lip.

'The great artist, I presume.'

'You know about Noel?'

'Andrea spoke about him, of course, and very loyal she was too, but it was quite obvious to me that the man was more albatross than swan, if you know what I mean.'

'Not really.'

'He had one show that was semi-successful, and he traded on it like he was the next Damien Hirst.'

'You met him?'

'Twice, and I found him to be a very unpleasant fellow, very insecure. You should talk to Dy about him; he gave the staff at Albas no end of trouble.'

'Dy Anderson, as in Andrea's boss?'

'That's right.'

'How long have you been with Albas, Dr Milton?'

'Oh, years. Dy's a personal friend. We met at college.'

'Who was your PR before Andrea?'

She threw the question from left field and hit a home run. Milton hesitated for a split second, even looked a little uneasy. It was a tiny flicker, but she noticed.

'Don't you remember?'

'Oh, it was another young woman … Della, Delia? Yes, I think that's it, Delia.'

'She worked for Mr Anderson too, did she?'

'I believe so.'

'Only I don't recall seeing her name on the list of contacts.'

'Oh well, she's not there any longer.' He smiled. 'PR is not for the faint-hearted. People leave all the time.'

Roxy wrote the name down and put an asterisk next to it.

'Was she faint-hearted?'

'Oh goodness, Sergeant, I didn't mean anything by that.' He laughed heartily, showing a lot of teeth. Roxy wondered if he had any idea how phoney he sounded.

They talked for a little while longer, but Milton had recovered and kept his bases covered. He even managed to present an alibi for the day Andrea was murdered, though Roxy hadn't asked for one.

On her way back to the station, she thought about the performance and decided he gave her the absolute creeps.

She sent her notes to Miranda and sat chewing her thumbnail. Delia.

Where had she heard that name before if it wasn't in the employee information?

It came to her after a few minutes. The interview with Noel Furlong, the one Quinn had asked her to transcribe. Furlong had mentioned a Delia, she was sure of it.

She glanced at her watch. It was almost knocking-off time.

Quinn could hardly complain about what she did on her own time.

Decision made, she grabbed her jacket.

CHAPTER FORTY-SIX

Edwina King was a shrewd woman and understood only too well how the wheels turned, so she had been expecting the call ever since her findings in the autopsy. Nevertheless, when it came, she was angry and insulted and let her feelings be known.

'This is ludicrous,' she said. 'It's unlikely to stand up in court.'

'Oh come now.' The Garda Commissioner's voice was so oily it practically slithered down the line. 'You said yourself the dating process was inconclusive.'

'What I *said* was that in my opinion the foetus came under the twelve-week gestational age period.'

'You were to get a second opinion, I believe.'

'That's right. My colleague is unwell at the moment.'

'Well then, this is a serendipitous solution. Dr Porter will be with you within the hour.'

'Is he at least an obstetrician?'

'He is eminently qualified.'

'How did you learn about this? I asked for the information to be contained until we had conformation.'

The Commissioner made a strange sound. 'Dear me, Dr King, I never took you for a naïf.'

'Why are you interested in this case?'

'Let's just say there are interested parties and leave it at that.'

Edwina looked up at the ceiling and took a breath.

'Goodbye, sir.'

'Goodbye, Doctor.'

Porter arrived shortly before midday. He was an elderly man with thin wispy hair and a pronounced stoop. When he offered Edwina his credentials, which were numerous, albeit long out of date, she noticed he had a tremor in both hands.

Where did he dig you up? she wondered, slowing her gait so that he could keep up with her as they went to theatre.

An hour later, the ridiculous charade was over. Without making any eye contact, Dr Porter announced that in his professional opinion, the foetus was twelve weeks and five days old, and deserving of the status of personhood.

Edwina didn't bother arguing with the man. He was as much a puppet as she was, and it seemed almost indecent to belittle a man of his advanced years further.

Later on, when filing her report, she considered making a complaint, but good sense prevailed.

After all, the fish rots from the head down.

She signed her report and sent it directly to Detective Eli Quinn. The DNA of pre-born Baby Colgan was now available.

CHAPTER FORTY-SEVEN

If Caroline Furlong had been frosty before, she was downright glacial when she opened the door and saw Roxy standing there.

'You have some nerve showing your face.'

'I know that, but I really need to speak to Noel.'

'No, he's been through enough.'

'Look,' Roxy said, 'I don't blame you for being angry. I'd be angry too.'

'Angry?' Caroline's nostrils flared with indignation. 'I'm not angry, Sergeant; I expected nothing more from a corrupt group of despicable bullies and thugs. You dragged our name into the mud, terrorised an innocent grieving man, and now here you are, not blaming me for being angry. How very gracious of you.'

Roxy didn't try to deny any of it.

'You're right.' She shrugged. 'There's been a cock-up of epic proportions and you and your brother have borne the brunt of it. I can't change any of that. I don't seem to have the necessary skills to spin you some kind of yarn either. The truth is, I shouldn't even be here and Quinn would probably have my guts for garters if he knew.'

'Then why *are* you here?'

'Something about Andrea's death didn't sit right with me from the beginning. I'm missing something, something obvious, but I have no idea what it is. I was hoping Noel might be able to fill in some of the blanks.'

Caroline pulled her cardigan tighter around her body.

'Why should he help you?'

'Because he loved Andrea, at least for a time.'

Silence descended. Roxy kept her yap firmly shut as she watched Caroline Furlong's brain go to war with itself. If she said no, that was it, but she really hoped she wouldn't.

'All right,' she said, snapping the words out as if they cost her a great deal. 'But I'll be with him the whole time. If you try to pin anything on him, I will call my solicitor and bring charges against you for harassment.'

Roxy followed her down the hall into the pine-nightmare kitchen. As before, the dog was in his basket by the stove, and the teapot was on the table, a cup beside it. When Noel Furlong saw her enter the room behind his sister, he leaped to his feet.

'No, no, get her out of here.'

'Noel, please, she only wants to talk.'

Roxy gaped at him, and probably quite rudely. It was hard to reconcile the broken, bald creature before her with the handsome rogue she had first seen in the photograph at Andrea's apartment.

'Mr Furlong, I won't take up a lot of your time.'

'I told the other cop everything. Please …' He looked terrified, close to tears. What the hell had happened to this man?

'I'm not here about Andrea – well, I am, but not her specifically. May I sit down?'

Without waiting to see if he said yes, she pulled up a chair and sat down with a sigh.

Furlong, with an agonised glance towards his sister, sank down too.

'Mr Furlong, I'm sorry about what you've been through these last few days.'

He darted a glance her way and looked back down at his hands. He was trembling, and again Roxy felt a deep sense of unease and guilt.

'I read your statement—'

'I told him everything. I didn't lie, I told him everything I knew.'

'Yes, it was very ... comprehensive.'

That was something of an understatement. Furlong had admitted to things that had no relevance to the case whatsoever. Had Quinn pushed even slightly, he might have gone all the way back to his childhood and dug up some old crimes from the memory banks to confess to.

'You mentioned a name in your statement; somebody called Delia. I was wondering if you could tell me about her.'

'Delia?' He looked at her blankly for a moment, then said: 'Oh, Delia, right, what about her?'

'Who is she, please?'

He glanced at Caroline again, looking less agitated but more confused by the second.

'She worked with Andrea at Albas; they were friends.'

'I've gone back over everything we have, and her name hasn't come up anywhere except in your statement.'

Noel shrugged, picked at a piece of loose skin on his ring finger.

'I think maybe they had some kind of falling-out.'

'Oh?'

'Yeah, she stopped coming round and Andrea stopped talking about her.'

'When was this?'

He screwed his face up. 'I don't know exactly. A while back; sometime early last year.'

'Do you know what happened between them?'

'No.' He shook his head. 'I know Andrea was pretty upset over it, but she didn't tell me what it was about. Shame really. I liked Delia, she was a funny bird.'

'Do you know her surname?'

'Shawcross.'

She questioned him a little while longer, but he really didn't know much more about Delia other than what he'd already told her.

Back in the car, Roxy ran Delia's name through the residential property index and came up with two addresses, one in Lucan and another in Clontarf. She drove out to Lucan first as it was closer and found herself looking through the windows of a vacant property. She had a quick chat with the next door neighbour and learned that Delia Shawcross had not been seen at the address for quite some time, over a year at least.

'Don't blame her, really,' the neighbour said, leaning on the doorframe.

'Why's that?'

'Well I wouldn't like to live in a house where my partner hung himself neither,' she said with a shudder. 'Got to be bad luck, that.'

Yes,' Roxy said. 'I imagine it is.'

CHAPTER FORTY-EIGHT

The wolf cracked his knuckles and began to type.

> For much of human history, men have claimed what is rightfully theirs. Now, though, we have allowed ourselves to be deceived by an ideology that has all but destroyed the imperative. We are at war! Society has forced our hand and driven us to this point. For too long rampant feminism has been allowed to poison the well. We are forced to drink from this well, forced to swallow a steady stream of abuse that tells us we are not *handsome* enough, not *wealthy* enough, not *smart* enough; we are told we have nothing to offer, nothing of value to contribute to a society that bends over backwards to accommodate the weaker sex. Today I reclaim my biological right. Today I stamp my will on the world.
>
> Today I will reclaim the Imperative.

He finished with a flourish and toasted his brilliance by opening a fresh tub of cookie dough ice cream.

*

Two things were bothering Samantha Mullins: she was late and she had had another stupid row with her husband.

She ran across the road, crossing two lines of traffic and trying to ignore the blaring horns and the unpleasant insults aimed at her. By the time she reached the pavement, there were tears in her eyes and she was breathless.

Yvonne Hershey glanced up from her phone.

'Where's the fire?'

'Christ.' Samantha leaned on the railing beside her friend and rested her hands on her knees with her head down. 'I think I'm going to be sick.'

'Relax, hen, the bell hasn't even rung yet.'

Yvonne put her phone away and lit a cigarette with a flamboyant flip of her Zippo lighter, drawing disapproving looks from the other mothers, which she ignored. Samantha watched her for a moment and wished she could be more like her. Yvonne didn't give a shit what anyone else thought and wasn't remotely interested in school-gate politics. She turned up wearing her gym gear, Lycra-clad legs, toned, just the right ratio of muscle to fat. Her dark-red hair shone in the winter sunlight, healthy and vibrant, not a single trace of grey anywhere.

By comparison, Samantha felt downright dowdy, but then again, Yvonne made *everyone* feel dowdy.

'We're still on for tonight, right?'

'I guess.' Samantha pulled her ponytail tighter and readjusted her scarf.

Yvonne, always hawk keen, caught the undertone immediately.

'What's wrong, have you changed your mind?'

'No.' She took a long breath. 'It's … I had a row with Michael this morning and … I don't know, it's stupid really.'

'Listen to me, hen.' Yvonne reached out and laid a hand on her arm. 'You've got to stop letting that man waltz in and out of your life when he feels like it, okay?'

'I know.'

'Don't let him call the shots. You're a fucking saint taking him back. If it was me, I'd have told him he made his bed with that tramp and now he can lie in it. You still have time, you know. Tell him you've changed your mind about reconciliation. Tell him you're tired of his saggy old balls and you have your eye on a younger model.'

Samantha laughed, feeling a little better.

'It has been nice having the whole bed to myself.'

'God, I can't remember the last time I had a full night's sleep,' Yvonne said with a sigh. 'Colin snores like a chainsaw.' She glanced at her friend, serious. 'I mean it, Sam, don't let him call the shots. He fucked up; never let him forget it.'

'I know, but it's going to be different this time. The therapist even got him to admit that what he did was an act of self-sabotage.'

'Act of being a middle-aged prick, more like.'

'He's thirty-five!'

'Exactly, old enough to know better.' Yvonne pulled a face. 'If Colin ever steps out on me, he'll wish he was never born.'

Samantha rolled her eyes. 'Colin? Don't be stupid, that man adores you!'

'It's hard to tell sometimes. He's not big on romantic gestures.'

'To be fair, he did buy you a cracking big house.'

'Well there is that,' Yvonne said sagely. 'Don't get me wrong, hen, I love the man, but a little spice now and then adds flavour to the meat and two veg, you know?' She winked, and Samantha grinned.

Inside the school, a bell pealed. Yvonne pitched the cigarette butt down and ground it out under her heel.

'Incoming.'

The children came out as a trickle, then a flood. Loud, happy, catcalling, running with huge brightly coloured bags bouncing on too-small backs (really, why did they need so many books at this age?). Samantha saw Mason first, walking along shoulder to shoulder with his best friend Maki. The boys were deep in conversation, wearing serious faces. She felt her heart swell in her chest at the sight of him, her little miracle baby, born four weeks early, eager to be part of the world.

Yvonne's daughter Grace came next. She was a funny auburn-haired child with big brown eyes and the same dimples as her mother. She was five years old and cute as a button. Samantha was her godmother.

'There's my girl!' Yvonne said, beaming. 'Good day?'

'We made posters!'

'You did? That's great. Hi, Mason, hi, Maki – wow, I love your new haircut.'

Maki smiled shyly. He was seven, the same age as Mason, but smaller, slighter in build, and obsessed with football.

'Hello, sweetheart.' Samantha leaned down and kissed Mason on the top of his head, catching his scent in her nostrils. 'Where's your brother?'

'He got held back.'

'He did?' Samantha frowned, her hand on Mason's shoulder, drawing him in closer to her. 'Why?'

'Dunno. Missus Chambers called him in.'

Samantha tensed. Mrs Chambers was the principal, a kind but firm woman who made Samantha a little nervous, if she was honest.

'Right,' Yvonne said. 'We'd better get moving. See you later on.'

Most of the mothers had dispersed by the time MJ appeared, swinging his school bag from one arm. Samantha raised a hand to him and saw his look of displeasure. His walk was so like his father's, it sometimes hurt her heart to watch him.

No, she was not going down that mental road again, not now. None of what had happened had been her fault, and she was tired of shouldering the lion's share of the blame.

'What did Mrs Chambers want?' she asked, trying to keep her voice light, non-judgemental, non-accusatory.'

Immediately he scowled at Mason. 'Tattle.'

'Am not.'

'Okay.' Samantha put her hand to her forehead, tried to keep her smile in place. 'Is everything okay?'

MJ shrugged one shoulder, another legacy from his father: dismissive, impatient, more than a little defiant. Samantha decided not to press, not now at any rate.

'You remember you're staying at Granny's house tonight, right?'

'You're going out *again?*'

She was stung by the accusation. Her son was acting like he was some kind of latch-key kid.

'Granny said she's going to make your favourite, lasagne.' Hoping she sounded more positive than she felt, she scanned their faces for even a hint that she was making a mistake; that she was failing.

'Can we have ice cream?' MJ wanted to know, always so quick to pounce on a bartering position. Definitely his father's son, she thought before pushing the thought away.

'Sure.'

Samantha smiled at her boys, grateful that she had managed to navigate another moment in their lives with falling apart at the seams.

God, she thought, she could really do with a night out.

*

When Samantha didn't show up at the cocktail bar, Yvonne didn't think too much of it. They'd known each other almost ten years, and in all that time, her friend had never been on time. She was the kind of woman who'd turn up late for her own funeral.

Even so, when she went outside to grab a cheeky smoke, leaving Colin in the booth, she took the opportunity to call Sam's mobile. The phone rang out. It was probably in the bottom of her bag or something. She left a message anyway.

'Hey, it's me. You better be on your way. I'm getting wasted and Colin's getting fed up talking to me.'

She hung up, smoked her cigarette and went back inside.

A little after eight, they went across the road to the restaurant. They each had a glass of Prosecco while they looked over the menu.

There was still no sign of Samantha.

'Maybe one of the boys is sick,' Colin said, watching her send another text.

'Unless he has bubonic plague, I'm not interested.'

'Come on,' he said, waving a hand. 'You know she's been through the mill lately.'

'So?' Yvonne said, tilting her head.

'Have you ever ordered the terrine here before?' Colin said, changing the subject.

Dinner was nice. They ate, shared a bottle of wine. When Colin went to the bathroom, Yvonne checked her phone.

After dinner, he helped her into her coat and they went outside. He was yawning as he put his hand out for a taxi.

'Let's go home.'

'You go if you want. I'm going to swing by Samantha's house.'

Colin looked at his watch pointedly.

'It's half ten on a school night.'

'Exactly.'

Her husband looked at her, saw her expression and knew he was never going to win this argument. Besides, Samantha's house was on the way, in a fashion, a circular, convoluted fashion.

It wasn't that she was cross, Yvonne told herself on the way there, though she *was* actually, and a little hurt. She was also a little worried: it wasn't like Sam to be a total no-show without at least one text message.

Outside Samantha's gate (honestly, it was such an ugly house, she thought, so like Michael, all money and not a screed of taste), she asked Colin to wait, telling him she'd only be a moment.

She walked up the drive, taking care not to stumble on the gravel in her heels. The curtains at the downstairs windows were drawn, but the lights were on behind them. The slide door on the porch was unlocked, so she yanked it open and stepped in to ring the doorbell. When nobody answered, she bent down and yelled through the letter box.

'Samantha?'

She could hear music from inside the house, but it felt wrong, all of it. *Go back*, a small voice in Yvonne's head warned. *Turn around and get Colin.*

Yvonne Hershey was a lot of things: pushy, competitive, sometimes a little inconsiderate of people's feelings. But she was also brave, and it was this that decided her next course of action. She set her jaw, fully prepared for Samantha to be angry with her for the intrusion. She would accept a telling-off, she decided. It would be worth it. They'd probably laugh about it later, when she stopped being angry about being stood up.

The spare key was under the half-dead cactus; the same place Samantha, somewhat unimaginatively, always left it. With increasing unease, Yvonne let herself into the house and stood in the hall, the walls of which were adorned with pictures of the boys.

'Samantha?' Her voice sounded strange to her own ears: too many false notes, too much emotion in the vocal cords.

Cautiously she pushed open the living room door, and immediately backed up so hard she slammed into the under-stairs cupboard, her hand pressed to her mouth in horror. She heard a strange sound and realised it was her own voice, keening in the back of her throat.

Something thumped upstairs, breaking the spell. In terror she ran from the house and down the drive, screaming Colin's name. He got out of the cab and came running, managing to catch her as she pitched forward, hysterical, pointing back towards the house.

The taxi driver got out too.

'What's happening?'

'Ring the Guards,' Colin ordered, taking control. 'Yvonne, stay here, do you hear me?'

'Hold on, mate.' The driver reached under his seat and produced a nasty-looking wooden club. 'You'd better take this with you.'

Colin accepted the weapon and set off towards the house.

The living room was a horror show. He stared at blood-spattered walls and a body he recognised as Michael Mullins. He hadn't liked the man much in life, but seeing him this way made him feel sick to his stomach. Michael was half off the sofa, one hand on the floor, fingers curled. Colin knew there was nothing he could do for him. Quickly he checked the rest of the ground floor and then proceeded upstairs, very slowly, holding the club out in front of him in both hands.

'Samantha?'

She was in her bedroom, lying across the bed wearing a satin nightie. He crab-walked over to her and put his fingers to her neck; exhaled with relief when he felt a faint pulse.

With his back to the wall, he pulled his phone from the inside of his jacket and called for an ambulance. When he was done, he checked the boys' bedrooms, horrifically aware of his heart beating too hard and fast in his chest. He opened all the wardrobes, using the tip of the club, convinced he was about to be set upon any second. It wasn't until he heard the sirens that he relaxed and went back to Samantha, unsure what to do. His natural instinct was to cover her, protect her dignity. But he had watched enough late-night cop shows to know that contaminating a scene was a big no-no. He was still dithering when the bedroom door creaked open behind him.

The scream died in his throat when he saw Yvonne standing there, her face alabaster white.

'Is she … is she dead?'

She looked so small and scared he went to her immediately and wrapped his arms around her.

'She's alive, but I don't think we should touch her.'

'I heard him, the man who did this, he was here.'

'Well he's gone now, so we can—'

Samantha began to twitch, then to convulse.

'Colin!'

'Oh shit.'

Panicked, he grabbed Samantha and tried to roll her over, terrified that she would harm herself or choke. But as strong as he was, he could barely hold onto her. Suddenly she stiffened, made a strange rattling sound and was still.

'Oh my God, is she …'

Colin stared at his wife, stricken.

'She's not breathing.'

Yvonne Hershey screamed until her throat was raw.

CHAPTER FORTY-NINE

Eli Quinn got the call shortly after three a.m. He roused Miranda from her bed on the way.

Now they were sitting in Yvonne Hershey's kitchen, drinking coffee. Yvonne, still in her clothes from the night before, looked pale and shaken, but she insisted on talking to them while Colin, her husband, excused himself and went upstairs for a shower.

'I can't believe it, I just can't.' Her left leg jiggled up and down non-stop as she spoke.

They were sitting on either side of a long table. Even Miranda, who had almost no interest in interior design, could see that it was a beautiful room. She marvelled that people owned homes like this one in real life. The kitchen alone was probably almost the size of her entire apartment.

'She was so fucking sweet; she was the sweetest person you will ever meet. She didn't deserve this, she didn't deserve any of the shit she had to put up with.'

'No,' Quinn said, reaching for his coffee. It was good, as were the fancy lemon butter cookies. So far he had eaten two and was considering another, though he didn't want to look greedy.

'You mind if I smoke?' Yvonne asked.

'It's your house.'

'You want one?'

'No thank you.'

'I'm trying to quit,' Miranda said.

'Oh yeah? I tried once, it was shit.' She lit a cigarette, blew the match out and took a deep drag. Her hand shook badly.

'I'm very sorry about your friend,' Quinn said. Word had come through from the hospital that Samantha Mullins had died.

Yvonne's bottom lip wobbled and tears spilled down her cheek.

'She … she didn't deserve that,' she repeated.

'No one does.'

'Every time I close my eyes, I see her, you know? I keep thinking I should have gone there sooner, I should have known something was wrong. I could have saved her.'

'You saw Samantha yesterday?'

She nodded. 'I met her at the school gate. Our children go to the same school.'

'How did she seem?'

'I don't know, a little distracted. Giddy.'

'Giddy?'

'Michael was moving back in.' Yvonne dashed at the tears with the heel of her hand. 'Poor cow thought it was a good thing.'

'They'd broken up?'

'He cheated on her, broke her heart into a million pieces, and she forgave him; she was giving the bastard a second chance.'

'You didn't like him.'

She gave him a look that would have withered a lesser mortal.

'That's a pretty accurate assumption, but even he didn't deserve what happened. Oh God, it's so awful.'

'Can you think of anything that had changed recently in Samantha's life? Anything that struck you as unusual?'

'Apart from taking Michael back?' Yvonne tried for a smile but couldn't pull it off. 'Not really. Well, she'd got a job, part-time gig, nothing special. Just answering phones, but she liked it.'

'Where was this?'

'For a printing company, three mornings a week.'

Miranda and Quinn exchanged a look.

'When did she start there?'

'About four months ago. Look, it was a shitty job and the wages were crap, but she liked having some financial independence, you know. It gave her a bit of confidence back, and God knows she needed that after the crap Michael put her through.'

'Do you know the name of the company?'

She told them. Quinn entered it into a search engine and felt a genuine gut-punch when it turned up the company address.

He showed it to Miranda. Her eyes widened.

'She was so happy, you know; for the first time in so long she was really fucking happy. This is all so surreal.' Yvonne put her head in her hands and began crying openly. 'You hear about these things, read about them, but you never think it will happen to you, to someone you love.'

'No,' Miranda said. 'You never do.'

'I mean, why her? She was one of the nicest people you could ever meet.'

'A real sweetheart,' Quinn said softly.

CHAPTER FIFTY

Delia Shawcross's family home was a large house set well back from the road with an unusually long front garden. The exterior was covered in ivy and there was a metal balcony over the front porch, looking out to the Irish Sea.

Margaret Shawcross had answered the door wearing an apron and a smile. Now, as she and Roxy sat down in the living room, she wore neither.

'I'm afraid you've had a wasted trip, Sergeant. Delia no longer lives here.'

Roxy, perched on the edge of the high-backed sofa, regarded Margaret Shawcross with professional interest. The older woman had a pretty decent poker face, she was willing to grant her that, but her eyes told a different story; she looked petrified.

'Can you tell me where she lives now? I'd like to speak to her.'

'What is this in relation to?'

'Delia was a friend of Andrea Colgan. I'm part of the team investigating her murder.'

'They *worked* together,' Margaret said firmly. 'I wouldn't have said they were friends. Look.' She tried to smile, but it was a ghastly effort. 'I don't want you to think I'm being rude. It's just … Delia had a horrific time last year. She lost her fiancé and had a very short but painful breakdown. I want you to know that I think it's terrible what happened to Andrea, but I don't think Delia would be of any use to you. I think talking to her could possibly be detrimental to her health.'

'I'm sorry to hear that. When you say she lost her fiancé …'

'He died, Sergeant.'

'Ah, my condolences.'

'Thank you, it was very sudden.'

'Accident was it?'

Margaret crossed her legs and hugged her knees. Move on, her body language said.

'How long did Delia work for Albas Entertainment?'

'Three years.'

'What does she do now?'

'She's currently between jobs.'

'I see.' Roxy nodded thoughtfully. 'Grief has a way of knocking us for six, doesn't it?'

'Yes, yes it does.' Margaret Shawcross looked at her watch.

'So where is she living these days? I went by her old house, she's not been there for a while I take it.'

'When Declan died, she felt it was too painful to stay there, too many memories.'

'I can understand that. I'd still like to talk to her though. Do you have an address for her?'

'If you leave me your number, I'll get her to call you.'

'Okay, we can do that.'

Margaret left the room to fetch a pen and paper. While she was gone, Roxy got to her feet and looked around. There were numerous photos of what she assumed were various members of the Shawcross family dotted about. She picked up one that looked pretty recent and studied it. In it, a young woman with shoulder-length dark hair was helping a baby toddle over some grass. Roxy had looked up Delia's national ID before she had paid this visit and knew this was her.

'The baby's cute, what's his name?' she asked Margaret when she came back.

Margaret took the photo from Roxy's hand and looked at it. Her expression softened.

'Charlie, his name is Charlie.'

'How old is he?'

'He's one and a half.'

There it was, the flutter of fear again. Now why on earth was this woman so afraid to talk about a baby she clearly loved?

'They're a handful at that age, aren't they?'

'I'm sorry, Sergeant, I don't wish to be rude, but I really have to get on.'

'Then I won't keep you. Here, let me write my number down for you and I'll get out of your hair.'

A few minutes later, Roxy had left the house and was walking down the path back towards the road when a man wearing wellington boots and a floppy green hat entered the garden. He was accompanied by a very chubby brown Labrador.

'Oh hello,' he said when he saw her. 'Don't mind Flossie, she won't bite.'

Roxy reached down and patted the dog on the head.

'She likes to go down onto the beach when the tide's out.' The man pushed his hat back on his head and scratched his forehead.

'You must be Delia's father.'

'That's right.'

'My name is Sergeant Roxanne Malloy.'

She held out her hand and he shook it firmly.

'Malloy, eh? Used to work with a Seamus Malloy, any relation?'

'Not that I know of. I was here to talk to Delia.'

'Delia?' He looked puzzled. 'Delia doesn't live—'

'Ned!'

Roxy and the man turned towards the house. Margaret Shawcross was standing at the front door, her hand to her throat. She looked like she was going to have a nervous breakdown. The Labrador ambled up to her and went inside.

'What?'

'You're wanted on the phone right away, right now.'

'Oh.' He threw his eyes up to heaven and grinned at Roxy. 'There's never a dull moment, and don't let anyone tell you otherwise.'

'I won't,' Roxy said, watching Margaret Shawcross frantically beckoning him into the house.

Charlie, she thought, a year and a half. Delia might be off the books, but it was unlikely her son was. He'd need vaccinations, for a start.

She looked back at the house. Ned had gone inside, but Margaret Shawcross was staring at her with a strange intensity. Roxy couldn't leave fast enough.

CHAPTER FIFTY-ONE

The wolf was wounded.

Getting out of bed was agony. His back hurt, and when he stood up, his right ankle was so badly swollen he could barely put weight on it.

The pain was incredible.

Hobbling, he made it from the bed to his desk and dropped into his chair. As soon as he switched on his computer, he felt a surge of anger and disquiet.

Weakness was not acceptable, and he had failed.

She would have been perfect. She had such warmth and natural kindness. It was abundantly clear that she was worthy of his love. She was maternal too; she understood the needs of boys and men.

Celine … He thought of her now, felt her ghost in the air mocking him, enjoying *Schadenfreude*. Balling his fists and pressing them to his temples, he rocked back and forth, moaning softly.

None of this was his fault. It was the women; they held all the cards, they were biological blackmailers. They tempted and teased, inflaming emotions and passions beyond boiling point, and then …

And then they did not deliver.

What did they expect?

Was he supposed to just *take* it?

Take it for ever?

He had not meant to harm Celine – he truly believed that. If she hadn't laughed, if she had let him explain his feelings, things would have turned out differently.

That afternoon stood out in his mind now in stark relief. The funeral: dry-eyed relatives patting him on the shoulder, his bitch mother, fetching in her widow's weeds, holding the arm of her *companion*, a sloe-eyed creep with pockmarked cheeks. He knew from their body language that they were fucking, the wanton whore. When she hugged him, he swore at her, and was glad when she recoiled.

'Easy there, big man,' the creep said, no doubt protecting his meal ticket.

Later, back at the house, he'd stood in the doorway of his father's bedroom, staring at his bed. He was gone; his mother was gone.

Celine was gone.

The emptiness washed over him, unmoored him.

Then the doorbell rang, and there on the step was Celine, carrying a shopping bag.

'I thought we'd wake the dead,' she said.

The wolf didn't understand the expression, but he was so happy to see her it didn't matter.

The next three hours were the happiest of his life. They sat in the kitchen, listening to music on the radio, drinking spiced rum from crystal glasses. Alcohol loosened the wolf's tongue, and near the end of the bottle he found himself telling her his true feelings; painting for her the future he had planned for them both.

At first she had smiled, patted his hand, but gradually she withdrew, her brow furrowed, her expression one of ... what had it been? Pity?

Then he tried to kiss her.

Even thinking how he'd lunged at her filled him with anger and shame. When she finally squirmed free from his grasp, she wiped her mouth with the back of her hand.

And laughed.

Wounded, he reached for the empty bottle and swung it.

He had never meant to hurt her. He had never meant any of this.

Later, he rolled her body in a rug from the formal living room and dragged it downstairs and outside to the much-neglected garden. Frightened and crying, he put her in a wheelbarrow, brought her down to the bottom of the garden and buried her under the mulch pile his father had been cultivating for his roses for as long as he could remember.

He burned her bag and her shoes in the grate in the kitchen, and waited.

Days went by, then weeks. Nobody came. He began to wonder about this and made casual enquires with the agency she worked with, who told him she was under investigation for larceny. Apparently sunny, sweet Celine had been helping herself from the various old cripples she'd been working with.

He wondered what she had taken from this house.

Six months went by. Sometimes he stood at the kitchen window and looked down the garden, thinking about her mouldering there with the mulch, returning to nature.

It pleased him and gave him comfort. Later that year, he tended to his father's roses and was rewarded with a bumper grow of rich, tumbling yellow blooms.

It was a sign, he decided, a sign she had forgiven him.

Now he was not so sure.

He glanced at the empty space on the wall where his sword usually hung and felt a genuine stab of loss. It was a Shinwa Imperial Dragon Handmade Katana and he'd ordered it online many years before he birthed the Imperative. Since then it had become not just a weapon but also a symbol of his journey, a talisman of sorts.

Its loss was a source of intense anger and frustration.

He hung his head in his hands. They would find it; he knew that with absolute certainty. They would find it and they would come.

It was as inevitable as night following day.

But he would not succumb to their will, not now, not ever. He would show them what he was made of, and he would prove once and for all that nothing mattered, not them and not him.

Only the Imperative mattered.

His manifesto would make him a legend. His manifesto would change the world of men forever.

CHAPTER FIFTY-TWO

The moment Roxy arrived at the station, she felt it: there was almost a physical wave of nervous energy surrounding the place.

Curious, she went directly to the incident room and found it packed.

Cora waved when she saw her, looking both nervous and excited. Roxy squeezed between the extra bodies and make her way towards her.

'What's going on?'

'Didn't you hear what happened?'

'No, what?'

'The Sweetheart Killer struck again last night, only this time he was disturbed and nearly caught. Apparently he jumped from a window to get away, and after a search they found a sword hidden in some bushes near the house. They reckon it's what killed Kilbride and Bannon and the man from last night.'

'So what's the plan?'

'I don't know. Word went out half an hour ago that Quinn wants all available hands on deck.'

The incident room door opened and Quinn and Miranda entered. They both looked like they needed a good night's sleep, but when Miranda scanned the assembled officers, Roxy saw the determined gleam in her eyes and knew this was it.

Show time.

'Listen up, people.' Quinn clapped his hands together to quieten the room. 'As you know, last night the killer struck again.

He killed two innocent people and destroyed the lives of two more families.' He looked around, a muscle in his jaw bunching. 'This stops here. This morning Sergeant Lynn and I made a series of calls and have come up with a list of people we are going to interview today. That list will be sent to your ENs at the end of this briefing, as will our most recent profile. You will work in pairs. You will report back to me or Sergeant Lynn as you work through the names assigned to you.'

'What are we dealing with here?' an officer asked.

'Samantha Mullins, Lorraine Dell and Estelle Roberts all worked in the Park West Business Park, but they worked for different companies. What connects them? We ruled out couriers, because they stop at reception. Who does that leave? Maintenance guys, security, building managers, who else is there?'

'Food delivery,' Fletcher said. 'A lot of these places order lunch in daily. Nobody takes much notice of the delivery guys, and they could be in and out of every building every single day.'

'Unusual hours,' Roxy muttered under her breath.

'We also turned up a weapon, a bloodstained sword found in a garden three houses down from the Mullins residence. Forensics have it now; as soon as we know anything, you will too.'

Quinn leaned his hands on the podium. 'This man, whoever he is, has killed six, possibly seven people. Do not underestimate him. If you speak to anyone who gives you pause or sets off any alarm bells, call for backup immediately.'

He looked around.

'Are we clear?'

'Yes, sir,' the squad replied as one.

Quinn nodded. 'Make sure you are properly attired; stab vests are mandatory, so wear them. I don't want to hear any bullshit about them being uncomfortable.' He took a breath, drew himself up to his full height. 'I will assign your partners within the hour. I want everyone ready, no exception. We leave as one.'

He nodded to the group and walked out.

Cora grabbed Roxy's arm and squeezed so tight it hurt.

'This is it, we're going to be part of history.' She made a strange little squeaking sound. 'Oh my God, I've got to call Joe.'

'You ready, Malloy?' Miranda was watching her.

'You mean the big chief thinks I'm up to asking questions?'

'You rather stay here, type up more reports?'

'Hell, no!'

'Then take a note from Simmons' playbook. Put your big-girl pants on, and don't forget your stab vest.'

'You really think we'll catch him?'

'We're going to shake the nest and see what falls out.'

Lynn pulled her own stab vest over her shoulders and fastened the Velcro straps as tight as they could possibly go.

When the teams were announced half an hour later, Roxy was astounded to see that she was partnered with Quinn.

CHAPTER FIFTY-THREE

'Ready? Quinn asked Roxy as they pulled into a parking spot. They were in Park West Business Park, a vast purpose-built community of over a hundred businesses, all operating out of identical blank two-storey flat-roofed buildings. Soulless, Roxy thought as she unbuckled her belt and got out, stretching her back and shoulders. She'd absolutely hate to have to come here every day.

This was the third food delivery service they had visited that morning, and so far, nothing. Quinn had said he wasn't interested in anyone complaining about the stab vests, so she didn't, but damn, they *were* uncomfortable.

Quinn checked his EN.

'This is the place. Come on.'

Roxy followed him inside.

'Hi,' he said to the bored-looking girl behind the counter. 'We've an appointment with Mr Dwami.'

'Take a seat.' She leaned her lips to a thin microphone and bellowed, 'Mr Dwami, reception!'

Shortly afterwards, a squat, sweaty man wearing an olive-green suit that needed a good dry-cleaning burst through a door and bore down on them at a frightening pace. He was dark-skinned, badly shaven and had the air of a man who thought having only twenty-four hours in a single day was a bloody rip-off.

Quinn introduced them and showed his identification. Dwami barely looked at it.

'You're the owner of Nom-Noms?' Quinn asked. 'Food delivery?'

'Yes, yes, but I told you everything on the phone. I don't have anything more to add to what I already said!'

'Still, we have questions.'

'You have to do this now?' Dwami said, wringing his hands. 'I have a full docket.'

'We can do it here or back at the station,' Quinn said, smiling.

Dwami's face fell. 'All right all right, you come with me.'

He barked something at the receptionist and led them back through the door he'd come through, along a short corridor and into an open-plan kitchen.

It was a long, thin room, devoid of any natural light. Rows of stainless-steel tables lined the walls between shelves containing endless containers of food and condiments. At the centre of the room were four stoves, back to back, the rings occupied by bubbling pots and sizzling pans. The heat and smell of cooking was so overpowering Roxy broke into a sweat almost immediately.

'Come!' Dwami said over his shoulder, and they followed him up a set of metal steps into a cluttered office that overlooked the floor below.

Dwami flopped into a desk chair, pulled a red hanky from his pocket and dabbed at his face.

'Sit, sit.'

Quinn and Roxy sat on plastic garden chairs. Roxy looked around. The office reminded her a little of Jerome Falstaff's apartment: stacks of paper, boxes and cartons everywhere.

'Now.' Dwami leaned forward, straining the buttons on his jacket to breaking point. 'What you want?'

It took a while and a lot of backtracking to explain. Roxy watched Dwami carefully as he listened to Quinn outline the case using broad strokes, offering a slightly tempered profile of the man they were looking for.

'It's a long shot,' Quinn said.

'Uh,' Dwami said, and made a scornful face. 'Sounds like Harry Potter.'

'I assure you this person is very real,' Roxy said, a little annoyed.

'No, no, is real, it's Harry Potter.'

Quinn and Roxy exchanged a puzzled glance.

'Ach.' Dwami struggled to his feet, opened the door and bellowed, 'Jasmine!'

After a minute, a rather pretty girl entered the office, nodded to Quinn and Roxy and looked at her boss, who was back behind his desk. She wore white overalls, and a hairnet covered her blonde hair.

'Is everything all right, Mr Dwami?'

'Tell, tell about Harry Potter.'

She looked at Quinn and Roxy again and in an irked but resigned voice said, 'What's he done now?'

'Who?' Quinn wanted to know.

'Quentin, Quentin Williams. That's who you're looking for, right?'

'That depends. What's he like?'

'Creepy,' Jasmine said, and there was no mistaking the conviction with which she spoke.

'Creepy how?'

'He's always staring, you know? Doesn't talk much, complete weirdo.'

'Does he do the food deliveries?'

'Yeah, him and Anto.'

'Anto?'

'Anthony Collins; he'd be the guy you should speak to.'

'Is he here now?'

'Downstairs.' She glanced at her boss. 'Will I get him?'

She got him. Anto was a skinny kid with a quiff.

'Harry?' Anto asked. 'What's he done?'

'We'd just like to talk to him.'

Anto shrugged. 'He's not in today.'

'He called in sick,' Mr Dwami said.

'You could have told us that at the start,' Quinn said. 'Go on, Anto, what kind of guy is Mr Williams?'

'Dunno. Quiet, big gamer, plays in all them crazy online tournaments. Won a shitload of them … oh, sorry, Mr Dwami.'

'You ever hear him talk about women?'

'Are you serious?' Anto grinned. 'Harry's afraid of his own shadow; no way he'd go near a woman in real life.'

'I didn't ask if he went near them, I asked if he talked about them.'

'Not to me. He doesn't talk much to anyone. I don't think he likes people much.'

'Why?'

'He gets twitchy around groups. Sometimes the lads slag him off a bit, nothing to it, bit of banter, but he goes real red in the face, you know?'

Roxy, who had endured plenty of people gossiping about her behind her back, and to her face at times, could imagine exactly how it made Williams feel.

'You bully him,' she said.

'Nah.' Anto shook his head. 'Like I said, banter.'

'Does he ever ask you to stop?'

That rattled him.

'Here, don't be making this into a big thing. *Everyone* here gets a slagging, it's part of the bleeding job.'

'What kind of slagging did you subject him to?'

'What is this?' Anto looked at his boss. 'What's the deal here? I didn't do nuthin' wrong.'

'Please, answer question so we can get back to work.'

'Jesus, I don't know. 'Bout how he was always wearing black and shit. One of the lads found a comic he was reading, mad porn with monsters and shit like that, so he got a bit of ribbing about that, you know, the usual.'

Quinn raised an eyebrow. 'Did he ever laugh along?'

Anto shrugged. 'He never said stop, okay. He never said nuthin'.'

No, Roxy thought, he wouldn't, because to a pack of wolves like you lot it wouldn't have made any damn difference.

Back at the car, Roxy sat in and put her belt on.

'Do you think he's our guy?' she asked Quinn.

He shrugged and started the engine. 'Probably not. He's probably just some lonely kid. I'll give his name to Sergeant Lynn and get her to pay him a visit, rule him out.' He sighed. 'Right, where to next?'

CHAPTER FIFTY-FOUR

Miranda parked the car under a horse-chestnut tree and got out, savouring the brief respite from chatter. And brief it was, for the very second Cora climbed out, she was off again. Miranda was finding new admiration for Roxy Malloy. If she herself had been partnered with Cora, she would have throttled the junior officer long ago.

'This is nice, isn't it?' Cora said, hitching up her trousers. 'I've never been over in this part of town before. Do you reckon these are all one-family homes?'

'I imagine so.'

'How much do you think one of these would go for?' Cora asked.

'I think if you had to ask you couldn't afford one.'

'Size of the gardens! Mad how the city is always looking for land to build on and there's all this space just sitting here going to waste.'

Miranda put on her hat and checked the name on the land registry. Williams, Richard.

'Come on,' she said. 'Let's get this over with.'

'Can we go for lunch after this one? I'm starving.'

'We've still got another four names to check.'

'I'm a quick eater.'

'We'll see.' Miranda pushed open one of the tall iron gates and began to walk towards the house. Cora fell into step beside her.

'Don't look after their gardens very well, do they? If this was my house I'd cobble-lock the drive for a start; my Joe reckons cobble-lock's more hardwearing than concrete.'

Up close, Miranda could see the imposing house was badly neglected: gutters were hanging off, the paint was peeling, and many of the windows were boarded up.

'My nan had her drive done with tarmac.' Cora was still rambling on. 'Cracked the second year it was down, and it doesn't drain properly. Went to get the crowd that did it and the phone numbers were all deactivated.'

They climbed the stone steps to the huge front door. The wood was warped and one of the lower panels was missing. The doorbell was rusted and didn't work, so Miranda lifted the knocker and gave it a few hard smacks.

As soon as the young man opened the door, she knew something wasn't right; she could feel it, sense it. Instinctively she turned her body to the side and rested her hand on her gun.

'Good afternoon, I'm looking for Quentin Williams.'

The man looked at her. He was about twenty-seven or twenty-eight. Pale-skinned and considerably overweight. He wore glasses that were several years out of date and his clothes were grubby and ill-fitting.

'Sir?'

'That's me,' he said, his voice creaky as though from lack of use.

'Sir, my name is Sergeant Lynn, this is my colleague Officer Simmons. We were hoping to ask you a few questions.'

'You should come inside.'

Though it was the last thing she wanted to do, Miranda removed her hat and stepped through the door. Cora followed.

'This is a great house,' Cora said, trying to be friendly, but the man barely acknowledged her. Miranda stared at the huge mound of mail behind the door. There had to be at least eight months' worth spread out across the black-and-white floor tiles.

'Sir,' she said. 'Maybe it would be better if we talked down at the station.'

'Sure, I'll go get my coat.' He began to limp away.

'You hurt, Mr Williams?' Miranda asked.

He didn't answer and disappeared around a bend at the end of the hallway.

Cora looked around, wrinkling her nose.

'It smells weird in here, like … mouldy or something.'

She entered the room on the left. Miranda, feeling more and more uneasy, followed. It was, she guessed after her eyes had adjusted to the gloom, a living room of some kind, rather formal: a chaise longue, bookcases, a large piano in one corner. It smelled of dust and mouse droppings, and there were cobwebs everywhere.

'Hate seeing these old places fall to rack and ruin, don't you?' Cora was saying. But Miranda said nothing. She was thinking. Quentin Williams hadn't asked what they wanted to talk about; in fact, it seemed as though he had been expecting them. Now why was that?

'Cora,' she said softly, reaching for her arm.

'Must take an absolute fortune to heat, though—'

'Cora, shut up.'

Cora looked at her. Miranda put her finger to her lips.

'Mr Williams?'

No answer.

Keeping her eyes on where she had last seen him, Miranda took her radio from her belt and spoke quietly into it.

'Dispatch, this is Sergeant Lynn. Officer Simmons are I are at 48 Temple Road, repeat, 48 Temple Road, we request backup.'

She glanced at Cora. She looked scared stiff.

'Simmons, listen to me. Go outside and wait for the backup.' Miranda put her radio back into its holder and undid her gun clip.

'What are you going to do?'

'I'm going to see where Mr Williams has gone.'

'I'm not leaving you, Sergeant.'

'I'm giving you a direct order, Simmons. Go outside and wait.'

Cora was as white as a sheet and looked like she was going to burst into tears any second, but still she shook her head. 'No.'

Goddammit, Miranda thought, chatty *and* brave, what were the odds?

'All right, then draw your weapon and stick close to me, okay? And for God's sake, Simmons, don't shoot me by mistake.' She gave the younger woman's arm a squeeze. 'Let's go.'

They crept down the hall, rubber-soled shoes soft on the tiles, their ear pricked for any sign of movement. They passed three doors, two on the right, one on the left. Miranda tried the handles; they were all locked.

At the end of the hall, she walked down two steps and paused, gun raised. There were stairs going down to her right, and what looked like a kitchen ahead. She pushed open the door, found a greasy light switch and flipped it on. The room was filthy and, like the rest of the house, didn't look like it had been used in a very long time. Plates were piled in the sink and there were takeaway cartons everywhere.

'Sergeant,' Cora whispered, and pointed.

Miranda saw what she was looking at: a large stain on the floor by the kitchen table, very old, very dark.

Blood.

'Stay close.'

That just left the basement. Every fibre in Miranda's body told her not to go down there.

'I'm going down there,' she said, pointing with her gun.

Down they went, slowly, step by step, until they reached the basement floor. Five doors led off the little hall, and it was so gloomy Miranda could barely see two feet in front of her.

Which one?

She inched forward, Cora right on her heels, breathing so loudly the neighbours could probably hear her.

The room to the front looked like an old surgery or something. It was large, tiled, with a sink at one end and a metal surgical table at the other. Miranda swept the room and pulled open one of the window shutters. Ancient charts of dogs and cats hung from the walls.

'What is this place?' She lowered her weapon and looked around.

Cora wrinkled her nose again.

'Lynn, I think I can smell—'

The door behind them slammed shut. Cora spun round as Quentin Williams leaped from his hiding place with a blood-curdling scream and plunged a knife into her chest.

'Cora!'

Cora staggered backwards. Miranda could see the blade was buried so deep only the handle was visible.

'Sergeant?' Cora said, her voice small, like a child's. Blood bubbled over her lip and she collapsed sideways onto the floor.

Miranda had a clear shot on Williams. Without thinking, she raised her weapon, closed one eye and squeezed the trigger.

The shot caught Williams right in the chest, slamming him against the door. He smiled as he slid to the floor. Miranda had never before seen such a look of triumph and hate. She had a split second to wonder what the hell he was smiling about when the basement exploded.

CHAPTER FIFTY-FIVE

The blast had blown out the basement window and damaged some of the ground floor, but the house was old and sturdy and the upper floors were relatively unscathed.

The fire crew found Miranda under a pile of rubble, injured but alive. The heavy ceramic sink had saved her life.

She drifted in and out of consciousness as she was carried outside, her ears ringing, half deaf, coughing up blood and dirt.

'Cora?' she asked every blurred face she saw. 'Cora?'

Nobody answered. She wasn't sure if she was speaking properly; shook her head to clear it and could not.

Someone wiped blood and dust from her face and put a mask over her mouth. It helped, made it easier to breathe. Good: she had to get up and find Cora.

Somebody rested a hand on her shoulder, pushed her back down. She tried to bat it away.

Then Quinn was there. She tried to focus on him, could see his mouth moving. After a few tries, she shook her head, pointed to her ears. Over his shoulder she could see Roxy Malloy standing on the patchy grass. She was crying, tears tracking streaks through the dirt on her face.

Dazed, Miranda lifted her hand to the side of her head. Her fingers came away bloody. Blood was running down her face from somewhere in her scalp. She turned her head in the opposite direction and witnessed something that would stay with her for the rest of her life.

A firefighter was kneeling on the grass, working on Cora. He moved from chest compressions to mouth-to-mouth and back to compressions. Miranda watched, feeling useless. Lights flashed, more people arrived, paramedics. Everyone was showered in dust and debris; the air was full of particles and white dust. Still the man worked, mouth, chest, mouth, chest.

Someone leaned over Miranda and began to speak to her. Miranda blinked slowly, tried to concentrate, tried to force her mind to work, to think.

The man shone a light in her eyes, held up a finger. She tried to follow it as best she could, but it blurred and she was no longer sure what she was supposed to do.

More people came. A woman with a ponytail put a different mask over her face and a brace around her neck. Another man helped slide her onto a stretcher. The first man was gesturing to them, then to her. She could still see Quinn's mouth moving.

Her vision began to fade, starting with the edges. She wanted to tell the man about it, thought about tapping him on the back, but she couldn't move her arms.

She couldn't do anything.

Except lose consciousness.

When she opened her eyes, she was lying in a hospital bed. Her mouth was dry and her head ached so badly it hurt to move her eyes.

'Hey.'

She managed to roll her eyes to the right. Quinn was sitting in a chair by her bed with a magazine on his lap. He looked filthy and exhausted. She tried a word, failed, and got it the second time.

'Cora?'

He looked at her, shook his head.

'She didn't make it.'

Miranda closed her eyes for a long time. When she opened them again, she had only one question.

'What happened?'

'The prick had the basement rigged, booby-trapped with old gas barrels. If you'd gone in through the conservatory out back, you'd have lost your head to a shotgun blast.'

He dug a photo from his pocket and held it up close to her face. It was of a couple, the man in his sixties, the woman much younger and unhappy-looking. Standing between them was a sullen-faced teenager. Miranda squinted, added a few years and a few pounds to the boy.

'That's him.'

'That's Quentin Williams, aka the Sweetheart Killer.'

'He's so young.'

'We found his "manifesto" in his bedroom. The guy was a fucking crackpot.'

'His manifesto?'

'Nothing but reams and reams of self-obsessed weaponised misogyny. Do you know what an incel is?'

'No.'

'No, me neither until now, but apparently it stands for "involuntary celibate", shitheads who think society is to blame for their lack of a sex life, with women as the number one block to their happiness.' Quinn shook his head. He looked angry and a little sickened. 'I've been reading this guy's crap since yesterday; messed up doesn't even begin to cover it. He was escalating, too, Samantha Mullins was supposed to be his final single "rose"; he was planning to keep her, can you believe that? Like she was some kind of sexual pet. I mean, this guy was off the charts. If you and Simmons hadn't ...' He looked away. 'You did it, Miranda, you stopped this guy, you and Simmons.'

Miranda closed her eyes, saw the look on Cora's face; heard her say, 'Sergeant?' before she fell.

She did not open her eyes again until she was sure Quinn had left.

CHAPTER FIFTY-SIX

The house was easy to find. The old man from the local shop who had given Roxy directions had been spot on.

It was a small cottage surrounded by gorse at the end of a short lane, overlooking a rocky field that sloped down towards the Atlantic.

Roxy parked the car, got out and took a lungful of fresh sea air. Gulls screamed overhead and swooped below road level, riding eddies and gusts, effortless in their movements.

She walked up the short path and knocked on the door. She heard footsteps approaching and held up her ID.

The fear in Delia Shawcross's eyes was a visceral thing, and it bloomed the moment she opened the door and saw her standing there.

'I'm sorry,' she said. 'I can't talk now, I was about to go out.'

She tried to close the door, but Roxy blocked it with her foot.

If Quinn had been here, he might have tried reason, empathy, charm, flattery: all the gifts he had at his disposal, all the things it took to be a detective. Roxy knew right at that moment that she had none of those things. But she had other skills, like persistence, doggedness and physicality.

'Delia, you do have to talk to me; you *need* to talk to me.'

'Do you have a warrant?'

Roxy hardened her voice. 'You'll notice I'm not in uniform, but if that's how you want to play it, we can do that, get a judge involved and make this official. I can go away and come back with a colleague or two, a squad car the neighbours can gawk at, and a social worker for young Charlie. Do you want that?'

Hearing Roxy utter her son's name was like a slap. Delia's head jerked backwards, her eyes grew wide, her expression changed from one of anger to resignation.

'That is not fair,' she said, her voice almost a whisper.

'No, it's not.'

They stood, neither budging. Roxy heard a blackbird singing in the still bare branches of the tree behind her. Spring was coming, rebirth.

With a defeated moan, Delia opened the door, ushering Roxy into a hall with wooden beams in the ceiling, limestone tiles on the floor. She wrapped her mauve cardigan tight around her body. She was thin, a little gaunt. She looked like someone who didn't eat much, didn't sleep much, someone weighed down by unspoken burdens.

The kitchen to the rear of the house was a surprise. Roxy had been expecting something poky and dark, cottagey. Instead she entered a double-height room with an exposed brick wall at one end, a hi-tech ultra-modern kitchen at the other. Then again, she thought as she reassessed her thoughts, Delia could probably afford it.

She took a seat at the granite-topped island and watched as Delia walked to the double fridge, opened one side and pulled out a bottle of white wine.

'Want a drink?'

'No.'

'Do you mind if I have one?'

'It's your house.'

Delia made a strange sound, but she got a glass off a shelf, poured a very healthy measure and gulped half of it down immediately. Once she'd taken a second mouthful, she looked at Roxy with less fear and a lot more loathing.

'Where's your son?'

'He's upstairs, asleep.'

'You realise that if you lie to me, Delia, I'll get a court order for Charlie's DNA. I don't need much: a cheek swab, some of his hair with the root intact.'

'You're a bitch, you know that?'

'I've been called worse.'

'I'll bet.'

Delia gulped her wine and refilled her glass.

'How did you find me anyway?'

'Charlie's vaccination records. You used your mother's maiden name.'

'Shit.' Delia shook her head. 'I was never very good at subterfuge.'

Roxy leaned forward, resting her arms on the granite.

'Charlie is Gregory Milton's son, isn't he? The TV shrink?'

Delia's look could have stopped a charging bull elephant.

'No, he's *my* son.'

'Immaculate conception, was it?'

'Fuck you.'

'You were Milton's PR before Andrea.'

'So what?'

Did you have an affair with Milton? Did it go bad? Is that why you quit Albas?'

'No.'

'So what was it then? A one night stand?'

Delia took another drink and closed her eyes. Her hand holding the glass was shaking.

'Look Delia, I wouldn't be here if I had another option. Andrea Colgan was your friend, now she's dead and I'm trying to understand why. Talk to me, Delia. Tell me what you know. What happened between you and Milton?'

Delia pulled out a chair and sat down. After a moment she lowered her head.

'I can't.'

'Suit yourself.' Roxy got to her feet. 'The hard way then.'

'No – please don't do this.'

'I'm sorry, it's my job.'

'Jesus.' Delia glanced at the ceiling, took a long deep breath. 'You're a real bitch.'

'So you said.'

By the time she was done, Delia had finished the wine, though she showed no signs of drunkenness. She stared at Roxy, holding the stem of the empty glass in her right hand, her eyes clear.

'He's a rapist,' Roxy said, disgusted.

'He doesn't see it like that.'

'Bullshit. Sex without consent is rape.'

'How do you prove you didn't give consent?' Delia glanced at her sourly. 'You don't understand. Gregory Milton is a flirt, he's charming, you think he's on your side, you think he's your friend.' She shook her head. 'Next thing you know you wake up naked with no idea how you got there.'

'Why didn't you report him?'

'To who?'

'To us.'

Delia laughed bitterly.

'It would be my word against his. Please, I've seen what happens to women who accuse men like Milton of rape.

'You must have known he'd carry on attacking women.'

Delia looked down into her empty glass.

'What happened next?'

'I found out I was pregnant.'

'With Charlie.'

'Right, I knew right away it was because of him. Declan… Declan couldn't have children.'

'You decided to go ahead with the pregnancy.'

'Charlie is innocent in all this, none of this is his fault.'

'Why does he do it?' Roxy wanted to know. 'He's rich, famous, good-looking if you like that kind of thing. I don't get it.'

'The man is a monster,' Delia said, emphasising the word. 'When I confronted him he told me I was delusional, that I'd come on to him. He likes it, he likes the power. He likes knowing he has implanted his seed, he likes knowing his progeny are out there.'

'Do you have any idea how many children he's fathered?'

She shook her head. 'How would I know? He's fifty-five. God knows how long he's been doing this.'

'Tell me what happened when you went to Dy Anderson.'

Delia looked away.

'That was the worst part. I thought … Dy was always talking about the company as family, I really thought he would support me, I thought he'd … he'd *do* something about Milton.'

'And did he?'

'Sure, look around you. This is my reward for not saying anything; this is my gilded prison. Do you like it?'

Upstairs a child began to cry.

Delia stood up, brushed her hand back from her forehead and straightened her shoulder.

'My son needs me, Sergeant. I'm sure you can find your own way out.'

'I'm not leaving without Charlie's DNA.'

'After everything I told you, you're going to push this further?'

Roxy got to her feet too.

'After everything you told me I'm going to make sure that bastard never has an opportunity to hurt another woman again.' She looked grim. 'This is not a negotiation, Delia. Don't worry, I know, I'm a bitch.'

CHAPTER FIFTY-SEVEN

Ever since she was a kid, Roxy had hated the media, an industry that seemed to thrive so magnificently on the misery of others.

But now, as she watched the clip of Gregory Milton being led by Quinn to a waiting squad car, surrounded by a horde of photographers, she allowed herself a smile.

'I like that you parked the car across the street, sir: gave the scrum plenty of time to take pictures.'

'That was your collar,' Quinn said. 'Should have been you taking the pervert down. You got the DNA match from Delia Shawcross's son so we could match it against Andrea Colgan's foetus. He'd never have given his consent, that's for sure. It would have dragged on through the courts for ever.'

She glanced at him; he was sitting in a chair, feet up on the desk, eating something … something that looked disgusting.

'What are you eating?'

'This?' He waved the offending article. 'It's a coddle wrap.'

'A what?'

'Jaysus, Malloy, and I thought you were a Dub.'

'I am a Dub.'

'And you don't know what coddle is? What's the world coming to at all?'

The incident room door opened and Gussy's secretary Nancy stuck her head through the gap.

'Sergeant Malloy? The superintendent would like a word.'

Roxy glanced at Quinn.

'Don't keep the man waiting.'

Gussy was scribbling away when she entered.

'Ah, Sergeant Malloy, there you are, come in, come in, sit down.'

Roxy sat.

'I saw the news.'

'Yes, sir.'

Gussy's moustache twitched as he leaned back in his chair.

'I also saw your report.'

'Sir?'

'You want to arrest Dy Anderson, am I correct?'

'Yes, sir.'

'May I ask why?'

'I believe he killed Andrea Colgan.'

'Yes, I thought you'd say that. Though I find it hard to understand when your colleague hauled Gregory Milton in for the exact same crime.'

'I believe I'm wrong. Not about Milton being a rapist, but about him being a killer.'

'The evidence says otherwise. You know we found Andrea's phone and laptop after a search of his home.'

'Yes, how convenient.' Roxy looked at Gussy and spread her hands in exasperation. 'Sir, there's something wrong here. I can feel it.'

'So you've said.' Gussy rubbed his forehead. 'What more evidence do you need, Sergeant? A recording of Milton committing the act itself?'

'No, but—'

Gussy held up a hand. 'It might have escaped your notice, Sergeant, but what you have on your hands right now is a win. Your colleagues will benefit from it, you will benefit from it, and I will benefit from it. You had your detractors and you proved them wrong.' He shrugged. 'Even the Commissioner is happy.'

'Oh that will surely help me sleep better at night.'

'Don't be sarcastic, Sergeant.'

'My apologies.'

'You need to learn how to choose your battles and take your victories where you find them.'

'Where in the Bible does it say that?'

Gussy picked up his pen. 'Good afternoon, Sergeant, your request is denied. Do close the door on your way out.'

She left.

Downstairs, Miranda Lynn had arrived on crutches. She was still technically off duty, but nobody dared give her a hard time about being there.

'Hey,' Roxy said. 'How are you?'

'Getting there. Sore, still a little deaf, you know.'

'Sure, it's good to see you.'

'Thanks.' Miranda looked down, took a breath. 'Quinn said you went to Cora's funeral.'

'I did,' Roxy said, softening her voice.

'I wanted to be there.'

'I know, Miranda. Her family understood.'

'They sent me flowers in the hospital, can you believe that?'

'They seem like nice people.'

Miranda lowered herself carefully onto a chair.

'She was a good person, you know.'

'I know.'

'I should have made her wait outside.'

Roxy put her hands in her pockets.

'I knew Officer Simmons, Sergeant. When she made her mind up about something, nothing on this earth would have changed it.'

They were silent for a moment.

'How did it go with Gussy?' Miranda asked. 'Quinn said you have reservations about the Colgan killing.'

'I'm not to rock the win-win boat.' Roxy threw herself into her chair and kicked it backwards until it rolled to a stop at the wall.

'For what it's worth,' Miranda said, 'he's probably right.'

'Explain.'

'You have a guilty man bang to rights with evidence he cannot deny. If you introduce doubt, there's a possibility that a good barrister could use it and get Milton off, and no guarantee Anderson would be charged with anything at all.'

'I don't like it.'

'Of course you don't.' Miranda smiled. 'You don't see yourself, do you, Malloy?'

'Rhetorical question, does anyone?'

'Most people are self-aware to a certain degree, but not you.'

Roxy sighed. 'What have I done or not done to warrant another of your lectures?'

'You think that's what I do? Lecture?'

'Sometimes.'

'Maybe I do. It's how I make my thoughts known.' Miranda struggled to her feet again. 'You won, Sergeant Malloy. If you don't do something stupid in the meantime, Gussy will rubber-stamp your promotion because of this. Milton's been kicked off his show, his reputation is in tatters. He's not in a position of power any longer. He'll do jail time, isn't that enough?'

'Not for me.' Roxy said. 'Not even close.'

'You'll learn,' Miranda said, and hobbled towards the door. 'Pick your battles, Sergeant, it's the only way to survive.'

Roxy stood at the front of the ferry, watching as it approached the heavily guarded pier of Lambay Island, where the huge fortress prison overlooked the bay. When it docked, she made her way to administration, left her ID and weapons behind the desk, got a temporary index code imprinted on the back of her right hand, and accompanied an armed guard through a series of barriers, down a long hall that smelled strongly of disinfectant.

They stopped outside a metal door.

'You know the drill, right? No touching, no passing of items, no taking of items.'

Roxy nodded.

'Proceed.'

She raised her hand to a screen, waited for it to read her barcode and unlock the door.

She stepped inside.

It had been many years since she had laid eyes on her father. He had aged, but not dramatically so. His hair carried more white; his face, thin like hers, had a few more lines, but other than that he looked pretty much the same.

Prison life clearly suited him.

'Roxanne.'

Still, it was hard not to shiver, hearing her name on his lips.

She sat down in a chair on the other side of the metal table bolted to the floor.

'You're looking …' he tilted his head to one side, cool, appraising, like he was judging stock, 'a little—'

'I'm not interested in how you think I look.'

'I see,' he said. 'Then to what do I owe the honour?'

'How do you do it?'

'Can you be more specific?'

'How do you carry on, write, eat, sleep, walk, talk?'

'I imagine in much the same way you do, albeit with less variety of places to go.'

'I don't have blood on my hands, though.'

He sat very still, studying her intently.

'No,' he said, after a while. 'You don't.'

'You could have done things differently, you could have …' She faltered, suddenly aware that she had no idea if what she was going to say was true or not. 'You murdered Francis Hill in cold blood.'

'He deserved to die.'

She narrowed her eyes. 'You know they might consider letting you out some day if you'd show a little remorse.'

'Why would I do that?'

'Because that's what people do: they show remorse, they show that they have learned the error of their ways.'

He looked bemused, which infuriated her.

'We have a system in place, we have laws, we have protocol—'

'Protocol would have seen Francis Hill free in ten years; would have allowed him to rebuild his life. Tell me, what would it have given me?' He sat back again. 'Is that why you're here, Roxanne? To talk to me of protocol?'

'I'm here because I wanted to see for myself how deep the poison runs in our blood.'

He tapped his chest, over his heart.

'I still carry you both here.'

Roxy snorted.

'Why did you come here now, after all this time?'

'I wanted to ask you something,' she said softly. 'I wanted to know if you ever considered that what you did was a mistake.'

'If you crack the spine on a philosophy book, you'll learn there are no mistakes.'

'Are you laughing at me?'

'No.' He shook his head. 'There is nothing amusing here, Roxanne. You asked me a question when you came in: how do I live with myself, yes?'

Roxy nodded.

'Well I'll tell you.' He leaned a little closer, lowering his voice to almost a whisper. 'I think of the alternative. I think of Francis Hill sipping a cold beer on a warm summer day, I think of him enjoying the embrace of another human while my wife lies under the soil and my daughter looks at me as if I'm a stranger. I think of all these things and am glad I did what I did. I would do it again in a heartbeat.'

Roxy felt as though someone had walked over her grave wearing spiked heels.

'That's all it takes?'

'That's right,' he said firmly. 'That's all it takes.'

CHAPTER FIFTY-EIGHT

Roxy mulled the conversation with her father over for a few days, and then, against her better judgement, she made an appointment to see Dy Anderson on her next day off. First, though, she sent him a long and detailed email setting out her theories.

When she entered his office, he smirked, but his eyes were filled with such undisguised hatred it unnerved her slightly.

'I'm sorry,' he said. 'You expect me to lend credence to your ridiculous ideas? My God, I've heard some garbage in my time, but this takes the biscuit. Gregory Milton is accusing me of murder?'

'That's right.'

'Frankly, I'm baffled, Sergeant, but not at him, at you.'

'Me?'

'Gregory Milton is a degenerate and a liar; he abused my staff, my trust and our friendship for years, and now he's attempting to slander my reputation – and for what? Personal gain? A more lenient sentence?'

'I don't believe he killed Andrea Colgan,' Roxy said. 'I think he raped her like he raped Delia Shawcross, I think he was happy Andrea was carrying his child; I think he got off on it.'

'You do realise I was at a charity gala the evening Andrea was killed? For goodness' sake, there are multiple witnesses, including, if I'm not mistaken, the Minister for Justice.'

'So you're his alibi and he's yours.'

'That is how alibis work, Sergeant.'

'Milton must have been a loss to Albas Entertainment, although Maureen Kelly tells me they weren't going to renew his show, and his last book sort of tanked.'

'Ebbs and flows, that's the nature of show-business.'

'It would look really bad if it came out that he was raping women on your staff and you were covering it up, though, right? Perception is everything in PR, right?'

Anderson's eyes narrowed to slits.

'I wonder how many more little Miltons there are out there. I wonder if we threw out a big enough net what we might catch.'

'What you'd *catch* is a lawsuit that would cripple you and your entire enterprise.' He steepled his fingers before him. 'Besides, I am not my brother's keeper, Sergeant.'

'No, you were his shield. Delia Shawcross came to you when she found out she was pregnant and knew her fiancé could not be the father of her baby. She told you her fears. You bought her off, threated her, silenced her.'

'Delia Shawcross had a consensual relationship with my client. It was only after her partner discovered she was knocked up that she suddenly cried rape.'

Roxy laughed. 'That's how you're spinning it?'

'That's how it is.' He cocked his head. 'I very much doubt Delia would like to retell that story in court. If my memory is correct, she accepted a very handsome redundancy package and signed a non-disclosure contract. I'd hate to see her lose everything.'

'Delia might have let herself be coerced, but I'll bet you my last pay cheque Andrea Colgan wasn't so easily pushed around.' Roxy leaned forward, her eyes locked on his. 'What did she do, threaten to expose you? Go to her father? You thought you'd nip the problem in the bud, didn't you? Kill her before her pregnancy made it over the twelve weeks, but you messed it up. You tried to make it look like it was Quentin Williams, but you got the details wrong. Boy, she must have really rattled your cage.

Anderson brought his hands up and gave her a slow clap.

'Bravo, Sergeant, what an imagination you have. If you ever leave the Gardai, I can probably get you a position writing fiction on any number of shows, minus my commission, of course.'

'Jerome Falstaff, that's what I don't get. Did he know you did it? Did he try to blackmail you? He wasn't above blackmail, of course, or any other kind of sleaze.'

'Who?'

'Oh, don't you remember him? That's strange. He was Andrea's neighbour. Funnily enough, he died yesterday, threw himself off his balcony.'

'Oh, so now I'm responsible for his death too? Dear me, Sergeant, why don't you go through all your unsolved deaths and bring them to my door?'

Roxy smiled. He was being glib, or trying to be, but somehow she felt the weight of truth in what she was saying.

'You think you have it all figured out, don't you?' she said.

'I think what I have is an excellent lawyer but questionable taste in friends. I will try to choose better ones in future.'

Roxy got up to leave; by the door, she paused and put her hand out.

'What are you doing?'

'I'm admiring this coat. Cashmere, is it?'

'Yes.'

'Nice.' She brushed the sleeve with her fingers. 'Real nice.'

'Will that be all?'

'Sure.'

She left.

CHAPTER FIFTY-NINE

A few days after the conversation with Dy Anderson, Sergeant Eoin Fletcher stopped by Roxy's cubicle.

'I thought you'd like to know, I took Edgar, in case you were worried about him.'

Roxy leaned back in her chair and looked up at him.

'You took Falstaff's dog?'

'Yeah.'

'That was kind of you.'

He shrugged. 'He needed a home.'

'What about the cat?'

'Can't, my partner's allergic to cats. Had a hard enough time convincing him to take Edgar.'

'So where did it go?'

'The animal shelter took it. I called them.'

'Right.'

'Anyways, I thought you'd like to know.'

'I appreciate it.'

She worked for a while, trying to kill time while she waited for Briana Lu to get back to her regarding the samples of hair she had scraped off Anderson's coat while she was pretending to admire it.

Finally her inbox pinged. She held her breath while the email opened, read the result and sagged.

No match.

She couldn't believe it; she had been so sure.

*

That night, she lay on her back staring at the shadows on her ceiling, unable to sleep. After a few hours of thinking, she made a decision and dozed off almost immediately.

'What the hell is that?' Boy demanded the following day, when she arrived home carrying a large metal cage containing a yowling, hissing, hairy cat.

'This is Cucumber.'

'Shit, you said you were rescuing a cat! That's not a cat, that's a mountain lion!'

'I think it's mostly fur.'

Boy peered into the cage. Cucumber growled at him.

'That thing is probably going to kill us in our sleep.'

Roxy set the cage down and opened the door. Cucumber stayed exactly where she was.

'I guess she needs some time.'

Roxy went into the kitchen and made some coffee; after a moment, Boy followed.

'I forgot to tell you, I got a new job.'

'That's great, where?'

'Fontana.'

Roxy had never heard of it and said so.

'It's a snazzy little number off Parnell Street, two floors and get this, regular hours.'

'Nice. You pleased?'

'Very.'

He leaned his head out around the door.

'Hey, it's gone.'

Roxy hurried into the living room. He was right. Cucumber had vanished.

'We didn't leave any doors open, did …'

She spotted the cat sitting on the bookcase, looking out of the window with her huge tail curled around her feet.

'I thought it would be hiding,' Boy said, looking at Cucumber with something approaching awe. 'What's it doing?'

'How should I know? I've never owned a cat before.'

Roxy went a little closer, but not too close. The truth was, she was a little scared of Cucumber, though she would never admit it in a thousand years to Boy.

'It looks like she's thinking.'

'Cats don't think. They're cats!'

'Cucumber.'

The cat ignored her, though her ears flickered.

'Here, Cucumber.'

Nothing.

'You try.'

'Me?'

'Her last owner *was* a man.'

Boy pulled a face. 'Okay, but just so you know, I'm not exactly a cat person.'

He inched closer, sliding his bare feet across the floor.

'Cucumber? Here, girlie-girl.'

The cat turned her head and looked at him curiously.

'It's working!'

Emboldened, Boy went a little closer. 'Cu-cu! Come on now, come on, pretty kitty.' He lifted his hands to her. 'Let Uncle Boy find you a— Ow!'

He held up his right hand, showing Roxy the stripes filled with tiny beads of blood. They both looked at the cat. She gazed back, defiant and vaguely haughty, then yawned, displaying impressive fangs.

'Son of a bitch!'

'Come on, I've got some disinfectant somewhere.'

In the bathroom, Roxy helped Boy clean the scratches, trying not to roll her eyes every time he winced.

'I think we should leave her alone, let her settle in a bit.'

'I think we should open a window, let her jump.'

'Boy!'

They went back to the living room. Cucumber was exactly where they had left her. She turned her orange eyes on them as they entered and watched them go about their business. After a while she lay down, curled her tail over her face and fell asleep.

*

When Cucumber woke an hour later, only the female human remained. She was reading a book with her legs folded over the arm of her chair.

The cat hesitated. This was all new to her: the place, the humans, the view from the window. She wasn't afraid, but she was cautious.

She stretched, arching her back.

The human paid no attention.

She groomed herself, pointing her toes skywards to reach the awkward spots.

Still nothing.

After a while, she got bored and jumped down. She kept one eye on the human as she left the room to investigate her surroundings. The space smelled funny, and there were not as many places to hide as before and nothing useful to sharpen her nails on.

Her ears flicked backwards and forwards, her nose twitched.

The human was moving.

She stood in the dark, listening, until curiosity got the better of her.

In the food room, the human was leaning against the preparation place reading the back of a tin, her features all scrunched up. Cucumber recognised the shape of the tin immediately and remembered she was hungry.

She rubbed her side against the door frame to indicate this, but the human wasn't paying attention.

'Marp,' she said.

The human looked at her.

'Are you hungry?'

A stupid question, but what could one expect from a human?

'Marp,' she said again, with a little more emphasis. This time the human understood.

There would be a period of adjustment, Cucumber thought, watching the human dump the entire tin into a ceramic bowl and place it on the floor without warming it or even breaking it up with a fork. Later, to show her displeasure, she would vomit a hairball onto something fabric and then they would be even.

Baby steps, Cucumber thought, baby steps.

CHAPTER SIXTY

Fat flakes of snow drifted down into the machinery yard. Smelling cigarette smoke, Dominic Travers changed direction and walked towards it, his coat billowing out behind him. He saw a figure standing in the shadows, the ember of his cigarette glowing like a beacon.

'What are you doing here?'

Eli Quinn pitched the cigarette into a puddle, where it hissed and went out.

'A long time ago you told me the law was for the sheep not the wolves.'

'I remember.'

'I didn't believe you at the time.' Eli inclined his head. 'I'm beginning to think I was wrong.'

'What do you want, Quinn?'

'Roxy Malloy, the kid I was telling you about before: she broke protocol and collected evidence she was told to leave alone.'

'The Commissioner warned you to keep that dog on a leash.'

'She did it because she believes in right and wrong; because she believes in justice.'

'She believes in a pipe dream. Jesus Christ, Quinn, of all the people in the world, you should know that.'

'What if she's right?'

'What are you saying?'

'You know the DNA we took from Andrea's unborn baby was a match to Milton.'

Dominic's face grew hard. 'I know that.'

'So Milton got off on having women carry his children, his progeny. When confronted by Delia Shawcross, he bought her off, had her sign a non-disclosure, let her keep the child, no questions asked; all she has to do is send him photos and an update once a year.'

He put his hand in his pocket, pulled out a sheet of paper and passed it to Travers.

'Read it.'

Travers tilted it towards the lamplight.

'What is this?'

'It's a mitochondrial DNA sequencing result.'

'For?'

'Cat hair.'

'What the hell do I want with—'

'It came from Jerome Falstaff's cat, to be exact. Malloy lifted it from Dy Anderson's coat.'

'Who the fuck is Jerome Falstaff and why would I give a shit about his damned cat?'

'Because it's Schrödinger's pointing finger.' Quinn smiled. 'Malloy doesn't believe Milton killed Andrea, same way as she never believed she was killed by the Sweetheart Killer. She thinks Dy Anderson killed Andrea and also Jerome Falstaff.'

'What do you think?'

'I think she has good instincts, that kid; if we can rein them in a little, she might make a fine detective some day.'

'Why are you telling me this?'

'I got the lab to tell Malloy it was a false read.'

'Why did you do that?'

'I don't know. Maybe I'm tired of all the bullshit; maybe to keep good kids like Malloy from turning into people like you and me.' Quinn rocked back on his heels, exhaled long and with some relief. 'I think a change is coming, Travers. I'd like to think she might be part of it.'

Dominic Travers folded the paper and put in his pocket.
'But not you?'
'This dog is too old to learn new tricks.'
Dominic grunted. 'Trick or not, I won't forget this.'
'I'll bear that in mind.'
'So long, Quinn.'

*

Quinn watched Travers walk across the yard, massive, brooding, a weapon of mass destruction launched on a course that nothing on this earth could possibly stop.

On the drive back to the city, he examined his own psyche. It was, he decided, like the inner tube of an old wheel, threadbare in places, patched together in others, softer than it should be, but still rolling. And as long as he could roll, he would keep on going.

CHAPTER SIXTY-ONE

Dy Anderson ended a long and triumphant conference call, leaned back in his chair and clapped his hands.

Nothing, he thought, nothing beat deal-making, nothing beat the thrust and parry of talking money. He would never grow tired of it.

His stomach rumbled, a reminder that he hadn't eaten anything since lunch. Maybe he'd go celebrate at that new restaurant down in the Docklands; he deserved it.

He left his office and walked through to reception, feeling lighter than he had done in years. Dublin was small, too small. The future of entertainment was the burgeoning market in East Asia.

He called goodnight to the cleaning lady emptying bins into her trolley, but she was wearing earbuds and didn't hear him. He could hear the tinny sound of music as he passed by.

In the car park, he was annoyed to see that two of the strip lights were broken. He made a note in his head to call maintenance about it when he got home.

Halfway to his car, something hit him on the back of the head, something hard.

He grunted and went down.

When he came to, he was in the boot of a moving car, bound and gagged.

He flexed his muscles, but whoever had tied him up knew what they were doing: there was little to no give anywhere.

It felt like a long time before the car slowed. He heard the rumble of wheels on a grate, and then it sped up again, but slower than before, and the terrain was rougher.

A few minutes later, he heard the crunch of gravel and felt the car slow to a stop. A dog barked; no, more than one. A door slammed, and he heard feet on gravel, more barking, high and excited, followed by silence.

It was very cold, and before long his muscles began to cramp. Pins and needles followed, and no matter which way he tried to move, his limbs ached.

Furious, he yelled behind the gag.

No one came.

Time passed.

The need to urinate became an issue, then a need, and then he had no choice. With the release came humiliation as the heat spread down his crotch and pooled under him.

If … no, *when* he got free, he would make his captors suffer; oh, how he would make them pay for this.

At some point he dozed off. When he opened his eyes again, he could detect faint traces of light between the minuscule gaps. Not long after that, he heard the dogs again and footsteps drawing close. A car door opened and something popped close to his ear.

Light blinded him as strong hands reached in and pulled him out. He hit the dirt with a wallop and tried to get to his knees. His captor kicked him over onto his back and dragged him across the gravel by his ankles.

Two dogs – he saw now they were German shepherds – danced around him, barking with excitement.

Hands grabbed him again and lifted him, depositing him onto the back of a flatbed truck. He heard a voice say, 'Up!' and the dogs were beside him, panting. He tried to flex his muscles against his restraints and realised he was weaker than he could have imagined.

The truck started up and they drove around the side of an old farmhouse and through a clump of tall fir trees before setting out across open ground. Anderson could do nothing but wince at every bump and watch the clouds drift across a red-streaked morning sky.

Finally the truck stopped and the engine was shut off.

His captor came to the back of the truck, hauled him down and dropped him for a second time onto the ground.

This time he stayed down. His eyes travelled from mud-encrusted boots, up a pair of legs and a torso to a hard, cold face.

'My name is Dominic Travers,' the man said.

Anderson frowned, confused.

'Andrea Colgan was my daughter. She was pregnant with my grandchild when she was murdered. I believe you know something about that.'

*

Travers left Anderson with the dogs watching over him and walked to the ancient oak tree. His great-great-great-grandfather had planted the tree with an acorn taken from a war-torn blood-soaked field in Poland, or so the story went. It was sturdy and forbidding, a great giant, and a favourite resting place in summer when the sun beat down.

Travers rested his hand on the gnarled trunk, tracing his thumb over a name grown silver in time. *Andrea.* He had hung a swing from a low branch for her as a child and she had spent many an afternoon swaying back and forth on a warm breeze while he drank tea from a flask. Those memories were stored in a private place in his brain and he cherished them. When Andrea got too old for swings, and no longer came to the farm, the swing had rotted from neglect and fallen away. He supposed he could find parts of it still if he cared to look, but he did not.

Now a different item swung from the branch, and it was this that he turned his attention to.

The gibbet cage too had been in the family for a long time. It was a peculiar item, long forgotten about in one of the sheds. He had found it years before during a renovation and kept it, more out of a strange morbid curiosity than anything else. Now he wondered if it had been destiny. Certainly this medieval contraption would bring him what he sought most.

He dragged Anderson to the base of the tree, ignoring his repeated efforts to bargain and plead from behind the gag. Using a sharp hunting knife, he sliced through the man's bonds, then kneeled on his chest and began to enclose his limbs inside the bars.

Before he clamped on the helmet, he removed the gag from Anderson's mouth and pocketed it. Anderson immediately began to babble, though his voice was rusty, dry, his vocal cords strained.

'You have this all wrong, I didn't do anything to Andrea, she was—'

Travers drew back his fist and punched him square in the face, so hard his nose broke on impact. Anderson blacked out.

Travers grabbed the metal sides of the helmet, brought them around Anderson's head and bolted them into place. Blood dribbled down Anderson's throat, causing him to gag and cough as he came round again.

'Stop, please … wait …'

Travers locked the helmet to the chest cage and yanked Anderson forward to check the D-ring on the back of the contraption was secure. He grunted with satisfaction and hooked the ring to a chain hanging from the branch. Using a simple hand pulley, he winched Anderson to his feet and kept winching until he dangled eight feet off the ground, spinning lazily in the air.

Anderson grabbed the chest bars, spat blood to one side and glared down at him.

'You can't do this, I have rights.'

Travers wiped his hands on his jacket, then walked back to the truck, put his dogs in the back and drove away.

*

In many ways, the first day was the worst, because Anderson felt sure Travers would come back, but it was not to be. On the second day he suffered through a deluge of rain and a biting wind that chilled him to the bone. He screamed for help until his throat was raw and his voice was all but destroyed. By nightfall he was completely exhausted, but as the temperature plummeted, he found he was unable to stop shivering. By midnight, his entire body was racked with pain.

Numerous times throughout that second night his bowels loosened and voided, filling the material beneath his buttocks with a hot stinking mess that slowly dribbled down his legs.

His spirits rose slightly at dawn's first hesitant light. Surely Travers would return. Then he would confess, oh yes, beg for his life.

He would do anything.

But as each hour passed and the sky went from light to dark again, hope dwindled.

He dozed. His tongue grew dry and swollen, and after a while it hurt to move it. His eyes felt gritty, and when he tried to focus them on anything for too long, his vision shimmered and became grey around the edges. That night the cold was unbearable, and he shivered and rattled so badly his bones felt like they were crumbling to dust. Foxes crept out from the woods and watched him from the hedgerows, noses twitching at his rancid stench. Nearby an owl hooted and he wept to hear it.

He understood that he was dying. His tongue was so swollen he was having trouble breathing, and his skin felt odd and shrunken. He no longer made urine, and staying awake for more than a few minutes at a time was impossible. The skin around his fingernails cracked and peeled and the nails themselves grew loose. His teeth ached, but he no longer cared about those.

Around noon of the fourth day, a raven landed on a branch nearby and cocked its head in his direction. He stared at it blankly, trying to remember what kind of thing it was. After a while it flew away, but later that afternoon it came back, and this time it wasn't alone. Through cracked eyelids he watched the birds march back and forth on the branch, fluttering their coal-black feathers as they assessed the situation.

When he woke again, one of the birds was tearing a long sliver of skin from the ring finger on his right hand. He tried to bat it away but the effort was too much. All he could do was rest his forehead against the bars and close his eyes.

His heartbeat grew erratic.

Sleep took him. Pain brought him round. He flinched, drew his hand back as a bead of blood appeared and dripped onto the bars. The raven hopped onto a branch nearby to consume his flesh. It cocked its head, ruffled its feathers and watched him until he could no longer keep his eyes open. He heard the sound of wings beating against the bars, a querulous croak, and then he heard no more.

*

Dominic returned the following weekend and lowered what remained in the gibbet cage onto a tarpaulin he'd spread on the ground. One of the dogs, the big male, sniffed at it, then cocked his leg and urinated on it.

Dominic threw the remains onto the flatbed and drove across the farmland to a pit he'd dug to the rear of the property, near the old walled garden next to the greenhouse. He backed the truck up, threw the carcass into the hole and, using a small digger, filled the pit in. When he was done, he scattered the earth with grass and wildflower seeds, then he smacked his hands together, whistled to the dogs and drove back to the house.

It was done.

CHAPTER SIXTY-TWO

The sun was low in the sky by the time Roxy, unused to driving around this part of the country, found the entrance to the private nursing home.

The car crawled along a long, narrow driveway flanked by brambles until she reached a set of high metal gates set into an eight-foot wall. She let the window down and directed her voice to the wall monitor. After identifying herself and showing her badge, the gates opened inward. She noticed there were a number of CCTV cameras pointed at her as she drove into the courtyard.

She parked, got out and followed the signs to reception, where again she gave her name and showed her identification.

'Well now.' The receptionist, whose name tag read *Imelda*, studied her ID carefully. 'In all the time she's been here, you're only the third visitor she's ever had.'

'Is that so?'

'Her husband used to come a bit at first.' She smiled at the memory. 'Had a real way about him, you know?'

'Mm,' said Roxy, wondering how on earth Imelda had missed the news about Milton.

'He's a doctor himself, ever so handsome. He was always so keen to hear about her, how she was doing, if there was any sign of improvement at all. Used to think it was a crying shame when he stopped coming, but then I realised it didn't seem to bother her none, so why should it bother me?'

Roxy unwound her scarf.

'A friend of hers came, Maureen I think her name was, but she only came the once. Awful upset she was when she was leaving.' Imelda sighed. 'It's just, you know, you'd like to think they're not forgotten.'

'Yes,' Roxy said. 'You'd like to think that.'

She followed Imelda into a large, bright salon. A number of people sat in comfortable chairs, their lower legs draped in colourful blankets. Most were sound asleep, but a small group were gathered around a large television watching a black-and-white movie with the sound turned down low. Roxy wondered how on earth they could hear a word until she passed by and saw their expressions and understood that words were not important; familiarity was.

'She's probably in her room,' Imelda said. 'She doesn't like to be in the salon with the others. I think it makes her anxious.'

On they walked, down a short hall with walls covered in a cheery mural of daisies and sunflowers. They stopped outside a door marked 'N', the last on the left.

'I hope you don't mind me asking,' Imelda said, her hand resting on the handle. 'But are you a friend of hers … from before?'

'No, we've never met,' Roxy said. 'But I have a message for her.'

'Oh?' Imelda looked confused. 'Well, I hope you understand she's quite unresponsive. We've been trying, but she's in her own little world most of the time.'

'That's okay,' Roxy said, suddenly tired of talking to Imelda. 'Shall we?'

Imelda knocked as she opened the door.

'Nadine, honey, you have a visitor. Look now, somebody has come to see you, isn't that nice?'

Nadine was in a wheelchair by the window. Roxy walked towards her and looked down. She would have been a beautiful woman once; certainly the foundations were still there in her bone structure – her high cheekbones and aquiline nose – and her cornflower-blue eyes rimmed by long black lashes. But the skin around her throat sagged and her cheeks were hollowed to the point of sunken, and when Roxy fetched a chair and sat down, she saw that Nadine's eyes were blank and listless.

'If you need anything, anything at all, there's a bell by the side of her chair.'

'Thank you.'

Imelda backed out of the room and closed the door. Roxy glanced out of the window, staring into the deepening shadows, then leaned forward and took one of Nadine's hands in hers.

'You don't know me and I don't know you. I didn't even know you existed until a few weeks ago.' She cleared her throat and leaned a little closer. 'I want you to know that your husband, Gregory, is in jail.'

She looked at the motionless woman, saw the gentle rise and fall of her chest, felt how loose her fingers were, how papery her skin.

'He can't ever hurt you again; he can't hurt anyone again.'

A sigh, so slight she might have missed it, but she had not. She leaned closer still and lowered her voice in case Imelda had not gone far. Nadine's fingers tightened around hers, not much, but enough.

'I want you to know that it was a woman who took him down. I want you to know that he underestimated me, but I did not underestimate him.'

Was that a flicker of triumph in Nadine's eyes? Or was Roxy projecting, making something out of nothing?

'I want you to know that I'm sorry he was allowed to operate for so long.' She put Nadine's hand back on her lap, where it lay unresponsive and still. 'I want you to know I'm sorry no one believed he was cruel to you. He was a piece of shit, but now he's going to spend a long time behind bars.'

Feeling stupid, even indulgent, Roxy rose and began to walk towards the door. She had only taken a few steps when two words caused her to stop.

'Thank you.'

It was soft, barely a whisper, barely a breath.

'You're welcome,' Roxy said without turning back.

She found Imelda in the salon, straightening blankets and pillows, fussing gently over her charges.

'Oh, you're off already then?'

'Yes.'

'Hard, isn't it? Sometimes you don't know if they can even hear you or not. But I think they do.' She touched the hair of a sleeping woman, stroking it softly, almost absent-mindedly. 'Twilight, they call it. I used to think it was a strange expression when I started here first, but now I think it suits them.'

Roxy walked past the television watchers, then stopped and turned round. 'One thing I wanted to ask you about. The flowers, the roses?'

'Oh yes?'

'Where do they come from?'

'It's a standing order from her husband. She gets a delivery every month.'

'Can you change it?'

'I … Well I suppose I can. What did you have in mind?'

'Daisies, carnations, pick whatever you like.' Roxy wrapped her scarf about her neck. 'But not roses, anything but bloody roses.'

A LETTER FROM ARLENE

Since the inception of the internet way back in August 1991, this global information highway has revolutionised life on earth as we know it. These days the whole world is at our fingertips 24/7. We can connect with people from all walks of life, share information, passions and hobbies. We can talk in real time to friends in different countries and research everything from the mundane (the best recipe for sourdough bread) to the extreme (so, what's the best way to discard of a body in cold weather?).

I met one of my best friends, Kris, online over a decade ago; we had a shared interest in running that developed into a real-world friendship. My husband runs a huge website where hundreds of thousands of strangers stop by every day to chat and read about a London football team. It's a brilliant community and it could not have happened without the internet.

Go, technology!

But for every positive, there is a negative.

A few months before I began writing *Last Goodbye*, I read the ramblings of Elliot Rodger, a young 22 year-old man who, in 2014, shot six people to death in Isla Vista California. This in turn brought me to a very disturbing set of forums and down the rabbit hole into the world of the 'incel' (men who identify as involuntary celibates). What I read affected me so profoundly that 'the wolf' was born almost overnight. Unlike the majority of incels, who rage into the void, the wolf acts on his hatred.

If you enjoyed the book, and want to keep up-to-date with all my latest releases, just sign up at the following link. Your email address will never be shared and you can unsubscribe at any time.

www.bookouture.com/arlene-hunt

I'd love to hear some of my readers' views on the Sweetheart Killer. Did you feel any empathy towards him? Understand what drove him? Is our society becoming a colder, more remote one? Have we lost our way a little?

I'd like to think technology has brought us closer together, but then there are days of raging Twitter wars, Facebook spats, and acts of cyber-bullying that make me despair. I think of the Sweetheart Killer, alone in his room, festering, seething, lonely and filled with rage, and it scares me, because while my wolf is a work of fiction, there are many wolves out there who are not. I hope you loved *Last Goodbye* and if you did I would be very grateful if you could write a review. It makes such a difference helping new readers to discover one of my books for the first time. I'd love to know what you think.

Arlene Hunt
March 2018

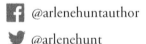 @arlenehuntauthor
@arlenehunt

ACKNOWLEDGEMENTS

The book you're reading right now is the result of intense collaboration. So thank you to my long-suffering agent, Faith O'Grady; thank you to the extremely kind and patient Jessie Botterill and Lydia Vassar-Smith; thank you and a million more to the one-woman dynamo that is Kim Nash. To the book bloggers of the world, I hope you know how much we appreciate all the hard work you do, book after book, year after year. On the home front, my thanks as always to my friends and family. Writing can be an insular gig at times, but when I do surface for air, it's nice to have real people to swim towards. Andrew, no words needed for you, ducky; you already know my heart. Lastly, thank you to my readers. I cannot fully express how much you mean to me. I am grateful for you, for the time you take to read my books, for the emails, the tweets, the reviews, the word-of-mouth. Without you, writing would be a pointless exercise, so thank you all.

Printed in Great Britain
by Amazon